MONDO KANE

MONDO KANE

GEORGE GOULD

Published by Pembury House Publishing
5 Henwoods Mount, Pembury, Kent TN2 4BH

First published in Great Britain 2014

A CIP catalogue record for this book is available from the British
Library

ISBN-13: 978-0992995607

PART ONE

The old Lakota was wise. He knew that away from nature a man's heart becomes hard.

Chief Standing Bear of the Oglala Sioux (1868-1939)

1

PFFT

Mad it was, right from the get-bloody-go. Just picture it, brother: it's past beer o'clock on a pissing down baltic bastard in the thick of January, all quiet on the western front, and there I am sat in the back of my boss's spanking new beemer with my nose to the glass like a prize ninny, totally oblivious to the Armageddon of shit that's about to swallow me up hook, line and stinker. It's a proper pea-and-misery-stew drive and no mistake: we're out on some grebby jumblegut in the middle of deepest darkest cowcountry, all grey mud and freshly-squeezed dung, headed I don't know where for some hush-hush meet with top reps from a new Manchester firm offering juicy percentages, and me I'm quietly minding my own bollocks as usual, staring out at nothing just counting the minutes to when I'll be back in the Smoke knobbing the doris on her frilly pink bed, when *WHAM*, like a clap of thunder out of a clear sky comes this snap crackle and pop and the 7 Series sedan gives an almighty great judder, rrrr. What this is is the first shot piercing the back door on the driver's side, the side where Frank 'the Tank' McBride is parked looking like the Buddha after a forty-course meal. Yes, brother, shot as in gunshot. Now you see he's built like a brick shithouse, is Frank, and tiny me I'm squeezed in with hardly no space at all for my scrawny little windmill, and as soon as we realise what's happening we both make a nosedive for the floor, at the eggzak same time, only somehow he gets there first, the fat biffa, and I land with my face on his pigging elbow. Whack.

Typical.

Next I know it's D-Day all over again: people screaming, metal tearing, bullets flying bloody everywhere: total mind-bending, nut-numbing chaos. And I'm wondering: we've got open field on one side, some empty cowsheds on the other, not a ruddy soul in sight, so where the shite is all this shatter coming from? I hear some revving and skidding so I'm guessing a motorbike, but the truth is it's bloody hairy and there's no time for much guessing or thinking of any sort —not on my part, anyway. More shots crack the windows on the Tank's side, then a couple more hit the door again, thwump thwump, missing him by a fluke impossible to explain with simple equations. The windscreen goes next. I hear a muffled cough and see Suki, the driver, double up over the steering wheel like a binbag full of jelly. A spray of blood a yard long squirts from his neck and paints the car in Technicolor. (It's like one of them Jackson Pollock abstracts, brother, only worse.) The beemer, which up till now has been cruising through this bloody blitzkrieg like nothing's happening, lurches suddenly and we tear sideways into hedges and a wooden fence at the same moment as our airbags pop out.

I can tell you now, it's a wonder I didn't piss myself.

Then the Tank starts shouting for someone to fucking do something just as another shot comes singing in through the smashed window on his side and destroys the rearview mirror, sprinkling silvery sharp shards fucking all over me. I make like super-sodding-turtle and press my head down as far as it'll go between my shoulders and somehow manage to say in a tiny piddly voice:

'Whoever it is, thank Christ they're such a fucking lousy shot.'

By this time the other two motors have ground to a halt somewhere just in front and behind us and I can hear our guardian angels gobbing it out proper hellsbells as they open fire.

'Flaming fucking Nora, what the fuck's going on out there?'

It's the Tank again, talking into the carpet. Then he raises his nut a couple of inches to gawp at me.

'Shit, Dodger, you're bleeding.'

I snite a hand across my jagger and look down at it. Yeah, it's blood all right.

'I'm okay, Frank,' I says. 'It was only you with your elbow.'

'This is a right clusterfuck, this is,' says Frank.

We don't move, speak or even breathe now, listening to the thrash metal of gunfire and wondering if we're going to make it out of this alive and with all our bits and bobs intact. We're still staring at each other like a couple of bollock-brains when the shooting stops and we hear the clop clop of someone running towards the car in heavy boots.

'Jesus bloody Christ,' Frank spits, 'they're coming for me. Where are those fuckwits? What do I fucking pay them for? Give me your gun, Dodger. — *Now!*'

I fumble for my barker but, wedged in tight as I am between the car seats, I can't move my arms or turn round fast enough.

Too bloody late: I hear the door on my side yank open and my nutmegs instantly shrink to nothing.

And I know, brother, I just know.

I've fucking had it.

***

Now let me just explain a thing or three. You see, Frank McBride — the gaffer, as you've no doubt worked out for yourself — ran a right tight little firm that had become spectacularly successful in a very short time. He was decades ahead of the competition, and had made more wonga from drug trafficking — his main line of trade — than you could shake your snake at, with a little protection, armed robbery and murder on the side, just to keep it lively.

Thanks to the Tank's level bizniss head, proactive attitude and excellent people skills, the firm had managed to evade repeated stings by the Old Bill, and the most any of us had ever served was a couple of months in nick for minor offences. The Tank had his method, and he stuck by it. He only worked with the best. If anyone cocked up, they were out. If they dreamt of cocking up, they were out. If a mush bubbled he either died or got a severe case of chronic amnesia before any real harm was done. Simple as bloody that.

But me, I was never a gunman. Sure, on Frank's orders I'd carried a barker on some rare — very rare — occasions, as a mere formality as it were, but I'd never needed to take the thing out of its nest, not ever, let alone fire it at anyone. You see, brother, the violence had never been a part of my duties, thank Gog, not directly. Truth is I wasn't suited to it, though you can believe it when I say that even back then if it had come down to it I'd have done what I had to do and done it good and proper, bingo bango bongo, no two ways about it. Frank knew that, of course, otherwise I wouldn't have been where I was. But that didn't mean the danger didn't get to me. It did. The threat was always there, you understand, hovering over your head, every minute of every hour of every bloody day, week in week out, all ruddy year round and non-bloody-stop. In this line of work, a bloke can be your best mate for twenty years and still turn his back on you at the drop of a hat, all it takes is a wrong word from the right quarter. You can take nothing for granted. We'd all heard stories, and everyone knew how one day a joe might go out to buy fags or give his doris the once-over or just like take the fido for a runaround maybe and never bloody come back, not on his feet and breathing any-way: the tide had turned, the winds had changed; someone at the top had taken a disliking to him. Whatever. And you also knew how next time it could be you, mate, vanished off the face of the bloody earth like spit on a hot stove, pfft.

I mean, I'd been in my share of sticky situations, believe me, and there had been at least two occasions when I'd been in it up to the bloody hilt — in very clear, unequivocal danger of losing my life. And let me tell you, brother, no matter how bleeding tough you think you are, these moments come back to haunt you. And after a while, it can become a sort of obsession, this coming to terms with your own death. Me, I'd imagined it many, many times: the moment, place and method of my execution. I'd become an expert on all the gruesome little details over which the true para-noiac likes to pore. I mean I just couldn't get over the fact that a simple hand-held mechanism that fired a projectile no bigger than a bloody fag-end could put an end to a person's life — my life — in the blink of a bloody eye, just like that. An irresistible force, an immovable object, and *pop!* That's it for you, mush. Better luck next time. And you know I once read somewhere that we're made up of like 80 per cent water and 90 per cent empty space between atoms. Think about it. Oh, yeah, it's a bloody miracle of physics. A terrible one, granted, but a miracle none the bloody less. I mean, do you know what actually happens when someone pulls the trigger on a handgun? In my Hollywood-conditioned and CGI-inspired funk I'd sometimes visualise the sequence as clearly as if I was watching a film of it on the telly, the scene captured from a combination of like microscopic cameras mounted round the weapon, even one on the actual bullet itself, all in sickening, ultra-slow motion: first, the finger squeezing down, then the hammer being released, then, with a hollow boom, the firing pin striking the cartridge — a sequence whose cold mathematical inevitability was almost beautiful in its deadly simplicity, brother. Just picture it a moment. There's a dry hiss, and a compact, intense orange flame bursts out, tiny and precise, igniting the powder charge in the cartridge. A cloud of gas erupts, a microscopic volcano, and the heat in the chamber soars to well over a thousand degrees, the intense pressure ejecting the 9mm calibre bullet from the barrel at roughly a thousand feet per second, spinning with lethal force. The bullet hangs a moment, shimmering, slicing through the air towards my forehead, nearer and nearer as I watch in paralysed fascination (and it has, as the cliché goes, my name on it, in clear silvery letters that I can read an instant before it pierces the skin between my eyes). The moment of impact is like an underwater ballet: the skin rippling before splitting to allow the projectile's entry; the tiny splinters of bone pirouetting through the air like itty circus acrobats; stringy petals of pink, lacerated flesh billowing out from the edges of the wound like the blossoming of some exotic tropical flower; and blood, a great fucking fountain of sticky crimson...

And in the time it takes to perform this deadly little watchamacallit *danse macabre,* the bullet passes through all them carefully trifled layers of soft pulpy flesh and smooth muscle and tangled nerves and diddy pulsing veins and hard shiny bone and sticky filmy membrane, fwwwooooom, finally reaching the Magic Centre, My Brain, to destroy every diddy thought and idea and memory and desire and fear and bloody dream I ever had or have or will have or would have had. Ever. And just like that it's gone, all of it. Where to? Fuck knows. Just EOT: End of Transmission, zzz, ciao. Nothing else. And in the place of all these billion wondrous multi-coloured many-splendoured bits and pieces that once were me, good ol' Dodger, who was like this and who liked that and who lived in such and such a place and loved this and hated that and hoped for whatever, a human being in all its puzzlement and pleasure and pain and happiness and sadness and fantastic like phantasmagoric trillion-stemmed complexifications — all that's left is a grey dead lump of meat to feed the sodding maggots.

Makes you think, don't it?

Well, again and again I'd lived it out in daymares, that final moment of total bollock-freezing horror. You would too, brother, believe me. Did you know, at close range a bullet will barely slow down as it makes a neat tunnel through your cranium? Full metal jacket bullets like the ones we used tend not to deform once they strike tissue, and usually pass straight through a person's nut more or less intact. You have more than a ninety per cent chance of dying, of course, but at longer ranges the trajectory of a bullet through the brain is in fact highly unpredictable. It can sometimes zigzag around your nut and ricochet off the inside of the skull in the strangest ways. A couple of years back, Jimmy O' Dwyer's youngest got shot just over the left eye and the bullet came out of his ear and he survived — a bit slow on the uptake and speech a little on the slurred side, if you know what I mean, but alive, brother. Now if the bullet goes through the thickest part of your bonce, you have about ten inches of brain matter for it to pass through, not to mention two sides of skull — unless it goes through the eye socket or nose cavity. From entry to death the whole thing takes no more than a second. Not too much pain and agony, at least.

Some ruddy consolation, eh brother? Well, you can see what I mean about the thing having become a sort of morbid obsession with me. So it was this nasty little sequence — or rather a fast-forward, fly-by, lickety-spit version of it — that flashed through my innermost the instant I heard the car door opening behind me, and I was about to start sobbing and like pleading for my life real doomsday when I recognised Derek's outsize lugs and orange freckles bending over me.

'Jesus bloody Christ, Derek,' I shouts, weak with a stupid glocky sort of joy and fuming furious at the same time, 'you scared the living sherbet out of me.'

He just looks straight past me at the Tank, not even listening. 'You all right, Frank?' he says, still panting hard from his run. I notice now how his lamps are big as bloody saucers and I think he must be beaked up cos I've never known Derek to have much bottle in him, least not enough to run out like this in the middle of the fucking Vietnam bloody War.

The Tank looks up.

'I'm fine, Derek, and so's the fucking missus, fuck you very much for asking. Now tell me this: what in fuck's name was that?'

'Couple of bikers,' Derek says, his wide staring lamps back on the road ahead, his barker still raised and ready for action.

'A couple of what? What the bleeding hell are you talking about?'

'They come at us out of the bushes, Frank. Like they was waiting for us. Well tooled they was, too. Makarovs, looked like, and a spray-and-pray. Real doomsday. We nailed 'em both, though.'

Derek looks down at Frank now, his lamps absolutely bloody huge like they're about to bungee out of their sockets.

'Keef got one of 'em in the gut, looked like. He went down over the fence. Des and Porker went after 'im. The other copped one in the canister. Dead as a fucking sausage roll. It's all good.'

Derek turns to me finally, blinks, then does a huge fly-catcher.

'Fucking hell, Dodger, you're hit, mate. Let me take a look at you...'

He leans further into the car to help me.

'I'm okay, Derek,' I says. 'Bumped me nose is all.' I point to the package slumped across the driver's seat. 'Check Suki.'

I watch as Derek crabs it round to the front of the car. Through the shattered windscreen I see Dave and Keef gallop towards us in the rain, barkers still steaming in their fists.

'Suki's had it,' Derek announces, and raises his bunched bloodstained prongs to prove it.

Frank is back on the seat now, breathing heavily, brushing down the three-bag South Molton Street bespoke ('you always got to look sharp, Dodger') that still looks cheap as chips on him, tucking his greased Grecian 2000 locks neatly behind little pink ears that are far too small for his massive lump of a bonce. For a moment he looks about him at the car with an air of little-kid hurt and bewilderment and says nothing. Then he turns to me and rolls his lamps real philosophical-like:

'Look what they've done to my fucking car, Dodger. Fucking barbarians. Brand fucking new.'

2

MISTER ARSEWIPE, TO YOU

That's Frank the Tank all over, that is. Cold as an Eskimo's tits, always calculating gains and losses, no matter the situation, no matter if the loss is material, monetary or human. No bloody wonder he's so successful. He rose through the ranks the hard way, from basher up, and reached the top roughly four years ago. His muscle, since he discovered his brains, has turned mostly to fat now, but that doesn't matter a toss because it's the brains that bring in the pigging bacon. Now don't get me wrong, brother, he is hard, as hard as they bloody come, totally fearless and ruthless. Cos tough, you see, is all in the mind. The rest is just window-bloody-dressing. And that was a lesson Frank learnt before he could tie his shoelaces.

The firm, well, we were what you might call commodity brokers — we supplied wholesale and didn't get involved in the street level retail at all. Our bizniss was strictly the devil's own dandruff, charlie. The brown we left to a mostly Albanian firm with which we had close ties — meaning we helped each other out on the logistics and security fronts and knew better than to step on each other's toes. I'd joined a little over a year and a half before. Unlike the Tank's, the story of my life is far from dramatic — no abuse as a nipper, no drug-related problems, no nick, not so much as a bloody parking ticket (and thank bloody Gog, too). Just the usual crippling poverty and zero prospects, especially bad for us growing up in Iron Maggie's new all-American supersonic Britain.

Mum worked like a dog and did what she could for me. My dad was a classic case of the walk-out: left Mum when she was about two months gone with me, the bastard, and was never seen or heard from again. To me he's just a blank.

Now, me being an only child, as a toddler I spent a lot of time on my own, as was like natural to the circumstance, but almost as soon as I was old enough to hit the streets I found there was strength in numbers. And what a discovery that was for me, brother. It was like at school: if you was picked on and bullied (and who wasn't, eh?) and were scared and angry and just hated your life, there was at least that bit of comfort in the group, looking out for each other and throwing the anger and hatred right back at the world. Out of school it worked the same way: if you're being fucked over, get together and bloody do something about it.

So I did. Like a lot of the kids I grew up with, I started shoplifting before I was in my teens, then did cars for a bit and quickly progressed to actual breaking and entering — shops and warehouses, mostly. I'm not justifying or making excuses, mind you, I'm just telling it like it was. The logic, in as much as there was one, was this: if people are stealing from me and getting away with it cos they have money and power, then I will bloody-well steal right bloody back, any way I can.

I took part in my first proper house burglary when I was seventeen. (Mum said I was never the same person after that. Well, that's what growing up is, innit, brother, that's what happens; I'm not the same person after a lot of things — we all aren't.) I joined my first firm a year later — admittedly a very sloppy outfit carrying out smaller jobs for bigger firms: the odd bit of graft, transport of merchandise, flogging knock-off gear, chasing up debtors, that sort of diddly shite.

Well it was on one such carry job that I first came into contact with Frank the Tank's outfit. This was about two years ago. I knew who they were, of course, but I never imagined that one day I'd be working for them. It was like this. We'd pulled off this fast job for a wheeler-dealer one of us knew, did what was asked, smooth as cream, no hassle, easy as piss. But come payday we're all like jellified to see these top heavy boys arrive for a meet at the same empty warehouse, all sharp suits and shiny shells and barkers under the arm. It's the Tank's organisation. And there he is, too, in poison, big as a bloody mountain. Looking us over, he is. Well, after we're paid comes the biggest surprise of all, brother: he singles me out from the group, and tells me he likes me. He must've noticed the tiswas in my eyes cos then he says, 'Not in that way, you moron. You think I'm a fucking bumbandit?' Well, when I've done the Dodger crawl and duly stammered out my arsefelt sorries he explains that he likes me cos I am efficient and I look discreet, unlike the rest of the fuckwits I am working with. He needs intelligent people around him, he says, with no files, no side, and no mouth on them, people who know how to keep a low profile and who know how to keep trade trim, neat and tidy. Can I do that? I say I can and make him believe it. He let me have lunch with him a couple of times after that, playing the good uncle. When he found out I also had a bit of a honey-tongue and a head for numbers, he took me on.

My duties for the Tank were manifold. I dealt, for instance, with the firm's accountant, laundering the dirty ready through various legit biznisses set up to keep the Inland Revenue from developing a chronic case of the curious. I also did practically all the Tank's PR work, sweetening old contacts, buttering the new, acting as spokesman at the minor meets when he couldn't attend or wouldn't, bigging him up, making him look important — bloody godlike, really — and making sure I always got the message across to everyone that he wasn't a man to be messed with — which he wasn't. I organised timetables, saw to payments, kept his agenda, organised his appointments, booked hotel rooms, made reservations, pre-selected the crumpet for bashes, took any calls to the general line, saw that he rested on the seventh day, and even, on occasion, made the tea. Such is life, brother. And of course I was never, ever, off duty.

My real name, the one my poor mother chose for me while I was still squirming inside her, God rest her soul, doesn't matter — not anymore. Perhaps it never did. They started calling me Dodger early on cos as a kid I bore a striking resemblance (by no means limited to the physical, mind you) to the character of the Artful Dodger as portrayed by the late Jack Wild in the film version of *Oliver!* I didn't mind the nickname, and got so used to it that I couldn't imagine going by any other tag. Of course back then I knew that because I worked as secretary-slash-all-purpose-do-it-all-pigging-doormat to Mr Frank the Tank they also called me Dodger Dogsbody — or worse, Dodger Arsewipe — behind my back, but who was complaining? Like I said, my position kept me out of the blood-and-guts end of the bizniss, and all in all the job was what you might call a moderately safe but more-than-moderately remunerative occupation. And I got no hassle from the bizzies, neither, which was more than I could say for those other sad bastards working the front end, right? Well, wrong, actually, because what I didn't know as I was sat there in the shot-up beemer beside my employer, nursing a bent nose and with blood all over my bonce like jam on ruddy toast, was that all this was about to change, brother — and real radical like.

3

THE DOG'S BOLLOCKS

The mop-up's quick — has to be. The three bodies go into the plastic-lined boots, one for each car. I take the wheel on the beemer, still sticky with Suki's life-juice. Derek's with us in the back now, for extra protection.

'Where to, Frank?' I ask.

'Just drive.'

The tone's dark as Satan and I make sure I say nothing else. I turn the key in the ignition and the shaken engine gurgles for a bit then starts with an old man's phlegmy cough. With no rear-view I have to look over my shoulder to back out of the trashed fence and mangled bushes, and as I catch the expression on the Tank's phiz I'm suddenly very glad I've not been told our destination before.

You see, he was studying this, was the Tank, working out just eggzakly who could have been behind the ambush, ticking off everyone who'd been in the know about the meet. When they were big like this was going to be they were always held out in cowcountry far away from city surveillance, but never in this neck o' the woods before, not to my knowledge. So whoever had called it would've been at the top of Frank's suspect list, certain, and you wouldn't have wanted to be in their toeshells for all the wonga in the world. But what would the Manchester firm have to gain from knocking off the Tank? Nothing, unless someone had paid them to do it. Who, then? Someone who'd known the route we'd be taking: in other words, someone inside. Blimey. So, of our team, who apart from the Tank had been in the know? Usually I was the only one with access to this kind of information, so I couldn't imagine any of the regular lads having being in on it. No one but Suki, that is.

So it's getting dark and still pissing down real doomsday. We reach a stretch of spooky woodland and the Tank tells me to hook a right into a narrow jumblegut winding through the trees. The other two cars follow and we drive on for a bit, everything getting darker and more deserted like the setting for a late-night screamer.

Five, ten minutes in and the Tank taps me on the shoulder.

'This'll do, Dodger.'

I kill the engine but leave the headlights on.

'No lights,' the Tanks says from the back. 'Get the flashes, Derek.'

We all get out of the car. The others, parked head-to-tail behind us along the leaf-n-muck track, follow suit. The Tank tells Keef, Porker and Derek to get the stiffs out and lay them on a bit of clear ground in front of him, one beside the other. When they're lined up, he beams the flashlight on their gory faces. One on the end still has his black biker's helmet on, looking like Darth bloody Vader.

'Right. Dodger, check their pockets. Suki's first.'

There's nothing in Suki's jacket but fags, his wallet and a set of keys on a ring that says 'I heart Paris'. I hand the lot to Frank.

He clumps back to the beemer and sits in the back with the door open. He goes through the contents of Suki's wallet meticulously, shining the light down on each item as he lays it out on his lap. We all stand there watching him, stomping our feet and blowing on our gropers cos of the cold. At one point he unfolds a little square of paper that's tucked away in one of the inner pockets, reads it, holds it up, reads it again, puts it down, then lets the air out very slowly through his nosewells. It's so bloody silent we can all hear the little hiss this makes. The Tank sits there for a long while, not looking at anyone, not moving even, and we all begin to get a bit jittery cos we've all seen this before and we know it's not good.

Suddenly he's out of the car coming towards me. I back away and he goes straight past me to where Suki's lying.

As we watch the Tank raises his right leg over Suki's head, a spotless Gucci shell glistening in the beam of the flashlight, and holds it there a moment, hovering-like. The movement is very smooth and deliberate, so for a second it's not obvious what he means to do. We're all standing there looking at his foot when suddenly he brings it down on Suki's face, hard as a bloody pile driver, and then again, over and over, and doesn't stop stomping till the features are all well pulped and nothing recognisable.

Nobody moves, nobody even fucking breathes. We'd never admit it, but this is going to give a few of us a right nasty nightmare or two, you can bet on it.

The Tank wipes his shoe clean on Suki's jacket after he's done and trolls back to the battlescarred beemer, saying to me on the way in a voice that's perfectly calm and level:

'Now the middle one, Dodger.'

The bikers have nothing on them but a little ready and some chewing gum. They're Slavs, by the look of them, and when Derek helps me undress them this is confirmed by their tattoos.

'Who are they?' asks the Tank.

'Russian,' I says. 'Definitely Russian.'

Behind me I hear Porker crack:

'Yeah, see, his rubles is hangin' out.'

Someone sniggers.

'Yeah, but who *are* they?' says the Tank.

That's when I notice the wrist-ribbon. It's a soiled and twisted little strip of cloth on Darth Vader's arm. You can tell he's had it for a while cos the original red has faded to a dirty pink and the edges are worn and frayed. I've seen one of these before. It's a Brazilian good luck charm. You make a wish when you tie it to your wrist and you're supposed to leave it on till it breaks off of its own accord and so your wish is granted, or some such bollocks.

I break it off to examine it. The writing on it says 'Lembrança do Senhor do Bonfim.' Of course back then I've no idea what this means, brother, but still I begin to suspect the presence of this ribbon on the Ivan's arm isn't just a coincidence.

'What's that, Dodger?'

The Tank's beside me, squizzing at the thing over my shoulder.

'I seen one of these before, Frank,' I says. 'On Captain America's wrist last time he came over. It's a Brazilian charm of some sort.'

The Tank takes it from my hand, turning it this way and that in his massive prongs for a bit, then gives me one of his inter-skull electromagnetic brainmatising Rasputin mindboggler zaps. Now understand, brother, they were very unnerving, these goglesome eyeballers, because the Tank made you feel like he was seeing right down inside of you, in and through your bonce like a pigging x-ray, reading you off like you was some molly magazine in a dentist's waiting room and downloading your thoughts. I tell you, it was bloody uncanny. Fucking turned me inside-out, it did.

So when he finally releases me from this head-zap he knows precisely what I'm thinking, and now he's thinking it too.

He turns to Derek and the others. 'Get rid of 'em,' he barks, then grips my arm and pulls me back towards the car.

When we're sat inside he fixes me dead serious.

'I want you to find someone for me, Dodger.'

I wait for him to say who. I wait some more then ask:

'Who, Frank?'

The Tank shrugs.

'The dog's bollocks, that's who.'

4

POWWOW

Believe it or not, brother, the party I'd been ordered to find went by the name of Chief Sitting Bill. Funny thing is when first I heard it I thought it was just another stupid nickname, picked up somewhere for no good reason, cos we all got 'em, haven't we, these daft like trade tags, and I didn't make the American Indian connection at all.

Well. So I'm sat there two days later twiddling my fiddlies at one of the smaller tables by the grubby window of Fast Freddy's in Croydon, waiting for Terry Tomlinson, aka Terry the Thomas, the one player in all England who might be able to help me locate this dirty harry, and he shows up forty-five sodding minutes late, the plonka, with some gimping bloody excuse about his anklebiter's tap-dancing lessons. Tap-what lessons? I ask you.

He rubs his nose by way of apology and sits down, giving off a smell of dirty underwear and last night's ashtrays.

'How you been, Dodger?'

'You don't look sorry, Terry.'

'Come on, mate, you know how it is. It's the kid's lessons. I'm a family man now.'

'Oh, is that what you are?'

Terry had one of those lived-in faces you knew had seen a bit of action a long long time ago and better days. The red lightning in his lamps matched the broken veins on his nose and puffy cheeks, and no matter what he did his hair looked like it was made out of old Weetabix.

So we order two cokes and some nibbles and catch up a little on the small talk. In the middle of a word I suddenly notice how Terry's fur-lined tongue is hanging halfway down his shirt-front like an old school tie. He's phased out of it, zapping the suicide blonde bent over our table serving the chow. He always was a bloody pervert. She's a right nuts-n-bolts, this one, built like a broken sofa, with baps on her like olympic-size water balloons and an arse wide enough to fit Terry, his missus and all their bloody kids in together.

I tut. 'Yeah, very fambly, Terry. You want me to ask her if she's on the bloody menu?'

The waitress gives me the evil eye and shoves off quick-sticks.

'I love 'em big,' Terry says, watching her and slathering into his coke. 'Don't you just love 'em big like that?'

'No,' I says.

I pull my sleeve back and tap the shiny platinum-cased Jaegre-LeCoultre Duometre a Chronographe (a b-day present from the Tank) with my nail.

'Look, we've wasted enough time, so wipe the drool off your chin. All I want is for you to tell me where I can find this geezer I asked you about.'

Terry tears his bloodshot lamps away from the waitress, points them down at his coke, then blinks them at me real twinkle-twinkle. The innocent look, it is. What an angel.

'Who says I know where he is?'

'Frank the fucking Tank, that's who.'

He pretends to digest this as if he didn't know already.

'He's not an easy man to find, Dodger. I told you that. Discovering his exact whereabouts... it might incur expenses.'

Always the pervert, and always the sneaksby, old Terry. A hundred years ago someone told him he was Jack the Lad and he believed it, the dirty little toerag.

'Yeah, I thought it might.'

He puts on the indignant mask, eyebushes up, mouthcorners down, shoulders up hugging the hairy chops.

'Think it's easy?' he says, whining. 'This johnny's a right billy-no-mates, Dodger, always on his jack, always away somewhere where he can't be bloody found. He's not on fucking Facebook and Twitter, I can tell you. He likes cowcountry, living it raw like some bloody pikey. You know, that whole Bear Grylls Ray Mears survival skills shite, only with him it's for bloody real — no moby, no iPod, no clocks, no nuffink. And he never leaves a fucking forwarding address, neither.'

'Yeah, Terry, but I bet you know something no one else does. Am I right?'

Now it comes, the thin slimy grin showing a glimpse of shitbrown choppers full of breakfast and pubic hair stuck in the cracks.

'I might, Dodger, I might. Now let me think...'

'Don't fret yourself too hard, Terry. You know you'll get what's coming to you sooner or later.'

The smile freezes and dies.

'What's that supposed to mean?'

'Let's cut the turd, Terry. It's not me talking, it's the Tank, so out with it. You'll get your pigging money if your gen on this geezer comes up trumps. If not, you can fucking forget it.'

He sips at his coke and nods, resigned. 'Furry muff,' he grumbles. He starts sipping at his coke again, pushing his lips out and slurping it right sewage-drain-like and true-to-nature, the uncouth boar, but not saying anything, and I can feel my patience strings getting just about ready to bloody snap.

'So where is he, Terry?'

He looks up blinking.

'I don't know, Dodger.'

'What?'

'But I know someone who might.'

'For fuck's sake.'

'I'm telling you, he's not one of the lads, this one. He's a queer fucking Easter egg and no joke, a right bloody psychotrack. He fought in Iraq, you know, and I think the experience really put a lot of worms in his can. Now he don't mix with no one, never, and he don't like to be bothered.'

'Oh, in that case I'll make sure to let him know it was you helped me find him, Terry. I'll give him your regards.'

Terry goes Monday-morning serious at this, and when he speaks the old songbox is quivering and warbling all over the pigging place.

'Don't fucking joke, Dodger. You don't know this geezer. D'you know, he was sectioned under the Mental Health Act once. Wrecked a restaurant cos the waiter got snooty or his soup was cold or something. Beat up the entire bloody staff, security and two cozzers into the bargain before they got a pair of ruffles on him. There was a lot of heads through windows that day. Two I heard needed the blood bank after and the waiter's probably still on a fucking drip as we speak.' Saying which Terry crumples up in his chair like the wet lettuce he is, soiling his underkeks. 'Look. I've changed me mind. Forget paying me. Tell the Tank this one's on the house. Just don't get me mixed up in it, Dodger. All right?'

'Yeah, all right, Terry,' I says, all chumly-like and soothing.

'Right. Here it is, then. There's this bird, see, lives up in Holland Park, real nice gaff, and far as I know she's the only one might have a clue to where he's holed up. He was married to her sister. Was, past tense. But you'll have to come up with a good story. — Here, I'll write the address down for you.'

He produces a stub of pencil that looks like it's been living up his khyber for a year and jots down a few crooked squiggles on the napkin.

'What d'you mean, "story"?' I says.

'They're a close lot, I tell you. There's no way she'll tell you what you need to know unless you can supply a good reason. Convincing, it'll have to be. And you can't just say "I need him to top someone for me", now can you?'

'Can't I? You tell me, Terry, since you seem to have all the answers.'

'I haven't got jack-shit, Dodger. All I know is what I'm telling you, on the square.'

I shrug. 'So what should I tell her?'

'Say something like you share an interest in the plight of the native North American indigenous peoples.'

'The *what?*'

'He's a raving Scouser, see, and he thinks he's a Sioux Indian.'

I uncork a giggle. 'Fuck off. You tweaking the nipple?'

'I swear on the health of me sacred tadger, Dodger, it's God's truth. I told you, he's fucking all-in, round-the-twist, out-to-lunch, hatstand bonkers, this one. A fucking maniac.'

'You sure this is the right bloke?'

'There's only one of him, Dodger.'

'Well Gog's holy trousers, and here I was thinking I'd heard it ay-double-ell. A Scouse bloody Indian.' I shake my bonce. 'And called Chief Sitting Bill, for Gog's sake.'

Terry shakes his bonce. 'That's just to take the piss, Dodger. Don't go calling him that to his face. He won't like it one bit, I can tell you.'

'So by what name should I bloody call him, Terry?'

'He goes by William Kane. Plain Kane'll do.'

'That Caine as in Michael?'

'No. Kane as in Citizen, with a kay.'

'I see. Righty-right. And this Holland Park bird — or is it squaw — who's she when she's at home?'

'Name's Penny. I told you, he was married to her sister. A long while back, this was. I don't know about the ex, there was a lot of bad feeling there, but this sister-in-law's still in contact with him. If anyone knows where to get hold of him, it's her.'

I let a chip hang in the air between my plate and open jagger. 'How come you know all this, Terry? You bezzies with this bird, or what?'

The smile creeps back. 'Now, now, you know better than to ask, Dodger.'

'Okay then tell me this, if he's so bloody piff, how come I've never heard of him?'

Terry holds up a stringy groper and starts counting out on his prongs: 'One, he doesn't move in your circles; and three, it's the anonymity makes him what-you-might-call lethal.'

'You skipped two.'

'Two is you may think you know everyone in the game, Dodger, but you don't.'

'Please, Terry, you're hurting my feelings. — Let me put it this way, then: has he ever done a job for anyone I know?'

'If he has you wouldn't never have heard about it, no mistake. Anyway, he only takes on contracts that appeal to him personal, if you know what I mean.'

'No, I don't know what you mean. Enlighten me, Terry.'

The hand comes down. 'He's a nut, Dodger. How the fuck should I know?'

Silence. I try to think of anything more I should ask. The crickets start chirping. Then Terry looks up, smiling horribly.

'Maurice Micklewhite,' he says.

I stare at him.

'That's Michael Caine's real name. Did you know that? Maurice bloody Micklewhite.'

Right. Eggzakly.

C. U. Next Tuesday, Terry.

5

BRING ME THE HEAD OF CAPTAIN AMERICA

So what's going on then, you ask. Well, it's like this, brother: the aforementioned Captain America — one Clay Tobczyk by name (and if you're wondering, no, apart from the fact that he was a Yank, I have no idea why they called him that, maybe he was a fan of the comic book) — was what you might call Our Man in Rio, the main artery for all Frank McBride's grade-A operations. In other words, he was the feller tending the golden ruddy goose. But lately he'd been giving the Tank a great mucho earache and whinge, a whole lot of limp-cock about not getting his due share on the endgame over here where all the real profit was made, weighed and laid. He wasn't far wrong neither, brother, but that's how it rock-n-rolls. After all, it was the Tank's bloody firm and it was his brains what ran it and kept it greased and oiled. Of course Captain America was already skimming plenty down his end, take my word for it. But the hunger had got him right tight by the lychees, so he was on the line every other pigging day to the Tank, whining about how the cost of living was always on the up, proper rocketing, and what he was making was not enough. It was him running the hairy risks, weren't it, all he wanted was a fair cut for the sheer wear-and-tear of it all. Come on. After all. Put yourself in his position. Come on. Fair's fair, buddy. Come on.

So the Tank tells him, very politely, to go fuck himself.

Silence, click, buzz.

And that, as they say, was that.

Well, not quite, brother. It had been three weeks and a day we hadn't heard from the Cap, not a dickybird, he was sulking, the squinny sod, sorry for himself and the hole in his pocket. But Frank wasn't too bothered: Captain America was kosher, he was, he was all-the-way, only a tad overgreedy like all his fellow red-white-and-blues. Bizniss was still on as usual, weren't it? All right, then, it was laid to rest; it'd blow over, he'd come round, good sort that he was. Like brothers, they was. Wunnerful. Triffic.

And then the ambush happens. Fuck. Gets you thinking, don't it? Now as I saw it that wrist-ribbon on the Cossack package could only mean one thing. Know what I'm saying? What d'you think? Was I right — or was I right?

***

So I do what the Thomas says and tail it to Holland Park to see this clued-up ex-sister-in-law with some daft jiggery pokery bloody story about the would-you-believe-it Stepney Native American Culture Society, all sharp and shitshape from much careful rehearsing and going over, and believe it or not I'm dressed up to the chin like some molly marmite-sarnie nine-to-bloody-nine trouser-shitting library-virus, to get in character as it were (my own mother if she was alive wouldn't have recognised me, brother, not if I'd fallen arse-over-tit into her Sunday stew), and what's the silly bint do? She give me the once over like she's enjoying this bit of fringe theatre, she being so well headucated, it's good for a giggle, smiling all gloopy like she don't believe one ruddy word of it, and next thing I know, without so much as a fart or a blink, bang, she tells me where William Kane is. Scout's bloody honour.

I tell you, brother, I felt a right ruddy plank. Was Terry fucking having me on or what?

'Bill?' she says, blowing diddy smoke rings. 'Oh, you know how it is with him, he's out in the wild. You can't speak to him unless it's in person, I'm afraid.'

'Is there no way I can get a message to him?'

'I'm afraid not.'

Picture it: it's a big bright gaff all done up in pastels and light wood like the set for a health insurance commercial, if you know what I mean, very feng shui, but there's a funny ronk in the air like overnight ruby what's been left out of the fridge too long. And then to add to that she's all the while working her posh little muncher round this Indonesian roll-up stinks more than a camel's runny bunghole, no clinton, blowing the foul smoke straight up my nosewells and into my teary lamps.

'Was it urgent?'

I just grin like a git and go, 'No... Well, yes, a bit...'

'He won't be back for quite a while, I'm afraid...'

'I see...'

'You know, it's his *thing*...'

'Right, right... His thing?'

'Being at one with nature...'

So I say, 'Yes, of course, of course...' Then I let out a bent smile.

'It's how he...' She hesitates, then goes on. 'How he deals with the PTSD.'

I nod like very serious and understanding and try to remember what the letters stand for.

She pulls a thoughtful sad sort of pout and says, 'Do you know, they left it to a charity to look after him after he was discharged.'

'Discharged?'

'Yes. From the armed forces. He was in Iraq.'

'Oh, yes. I heard he was.'

'He was a different person when he came back, very unhappy and damaged.' Then she kind of freezes and cocks her bonce at me, saying, 'Are you really from the Stepney Native American Culture Society?'

I have to smile, brother.

'No,' I says. 'To be quite honest, it doesn't even exist.'

She takes a deep puff on the roll-up. 'No,' she says, breathing out the ronky smoke, 'I didn't think it did.'

A moment's silence, then I shuffle in my seat and ask:

'And, er, where would he be doing this nature thing, eggzakly...?'

And you know what, she tells me. Just like that. No mystery, no what-d'you-want-with-him-he-doesn't-want-to-be-found lard, no bleeding hassle what-so-bloody-ever. Near done me nut in.

Now of course the outside's all poker, brother, but inside I'm ticking over: being at one with nature? Oh my giddy fucking aunt, can this really be the same cunting loon the Tank says is the best in the bizniss? I mean, can it?

Well, apparently it is, brother, so I set off again, this time to meet this Chief Sitting Bill dude in poison, and I tell you I'm starting to feel like the army captain in the film who's sent off into the big bad bush to find the crazy colonel, you know the one, Kurtz the name was, cos now I'm going right into it, chum, the very Heart of Darkness.

Wales.

6

OFF THE Ms AND As

'd never been to the fair land of Cymru before, boy-o, home to rarebits and the legendary Howard Marks, not up, down nor sideways, and at first the idea of a trip Snowdonia-way don't seem too displeasing-like, if you know what I mean. Righty-right, I'm thinking. So come morning I get geared up and plot my itinerary on paper as I don't trust SatNavs further nor I can piss on 'em. The map and the moby and Internet route planner wossits all agree for once: take the M1, then the M6 then the M54 for Shrewsbury, Wrexham and then onto the A55 at Chester. That's when I scratch my nut real thoughtful-like, brother, cos I realise it's near 300 pigging miles all the way, or about a seven-hour drive depending on how you're counting. Smeg. The old Gary Glitter's already puckering up right sorry in like dread anticipation, but it's paid work after all, I tell myself, some poor sods do it just for jollies, coughing up top dollar for the sheer pleasure, screaming kids puking in the back and the swimbo (she-who-must-be-obeyed, that is) rabbitting on in front, and they call it a fambly bloody outing. Just fancy that, brother.

A leaflet I pick up tells me Conwy on the A470 is a great touring base for exploring the Snowdonia National Park, but that driving on Snowdon's narrow roads requires 'care at all times but especially in the winter when the weather conditions can be treacherous'. Per-leaze. Well, this being the case the motor I hire is a very off-road little number, plenty of grunt under the bonnet, just the thing for the job — last thing I want is to be taken out of action by treacherous weather conditions on some mingy beshittened cowtrack out in the middle of sorry pigging Wales, am I right? Course I am.

So as I was saying, the plummy-voiced bird on the SatNav — come to think of it she sounded a lot like the Holland Park item, maybe they was sisters — can be a right unreliable mong half the time, so I keep the road atlas marked with my route spread on the passenger seat just in case. Supplies is a couple of Tesco cheese-n-tomato sangwidges, four packets of crisps, three chocolate bars and a two-litre coke. (Yeah, and tell Jamie Oliver he can get stuffed.)

The Holland Park bint's griff is that Chief Sitting Bill's roughing it in some poxy campsite near a village and on a river whose names you have to be totally euaned to get your clapper round, just a string of letters like a toddler's banged it out random-like on a typewriter, so I don't even try. It's written down on paper for me and it's on the bloody map and that's all I need to know.

I've packed a change of togs and, in case I have to go native, my wellybobs. No weapons — unless you count a penknife, which of course I don't.

Right: all set. I ease the motor out onto the road real smooth-like and lean back on the comfy seat. I spark up a cancer (I'd given up but what with all the ag I'd bloody started again), take that long first neurone-numbing drag, and spread a smile. Oh yes. I punch the music on, a bit of light travelling lounge, all soft sexy saxes and tinkly ebony-ivory and jazzy cymbals, and you know it all starts to feel right hunkydory again.

The odyssey is on, brother, the quest for Chief Sitting Bill.

Let it roll.

Pity about the bloody weather.

* * *

The first two hours go by Oscar Kilo. I stop at a service station for a slash and a splosh and then keep going for another two. As I'm sure you know, once you're out of the perimeter of the urbs you're surrounded on all sides by fields, all fenced off into neat squares and rectangles, and though I'm sure there's some sods who find this pretty, I just think it's bloody depressing, everything a dirty browny-green and plotted out and boring and treeless this way. And of course it's raining again. And cold. I mean cowcountry's all right to look at as long as it ain't stripped too bare and all farmed up and humanised, especially if what you are after is just some unpolluted air and free-growing vegetation, a little piss and quiet as it were, but along the motorways it's just bloody devastation. Try sticking this scrubland for more than a couple of hours sober and in this bloody weather — yeah, sodding right, give me the dangerous dirty ol' Smoke any fucking day.

And on and on it went, brother, no bloody end to it.

***

A yonks time later I cross over into Wales. At bloody last. It's been a long cruise, and by the end of the Ms I'm curlywhirly with the sheer John-Major-grey bloody boredom of it. The bonce is aching and the old windmill's itchy and flattened out something horrid. By the time I'm off the As I'm worn silly and about ready for kingdom bleeding come.

Ah, but wait, these rolling hills, these majestic crags and crannies, these sweeping slopes and windswept valleys, these bright luxuriant meadows full of turdy sheep and sheepshagging gumbies....

I'm here, brother, and no mistake.

***

Truth is there's plenty of sheep all right but the bit about the gumbies I just added for flavour as it were, cos technically speaking there's not a sodding soul in sight anywhere, not for bloody miles, so I'm driving through this deserted landscape and I'm starting to get the feeling it's like the day after the Apocalypse, brother, real doomsday-like and grim, and there's only yours truly left in the whole wide, wide world.

Well eventually I manage to find the campsite. It's on the grounds of a farm whose name I forget, situated near some lakes, with a what-you-might-call panoramic view of the Snowdon Horseshoes. On the edge of the campsite I find the farmhouse itself, a working one, adjoining which there is a converted bunkhouse with mattresses and pillows on the bunks and basic cooking facilities and very little else. I am back in the Middle Ages. I mean who in their right mind comes to a pisstank like this for their holidays? I ask you.

None of the bunks is occupied and I can take my pick. In fact the whole bloody place is deserted at this time of year and it's a wonder they bother to open for bizniss at all. A limp-haired redhead with a phiz like a blocked toilet, the farmer's daughter, is all smiles and very sweet but thick as elephant shit. She's wearing a pink jumper and huge jogpants stained and sagging at the arse like you see on nippers who've shat themselves. She shows me round the gaff while I ply her with questions. Can I get any grub at the farmhouse? Maybe, she'll have to ask. Can I get a hot shower? She's not sure if the hot water's on in the camp shower room, she'll have to check. I didn't bring a sleeping bag, can they provide sheets and a blanket? It's not customary, but she'll see what she can do. Do they have anyone camping on the site? Her cheeks is all dimples and she shakes her bonce again: oh, she's not really sure...

No, it's not shit dangling at the bottom of her jogpants, brother, it's her bloody brains.

Well, it's getting dark and I'm already half-frozen and three-quarters starved so I decide to wait till morning to go out in search of ol' Chief Sitting Bill. And a good thing, too, cos who knows what he would've done to me if he'd found me nosing about his tent in the middle of the night, eh?

The redhead (she tells me her name is Fiona and I have half a mind to oblige her in the carnal way, she looks so bored out-of-it) breaks all the house rules and brings me two sheets and a blanket smells like a herd of water buffalo have been having a gangbang under it. She also makes me a present of a tin of baked beans.

I shed tears of like joy, brother.

7

WALKABOUT

So next ay-em at the crack of sparrow's-fart I am up up up, stomach churning out a Beethoven symphony of gutty crackles from hunger, and sweet Fiona saves the day again with a pint of freshly squeezed moo-juice, fried eggs and hot buttered slices of burnt toast. Oh, and there's a Granny Smith for later. If I hadn't felt so stuffed after I would have porked her right there and then, I really would, out of sheer gratitude as it were.

She also tells me that yes, there is someone camping on the site, arrived a few days ago, he did, registered under the name of Crane. Not Kane, mind you, but Crane. No one else? No. Sure? Absolutely. Righty-right.

I don my wellybobs, grab my Swiss penknife, wrap up warm and set off in the direction she points to, over yonder a-ways, and become aware of a vague fear mixing with the breakfarts in my gut right sickly-like. I mean, who in their right mind wants to meet a psycho-case like this joker alone out in the middle of shit-where, eh brother? Not me.

* * *

Plod plod plod. Mud, wind, rain and muck. Fuck this. The site is bloody huge. I mean you could be lost in it for sodding years before anybody found your carcass rotting among the prickly furze and dry sheep droppings, you really could, bones picked clean by scavenger ladybirds. I climb hills, wade through puddles the size of ponds, twist an ankle, swallow a fly, climb a tree to get a better view, give up, start again, eat the apple, take a shit, get chased by a cow, fall over tired, and still no ruddy sign of anyone, brother, not a bloody trace, nix.

It's a long day's yomp, proper knackering, and by mid-afternoon I'm beginning to wilt and droop right sorry and wondering if I can ever find my way back to civilisation. I crest a hill, asking myself if I've climbed it before (these hills all being like clones of each other, brother), and rolling over half-dead with my tongue a yard long scraping the sand I zap on the far side wedged between two tall outcrops of rock the tip of a triangular frame. A tent, it looks like.

Right.

I scramble down and inch my way cautiously towards it, lamps peeled and ears pricked for any sign or sound of movement.

The tent's not big, fits two at most. It's obviously seen a lot of action but still looks weatherproof and sturdy: the ropes are tight and the material, a soiled army-green, is very thick like industrial canvas.

Two, three steps from it I cough loudly, to make my presence known to whoever might be inside, get no response, bring my face close to the front opening (zipped up, of course) and ask politely if there's anybody home.

Nothing. I wait, then try again.

Nothing.

I slide the zip up and poke my bonce inside the tent.

There's a sleeping bag to one side, nobody in it, a kerosene lamp, a box of long matches, a thermos flask, some cooking utensils, a big flat drum looks African maybe, a lot of itty feathers and coloured beads hanging from everything, a sort of hoola-hoop thingamajig with feathers and threads crisscrossed over it hanging from the top of the tent on a string, a rucksack oozing old togs, a pile of tatty books, and a small leather holdall, very battered, jaws open, showing an assortment of odd-looking clobber and personal like knick-knacks.

On the floor next to the sleeping bag there's a dog-eared paperback open face-down on the floor. The title is *Bury My Heart at Wounded Knee*. Well, I think, what's the hell's that supposed to mean? The cover shows a bloke wrapped in a blanket sat on a horse in the snow. I turn it over and I find this scrawled across the page in biro, hard enough to tear through the paper on the hat-trick of exclamation marks:

No forgiveness!!!

Well. Is this his stuff? Must be. And I'm thinking I'll have a nose round, when *snap!*

I never heard a thing, brother, not even in the dead silence of that wilderness, and I've got sharp bloody ears, sharp enough to hear the neighbours at it across the bloody corridor back home.

Quick as a flick my head's pulled out of the tent, my arm's twisted round behind me between my shoulder blades, my wrist's travelling up my bloody spine, my neck's bent all the way back to my arse, and I am completely fucking immobilised and in blinding bloody pain.

Then, very close to my ear, a throaty BBC newsreader's voice like whispers:

'You have exactly fifteen seconds to convince me of your innocence.'

8

KILLS-MANY

This is GBH, brother, real bloody agony. I grunt and squirm for a bit, trying to twist out of it, but it just gets worse, and then worser, so I grit the gnashers real hard and determined not to skrike like, but still my wrist just keeps creeping up my back, inch by bloody inch, and my head keeps bending back to join it, neck stretching like a ruddy elastic band ready to snap. The pain in my spine-bones is like nothing I've ever felt, proper horror film and a right bloody screamer.

'William... K-Kane...?' I manage to crunch out.

'My name's Otaktay,' says the voice, sounding right mighty and proud-like. 'The *wasichu*, the white men, call me William Kane.'

Eh?

And then the twisting cranks up a notch or ten. Soon there's coloured blobs flashing and stars like popping out all over the place behind my lamps just like in one of them cat-n-mouse cartoons and a deep sorry sick feeling begins to like gurgle and rumble fast as flies up my gutpipes. In this position, if I ralph I'll choke, brother, sure as shite and water's wet. So just before it reaches no-return puke-point I spew out, real loud, half-shouting, half-howling, the Holland Park bird's name, what-was-it Penny, and for dessert I even manage to blurt some shit-brained system D jackanory about how it was her what sent me, not even thinking like.

In a flash the grip on my wrist's a little less tight, the arm's coming down, limp as a wrinklie's cock, but down, and soon my head's sitting more or less back where it belongs on my bloody shoulders. The Kane bastard's still got me in a two-and-three-quarters nelson variation body-knot pigging arm-lock, of course, making sure I don't have no room to get a snook sideways at him, let alone even dream of trying to get free, but he ain't fucking killing me, at least, thank bloody Gog and his bloody angels.

'Why did she send you?' says he.

I'm spitting feathers here, in a right two-n-eight, so all I manage to come up with is a glocky:

'Er, um.'

Wrong bloody answer, mate.

He shoves my face hard to the ground now, pressing it right down into the muck so I can taste the worms in the back of my puke-box. My lovely new iPhone falls out of my pocket face-down into the goo and is bloody ruined. But you know what, that's still all right cos the pain in my back's down to a dull throb-throb so weak now I can at last think straight again.

'What I mean was she told me where to find you,' I say quickly, flobbing out gribbles of mud and grass. (I figure there's no point in running no extra risk by having a daft useless little clinton like this found out, right? Not with this psychotronic fucknut about ready to like snap my spine in two.)

The pressure on the side of my bonce eases a little. I take this as a sign of as it were encouragement.

'I have a message for you, is all,' I go on warbling, innocent-like.

Silence. Breathing. Then:

'Who from?'

'Frank McBride.'

And then he just lets me have it, brother, whack, right on my bent pigging nose, still aching like a nail in the jacobs from the Tank's bloody elbow.

9

SEPTIC

A chunk of time later we were sat in his tent, I remember, me nursing my bloodied sniffer that was proper broke now all crusty and caked in claret, and he sitting crosslegged in his scruffies, buckskins and jesuscreepers like some spaced-out sixties hippie folk-singer. And I just couldn't understand, brother. I mean, he wasn't really much to look at, was William Kane. A bit of an anticipointment, if you get my drift. It was hard to credit him as an active member of the so-called criminal underworld at all, let alone the ace mashman rat-catcher he'd been made out to be. Five ten or eleven maybe, not broad, not the least bit wrong-looking in any way... He didn't even look too insane apart from these stony nobody's-home Charles Manson zaps that kind of froze his lamps every now and then in mid-sentence, eyes gaping so wide it was like looking down into a tunnel and I had to stop myself from like tumbling down inside. But, other than that, brother, Ordinary's the word, with a capital O, really, just your plain pigging cornershop tea-and-biscuits everyday law-abiding citizen. He was even wearing a pair of old-NHS-issue style specs, you know, like he was the third bloody Ronnie. I mean, after all I'd heard, I was expecting a right nightmare, big and drooling, dents in the skull, Chelsea smile and whatnot, but he looked a hundred per cent straight-edge, Kane did, more like some molly primary school teacher, with a longish dial and droopy lamps, sensible yogi grown long and gone prematurely grey over the ears, regular features, some might say almost goodlooking in an old-fashioned sort of way, like one of them Cary Grant-style heartthrob matinee idols from way back in the Battle of Hastings, everything very standard and as it were norman. A shower, a shave and a change of gear and he could have been taking the class out for a game of fucking rounders. I mean it. He talked this softspoken Queen's English too, with hardly no Scouse in it at all that I could notice, only sometimes it went a bit funny, and I reckon what was going on was he was imitating those fake Indians you see in the old black-n-white John Wayne westerns, you know the type, made-up white actors munching their grammar and using their gropers to like illustrate stuff in Mickey-Mouse sign language no one could understand if they bloody tried, brother. I almost expected him to go 'How' at me, if you know what I mean. And at the time I thought: Well, if it's all a big phony I can't say, but he does seem to be able to turn it on and off at will. Maybe he doesn't know himself...

Well, so we're sat there, and he's making some puking hell-brew out of rotten twigs, mouldy leaves, slimy roots and dead spider-legs he takes out of a diddy leather pouch, shaking his bonce and smiling at me like we was on a bloody picnic, and there's a long long silence before finally he looks up and says:

'I had a vision three nights ago. In it I saw a white man, a little man. He came to me to ask for guidance, and justice for his people.'

I'm not even sure he's talking to me or to himself here, so I just like nod vaguely and try not to look him in the eye.

'And I saw a long journey along the Black Road—' (he shows this by sticking both arms out straight like he was directing traffic) '—a journey that took us far away into the land of the dead. Black Elk, a great Holy Man of my people, said: "From where the giant lives, to where you always face, the Red Road goes, the road of good, and on it shall our nation walk. But the Black Road goes from where the thunder begins to where the sun always shines, a fearful road, a road of troubles, and of war..."'

I sort of just suck my teeth and think: Blimey.

Then he says, 'I think you may be the white man I saw in my vision.'

'Me?' (Gulp.)

He hangs his bonce, staring into the flame of the kerosene lamp. 'But I will have to decline your offer,' he says after a bit, almost like he's sorry.

I say nothing to this for the time being, brother, I'm too busy worrying about how the Tank's going to take the news. Not well, I'm thinking, not well at all.

Then he says, 'Don't touch it.'

I look up.

'What?'

He hands me a dirty clay bowl of this stinking potion he's made, he says is some sort of natural painkiller. Painkiller my arse, it's fucking snake-poison.

'Drink this and stop playing with your nose. You'll only make it worse.'

Well. I feel my rosies heat up a bit at this, brother, seeing as how it was him what clumped me in the first place. 'Make it worse?' I says. 'How can I fucking make it worse? It's fucking broken, ain't it? And *you* fucking broke it.'

All of a sudden the hand holding the bowl stops in mid-movement, going very still and marble-like, and he gives me a look that's what you might call a Bombay-mix of expressions, very odd and quite frankly fucking spooky, I mean like someone's got hold of the remote for his brain and is changing channels inside his nut proper live-o. Christ, I think, a little worried now, wondering what he's going to do, the yampy sod, but suddenly the phiz goes blank again and he just clears his throat very polite-like and says to me:

'When you move, what is it that causes you to move? Have you ever thought about that? What causes a stone to fall to the ground when you drop it? And I'm not talking about gravity and that. If an arrow is shot from a bow what causes it to move through the air? What causes smoke to go upward? What causes water to flow in a river? What causes the clouds to move over the world?'

I go on staring.

'It's Taku Skanskan. He's the spirit who causes everything to move.'

Jesus wept, I'm thinking, on what planet did this spinny bit of pond-life germinate? But you know what, I keep the smile in place now, brother. No, no messing with this joker, no bloody way.

'Yeah, right. I didn't know that. Interesting.'

He nods.

I relax again. 'Now to get back to this offer, Mr Kane... Might I ask you to reconsider? You see, the Tank — Mr McBride, that is — he'll pay top dollar for this job. I mean we're talking telephone numbers here. Straight up. And he says you're the best man for it, number one seed, cock o' the walk. No one else comes even close.'

He just hums in a way that could mean absolutely anything.

'Says you can have whatever you want on it,' I go on. 'Just say the word and it's done.'

'I've already given you my answer.'

'Well, perhaps we can still work something out,' I says, scratching the nut.

'You're wasting your time,' he says.

But not to worry, brother. This is where my special negotiating skills come in. I now says to him:

'Of course it's not about the money. Maybe your vision was right, cos that's what it's really about, ain't it, Mr Kane? Justice, I mean. Cos this Captain America's a right ruddy Judas. Frank McBride was like a brother to him. That's why he tells me to come to you. Cos you understand. At first, the Tank says no, it can't be, he trusts this joe with his life. But the evidence, well, it's what you might call in-con-tro-vertible. Of course we're all stunned to stone and proper gobsmacked. I mean, who wouldn't be? How could the man whose life Frank's saved not once but twice do this to him? And for what? Greed. Money. I'm not saying the Tank is a saint, no, but there's principles involved he holds dearer—' and here I place a groper on my heaver for effeck, '—dearer than life.'

'My answer is still no,' he says, his phiz like a block of wood.

But I'm not giving up yet, brother. I go on painting the picture of the monster for a couple more minutes, putting like a fast spin on it, and end with:

'Pardon the pun, Mr Kane, but this Captain America's gone septic. We found out he's not only taking from his brothers, double-dealing and betraying his colleagues and closest friends, sending Russian goons to top Mr McBride after all he's done for him, but biznisswise he's gone off the deep end completely, I mean into the scummiest, filthiest bag in the whole bloody trade—' I slip in the pregnant pause here before the punchline to give it the full heavyweight clout, '—Human Trafficking.'

It's hit home, too, brother. I can see the Chief like stiffen.

'I am talking about sexual slavery and child prostitution here, Mr Kane, sort of stuff to make you sick in your stomach and ashamed to be human, it is, doing a lot of serious harm down there in Brazil. I mean, the feller's a fucking tumour.'

I knew I had a winning hand here, brother, but, as they say, I also knew I still had to play my cards right if I wanted to win the jackpot. So I poured in a few nasty horrid details about what I'd heard had happened to these poor girls (all true, too, far as I was aware) and instantly I knew Kane was hooked. It was just a question of reeling him in now.

'So you see how it is, Mr Kane.'

Next he asked me how the bizniss was run, both our end and Captain America's, top to bottom and all the ins-and-outs in-between, and how much more I knew about these dirty sidelines of the Captain's in Rio de Janeiro.

Of course I opened the tap wide and told him all. And don't think it was just a matter of like naming a few members and their turf neither, brother, cos it's a bloody complex machine and no mistake, like this mahusive beehive sort of network of people and different firms, each with their smaller units within, and all of them with very like subtle connections and shifting all the bloody time so you need a proper corporate management structure to hold it all in place and not lose the thread. You see, brother, the days of family run firms like the Krays are dead dead dead. Nowanights gaffers like the Tank run their firms like they might be the CEO of a big company, with tailormade bizniss software in their laptops and an understanding of economics that would give a City trader a month-long pigging migraine. It's all about minimising risk and maximising profit. And let me tell you, a lot of these so-called legit execs think they're the wrinkles on the dragon's arse could learn a thing or two from the likes of Mr Frank McBride. I mean, it's *huge* bizniss. A recent Home Office and Cabinet report has it that organised crime is costing the economy up to forty billion nicker, with the drugs racket taking the lion's share at around eighteen bill. Not bad eh, brother? But it's more than that even, cos no way do these johnnies have the whole picture, not nearly. The main thing you got to understand about crime in Britain is that the 11,000-mile coastline is so bloody easy to breach. Security weak-nesses at sea ports means smuggling drugs, guns and counterfeit goods into the country is easy as piss if you have a bit of wonga to spread round and the right like connections. And another thing: technically speaking, law enforcement in this country has very little to do with what you might call the public interest. You see, British bizzies on the whole work in like individual specialised cells, with only superficial communication and very occasional collaboration. For the most part they work at it like they might be little village clubs working to score points off each other. When it comes to dealing with crime at our more sophisticated level of organisation, the poor sods are completely out-of-their-depth stumped. Not to mention the fact that being into the big money means we always have at least one or two well placed contacts on the inside who provide us — sell us, is the word — all sorts of so-called secret police information about operations and upcoming stings. We get it all, brother, from codenames to dates, times and locations. And we're only one firm. There exist well over one thousand criminal networks in all in the UK, mostly home-grown despite the recent flood of crime syndicates from places like Eastern Europe and Southeast Asia. And like all big bizniss these days, all the top firms have connections overseas. These might be anything from actual full-scale operations to work-alone links. Now Captain America had built up a pretty strong base in Rio, with connections all over South America. His lieu-tenant, PR officer, counsellor, secretary and close amigo, a Puerto Rican called Benício Quintana, was a real old-school persuader. Him and his younger brother, Miguel, acted as Captain America's Praetorian guard like, and together the three of them had got us associates in Bogota, La Paz, Lima, Asuncion, you name it, some of them proper premier-leaguers, in all. Not even the Tank knew the full extent of it. And of course what Captain America did on the side, as long as it didn't present a risk to the firm — I mean as long as it wasn't coming into Britain and didn't interfere with the firm's intake in any way — was his own bloody bizniss.

So Kane listens carefully and just squints at me throughout my long expoclariplification, not moving, not even blinking any more. Is he interested? You bloody bet he is.

'And if you knew about what this man was doing, why didn't you do something about it sooner?' he asks.

'But that's just it. We didn't. We only found out a few days ago when the Tank puts one of his informers down there into action to bring up the dirt.'

Kane narrows his lamps at me, hangs his bonce a moment, bobs it back up, smiles (he's got these droopy puppydog eyes that crinkle up real friendly-like when he smiles, and for a second I ask myself again if maybe I've got him gauged wrong, after all, I mean this sod can't be the cold-blooded arseassin everyone goes on about, can he?), then says very gentle-like:

'I have to go outside now.'

And leaves the tent. He's carrying with him a hollow stick with like shells and feathers on and a bit of paint, all red and blue spots and yellow squiggles. What is it? A bloody rattle, that's what.

I poke my head out of the tent and watch him climb a few yards up the nearest hill. At the top he takes off his shirt and I see he's got this nut-job tattoo on his back, a big circle quartered into four colours, black, yellow, red and white, with four arrows pointing in to the centre making a cross. Then he spreads his arms and, believe it or not, brother, starts chanting and howling in some off-sounding foreign lingo that I know is not French nor Spanish, more the papa-oom-mow-mow made-up variety, if you know what I mean, shaking his bonce and stomping his plates like some loony-arsed wriggle-your-bits bloody boogaloo hip-hop shuffle. Great, I'm thinking, all he needs now is a builder, a cowboy and a motorcycle cop and he can start his own bloody gay band.

Then it starts to rain.

A sight, brother, a real fucking sight.

Next he starts repeating one phrase over and over, loud as fucking sirens, and I have to grin cos it sounds like he's saying 'Wanker Plonka, Wanker Plonka'. I mean — *what*?

Quarter of an hour later he's back, sogging wet. Dripping all over me and droopy-smiling again he taps me on the marylebone and says:

'The white man in my vision was a little man, a man of no account, a half man. But I saw him walking beside me in battle, and then he grew, bigger and bigger, until he became a whole man.'

I have no idea what he's on about. I tell him as much, so he says:

'OK. You can tell Frank McBride that I accept.'

I do a triple-take.

Well. Fuck me.

10

THE MEDICINE PIPE

So there I was, totally like out of my depth, brother, trying to work it all out and coming up 404 every time. Maybe it's a prank they're pulling on me, I thought. Maybe there's like hidden cameras. I mean, I couldn't believe this was for real, I just couldn't. Who in their right fucking mind would hire a complete goo-gah like this for anything? Listen to him, I said to myself, just listen to him. Ol' Terry was right about one thing at least, this dude didn't half talk a load of mad bollocks.

Cos you got to understand that it took me a mucho long time to see through Kane's insanity, to see it for what it was, brother, and reach beyond it to the man's essential like wisdom underneath. I mean, anybody listening to him for the first time would've felt the same. It was just too bloody freak-o-rama. Know what I mean?

It went, I remember, something like this.

'The trail is clear now,' he says.

'What?' I says, trying not to giggle.

'Take off your shoes. You must let your skin come into contact with the earth. You don't know how to pray to your ancestors so you can be guided back in the dark. You'll have to spend the night here with me.'

'Eh?'

'Did you ever try to talk to a sheep? I mean actually communicate with one? They look just like they're listening, they really do. There was a time, long, long ago, when human beings knew how to talk to animals...'

And just picture it, brother: it's late, late darkmans now, we're outside, sitting by a campfire he's made, probably illegal in these parts, and I'm still freezing my tits off. Around us in the dark little creature noises and rustlings break through the eerie silence, adding to the atmosphere of like cheap horror. The flames flicker in the wind and throw shadows dancing up and down across Kane's grim clock giving him a proper like sinister Karloff look. I watch as he pushes a plug of brown crap into a long pipe looks like it's straight out of *Dances With Wolves*, long and red with tiny feathers dangling from it, sparks up with a brand, takes a quick puff, then shoves it under my broken nose.

'Smoke,' he says.

'I got my own fags, thanks.'

'No. Smoke.'

He nods at the pipe, smiling, but it's not what you would like call a friendly smile. Very distant; cold as a polar bear's balls after a long swim.

I sniff at the thing suspicious-like.

'Cheers,' I says, 'but I never do Bob on the job, Mr Kane.'

'Bob?'

'You know, dope.'

He's sneering now.

'This is tobacco. Black Cavendish and red sumac bark and red willow bark.' He nods down at it again. 'Smoke. The smoke coming out of your mouth symbolises the truth being spoken, and creates a path for your prayers to reach the Great Spirit.'

'It does what?'

'*Smoke.*'

The voice has dropped a key and there's no trace of a smile anymore. The classic frenemy expression.

I take a drag on the pipe, hold the smoke in my rosies for a bit, wondering what it is, and inhale. Cough, cough. It's strong, stings the songbox a bit, this Indian baccy, but not half bad, brother, very rich and leafy in an interesting kind of curious sort of way.

Another spell of silence, then I say:

'If you don't mind my asking, Mr Kane, what was that little dance you done earlier?'

'I was asking Wakan Tanka for guidance.'

'Who?'

'The Great Spirit. When He wants us to do something he makes His wishes known in a vision. And He loves music. He likes the sound of the drum and the rattle.'

Is this for real? I mean it doesn't sound like he's pulling my leg.

'You really an Indian, then?' I ask. 'I mean, a Native American?'

But this time he just screws up his eyes at me a long long time, not saying nothing, so long in fact uneasy don't do justice to what I'm starting to feel, brother, not bloody nearly.

Suddenly the eyes crinkle up again and he gives this diddy like howl before saying:

'Can you see? What do you see?'

'Me?' I have a quick look-round. 'Well, I see you, don't I, Mr Kane...' I swing the bonce the other way. 'And this fire here, and the tent there...'

'No. What do you *see*?'

I give up, brother.

'Sorry, I don't think I understand what you mean.'

'*Look* at me. What did they tell you about me? And don't lie. I'll know if you're lying.'

'Well, they just said you was like the number one contract player.'

'And?'

'Well, and that you was a bit, you know... odd. I mean you being an American Indian and all. From Liverpool.'

He stares at me, then says with his jagger screwing up like he's tasted something right nasty, says:

'All wrong. Wrong, wrong, wrong. Well, I don't think I'm very easy to talk about. I've got a very irregular head. And I'm not anything you think I am anyway.' Another long pause. 'I believe in something the Lakota call Ni. A man's Ni is his life and it gives him strength. It's the Ni which keeps a man clean inside. And do you know what a man's Ni is made of?'

Now I don't think for a second he expects an answer from me, but I swear to Gog I'm dying to say something like 'chewing gum'.

He breathes in, breathes out, cocks his bonce at me, stretching the pause for suspense a little longer, and finally answers himself:

'Memory. All the memories that gather as it passes from life to life. It's what holds us to the earth and binds us to the Great Spirit. But dust-beings like you, you live in a world without memory.'

Gog, I've got blisters starting on me brain.

'I was like you once. A white man living in the dust world. I couldn't see things for what they were then, and a lot of bad things happened because of it.'

And suddenly, I'm not sure why, the atmosphere like turns proper creepy.

11

SIOUX SOUL DOWNLOAD

Turns out William Kane once had a daughter, brother, born out of wedlock when he was still thinking with his cock and dangles and too young to know better, but the mother (the Holland Park number's sister, if you remember) was a Bad Mistake, a real fire-and-brimstone grade-Z bitch with hairy warts on that made fatherhood, let alone husbanding, totally bloody impossible, with the stress on the *im*—. Now he had a real soft spot for the kid, it seems, and done what he could to get her away from the Gorgon's dirty clutches, but the British legal system wouldn't hear of it, not no way, the mother always like coming first in a child custody battle as far as they're concerned, as any fool knows. So what happened was the little daughter, what with this dooly disturbed dysfunctional background to skew things, grew into a bit of a rebel without a cause, and was barely of age when she up and done an Amy Winehouse out of rehab after getting hooked on the heavy-heavy stuff, running off in the night to get webbed up with some crackhead boyfriend from Noo Yoik and his group of flat-arse hell bikers. It did not end well, brother, not well at all. Cos you see, what's the boyfriend do but take her away to the ol' Yoo Ess of Ay, North or was it South Dakota, one of those, where the gang has a dirty little drug biz going, and together they got into a lot of trouble they didn't know how to get out of again. That's right. At first it wasn't too bad, but, things being what they are, and they being such a bunch of babyshambles with no experience and no talent for bizniss, prostitution soon starts to figure among their activities cos they badly need the extra, and it's not long before Kane's baby gets roped in to help out on that front as well as with the actual peddling. Even bigger problem is, the gang leaders all being brain-dead from consuming their own sub-quality produce, strung out on dirty crack and meth and oxi and other rough junk, they make a right balls-up of it all and things soon take a fast downward tumble, with the result that Kane's daughter ends belly-up and trotters-in-the-air with two neat bullet holes in her canister. Oh, it's an ugly world, brother. Only nineteen years old, she was. Local heavies they was dealing for. Old story. Someone didn't pay up when they should have. Of course the boyfriend and his mates peg it before the blood's dry on the girl's body. Police do nothing about it, glad to see another low-life go six under. So Kane, just returned from Iraq and already with more than his fair share of loose screws clattering about in his pan, goes looking for her and loses what little's left of his marbles when they give him the news of her death. He flies across the pond, brother, wild as anything, goes on a fucking rampage and takes the lot down, hardcase dealers, bikers, boyfriend and all. Wipeout, it is. Singlehanded, too. And with what you might call triple x-treme violence. I guess what he had is what you might call a natural knack for killing, brother. Got a right taste for it, too, to judge by what come later. But the memory of his little girl was like a festering wound for ever after, always hurting, never healing. Poor bugger. I mean, this is one explanation for what happened to him, but of course however much information and insight you bring into trying to understand someone's life, they always stay, you know, somehow unknowable, don't they, brother? There's just too much going on.

Well, anyway, so it was after this daughter got done in, and he was going after everyone he thought was to blame — which from what I heard was a lot of bloody people — that he became an Oglala Sioux. That's what he said. It was like this: he'd tracked down the bloke who had actually pulled the trigger on her, and was chasing him down one of them dobbing straight long American highways that go on for ever through the middle of bumfuck, when the bloke tries a dodgy manoeuvre and crashes head-on into this ickle banged-up old jalopy coming the other way. The bloke's car goes up in a ball of flame real doomsday and he's instant rat-meat, but there's two people in the other car Kane manages to drag out of the wreck. One survives, but the other, this wrinkly old Indian, is dying right there in Kane's arms. Only the second before he snuffs it, guess what? Yeah, his spirit or was it his knee or something passed into Kane, all of it, complete, like it might be files on a memory stick copied from one poota to another, zippity-zip.

(And I think: hang on, ain't this that Jim Morrison story?)

Well, the fire's very low now and I can hardly see him in the dark, only his voice coming through, low and gravelly, filling the night.

'His name,' he says, meaning the old Indian, 'was Chankoowashtay, which means Good Road. He was a Holy Man, a spiritual leader and a Yuwipi medicine man from the Pine Ridge Indian Reservation. He was a descendant of the great Black Elk. His white name was Joseph. Old Joe. His family called him Pop. But his sacred and spirit names only I know, because now they are mine.'

Am I supposed to say something? I sort of nod and play with my fingers. For a while there's nothing but the sound of the crickets chirping in the night.

'Now we are one spirit,' Kane says after a long time, very solemn-like. 'Now his Sicun is mine. The entire memory of the Lakotas. But a man with a new Sicun must learn the songs that belong to it. Sicun is similar to what you would call spirit, or soul. But sometimes a Sicun is wakan. Anything may be wakan if a wakan spirit goes into it. Thus a madman is wakan because the bad spirit has gone into him.'

And now I'm thinking: then you're fucking wakan, mate, the wakanest wakan bloody ever.

'Again, if a person does something that can't be understood, that is also wakan. Anything that deprives a man of his sanity is wakan. That's what happened to me. The old man's Sicun was wakan.'

'Oh, right,' I say, not even trying to understand anymore.

Then he leans in, the fire lighting up his phiz, and zaps me real hard. After a bit he raises his two prongs to point at me.

'You've signed away your soul, little white man. It belongs to the bad spirits now. The drugs you sell for a living are wakan-sica. Unwholesome, evil. There are spirits in many plants that can take us into the spirit world, but we must be prepared, otherwise they possess us, and poison the mind. They are sacraments, not toys for wayward, spoilt children to play with. Treat them lightly and you bring only evil. Yes, you and Frank McBride and the rest are all wakan-sica. And I'll tell you something else.' He slaps one hand hard against the other. 'Maka, the earth, has grown tired of you. And Wi, the Sun, is fed up with you as well.'

I kind of stiffen at this, brother, and try to give nothing away in my expression that might like antagonise or offend him in any way, like one of them bomb disposal experts afraid any little jolt might set something off disastrous-like, cos I know how nutters like him can just go off at the least little thing.

He says finally:

'You move in a world of the eyes only—' with the same two prongs he's been pointing at me he mimes like beams coming out of his lamps now, '—greedy for the world, even though to you it's all dead. But in reality everything is alive, animals, water, earth and sky and everything that comes from them, but you don't see this. You don't know where the centre of things lies. This world you live in is a dark place, and it's all in the present, a now that never goes anywhere. You're blown about like dust in a strong wind, with no past and no future. Because it's memory that makes us human. But you're only meat, walking over the earth for a short time, leaving a wake of filth and ruin. And although you don't know it, all this time you're here you're really just waiting to die.'

Christ. I mean he's not physically threatening as he's saying all this, which is a bloody relief, glory be to Gog, but remembering Terry's story about the restaurant I'm thinking who knows what he might like do in a sudden fit of frenzy, brother, gibbering on like this about what a piece of dirt I am and how the world's sick of me and how I'm just waiting to snuff it. The idea that I will have to spend the night sausaged in a tent with this fucking loony-tune begins to sound like a very bad fucking joke on me and no two bloody ways about it.

I nod a little here, like agreeing, but very sheepish in case the Knight Who Says Ni thinks I'm taking the mick.

He's still facing me full on, brother, with a zap that sort of drills into me, like he is expecting some transformation to take place in me because of what he's just said, but I just go:

'What? I didn't say anything.'

Kane's dial goes a bit teddybear at this, the lamps come down, the droopy corners crinkle up like before. Finally, he shakes his bonce.

'The universe is older than anyone can imagine,' he says. 'The wakan live on, and they're all around us, always, good and bad.' He shakes his bonce again. 'But I don't expect someone like you to understand.'

Now you're talking, mush.

He's silent for a while, looking up at the huge sky. It's totally black. Even the really hardcore bats have gone to fucking sleep. Suddenly he turns to me again and in a very changed, chumly, almost normal sort of warble asks:

'Brazil, eh? I hear Rio's a pretty rough spot.'

I relax, and try to return the smile. 'Yeah,' I says, chumly back, 'but then so are a lot of other places nowadays.'

He squints at me. 'Have you heard the one about the Brazilian footballer who comes to play for Liverpool?'

I go no with my bonce.

'Liverpool's newest big-name signing, right, a Brazilian international, has just scored on his debut for the club and immediately after the match he phones his Mum:

"Hello Mum."

"Hello dear, how did the match go?"

"You didn't watch it? It went great. I scored in front of the Kop and we won 3-1."

"That's wonderful. But I'm afraid things here at home aren't so good."

"Why, what's happened?

"Well, this morning the neighbour got hit by a stray bullet on her doorstep and died on the way to hospital. Our car was set ablaze by a mob of drug-crazed thugs who then broke into our house and battered your brother to a pulp. They shot your father in the kneecaps, so he can't walk anymore, and then raped your sister before moving on to the dog."

"Jesus, that's terrible..."

"I know. Why couldn't you have left us in Rio instead of bringing us to Liverpool with you?"'

He throws his head back and has a good hard chuckle at this.

Ask me if I larfed, brother.

***

He finally clams up after that, thank Gog. Needless to say I sleep badly, but then there ain't much of the night left anyway.

It's very early next morning and still bloody brass monkeys when he starts packing his gear. For breakfarts he gives me a stick of cured beef jerky looks like the Pharaoh Tuten-wotsisname's 3000-year-old tadger. Tastes like it, in all.

And not another word is spoke, brother, not a sound, till after about an hour plodding through mother bleeding nature mad Kane pulls up short, squints at me crazy-like over his shoulder and, out of the blue, says:

'When I'm done with Clay Tobczyk, not even the worms will want to have anything to do with him.' Then he takes a couple more steps and pulls up again, only this time he turns his whole body round towards me. 'If you speak of me to anyone, how you found me, or why, or where, I'll kill you as well.'

And you know what, I could see he meant it, brother, and it just sort of gave me a funny feeling, not pleasant, like tiny creepies crawling over my nutmegs with their hairy little legs.

1 2

TWOSOMES

Well, brother, ol' Kane was what you might call a proper hard-case amateur and the wonga wasn't supposed to come into it, like I said, but it fucking well did for this assignment, by the bloody cartload. And I should know: it was me handed him the briefcase stuffed full of used high-denomination Queen's heads. And that was just for starters. The rest was coming later in like instalments, with a big dollop at the end when the job was over and diddly-done. I also booked his BA flight out to Rio, got him a nice hotel room for the first night and saw to one or two other necessities he had talked over privately with the Tank at their meet in London. And that, I thought, was that as far as I was concerned.

But what did I know, eh brother? I should have suspected something wasn't quite right when the Tank told me to book not one seat on the economy class ('keep it discreet, Dodger'), but two.

'Two, Frank?'

'Yes, Dodger, two. Like the number of times I've had to tell you.'

'Right, Frank.'

At first I think it's for Kane's extra luggage or something, maybe his tent and shit.

'And two rooms, same floor, but make sure they're not too close to each other.'

So it dawns on me.

'It's all right, Dodger,' says he. 'If it's winter here, that means it's summer over there. Bit of sun'll do you good. You look like you was made of yogurt, son.'

Well excuse me while I fall down larfing. Can you fucking believe it, the Tank's somehow convinced Kane that my presence on the job will be what you might call a 'major plus', cos clever crafty me I can be downright resourceful in a tight spot, can't I, he said, and I don't half know a lot of useful griff about Captain America, just the sort of information that can come in mucho handy on a manhunt. Considering Kane's reputation, I wouldn't be too surprised if Frank also wants me along as bloody damage control.

Well, I'm thinking, you can take your useful information and ram it up your sticky khyber, Frank you fat cunt. And you know I get in such a state when I realise I'm tagging along whether I want to or not that I go and get proper euaned that night, I mean bat-bloody-blind, brother, which is something I never do, and end up having to sleep it off on Derek's dirty carpet curled up next to his mingy mog. I can't even open my jagger to speak next morning, and barely manage to troll in a straight bloody line till late in the evening, I'm that hungover.

And in the few odd flashes of lucidity throughtout the night all I think about is how can I get out of this one, what excuse can I make? But the answer just never bloody comes, brother.

* * *

Now Vicky – that's the doris, FYI – ain't too happz when I come in next pee-em with a killing headache, dead-dog breath and a bad case of the brewers' droop. No bollocking, mind, she knows better than that, but near as bad, brother, cos she don't half know how to twist it in when she wants to torture your like overloaded conscience. I open the door and there she is, zapping me out of the steady bright lamps she has, honey-yellow and glowing like live coals, not saying a bloody word. I tell you, she could make you feel like the mummy's boy caught red-handed in the khazi doing the five-knuckle shuffle, could Vicky. She was a fit little thing, not athletic eggzakly but with the meat packed on solid in all the right places (plus she'd had a boob-job the year before what had left her a right juggernaut), and she had this fidgety way of moving or even just standing let you know at a glance she was a live one, with a boiling mass of stored-up energy inside her – sexual, most of it – impatient for release and always on the verge, if you get my drift. And, brother, didn't she know it. She could control this energy to broadcast messages with like her lamps or the tone of her warble, invisible beams they were, waves, not always of the pleasant variety neither, very often downright fucking nasty and poisonous, as a matter of fact, work on you like a bloody hex. This was especially effective against me back then cos she knew things about me no one else did, and used this knowledge to grub for all sorts of fears and regrets I had lurking in those really deep, dark smelly nooks of as it might be my soul or whatever you like to call it, the ghost in the machine, then bring the foul bloody things up out into the open for all to see, dangling them before me till I was sick and weak and about ready to fucking break down in tears. And I swear, she could do this with just a look or a word. Some fucking piece of work, eh brother? But I did like her. — Love? Oh, I don't know. Yeah, maybe that even, a little, whatever it is. We talked about marriage once, early on. I told her she was too fucking scary to be anyone's wife. She said she'd never marry me cos I was already Frank the Tank's bitch. Oh yeah, real cute. Not that this was ever too much of a problem for her, mind you, not even at the start. If anything, she thought going out with someone in the trade was a right turn on and no mistake. We met at a carboot sale – she was doing the selling, me the buying, and by the end of the day she'd squeezed upwards of a hundred nicker off me – and we went out two or three evenings before I kind of let on my line of work was not eggzakly on this side of law and order. She seemed to take the idea as a bit of a joke, initially, then went a bit quiet when she saw I was serious. But the closer we tangled and the older I aged and the deeper I got in with the Tank's outfit the more Vicky got used to the dirt and its attendant dangers; said it excited her, in fact. Understandable, I suppose. Of course she knew I was afraid something was going to happen to me, afraid that someday my luck was going to run out, but she played it down.

But, brother, the truth was to me it really looked like it had run out now. My luck, I mean.

Well, so there I was, red-eyed and staggering, and before I'd even opened my gummed-up jagger to explain, Vicky knew straight away something was not right.

Long silence. Then, very dry:

'Where were you, Dodger? I was worried sick.'

'Not as worried as I was. And not half as bloody sick.'

'Why didn't you call?'

'I was too pissed.'

Her most efficient method of attack was not anger, brother, it was a sort of superior contempt. So she laid it on me thick now, this secret weapon of hers, and pretty soon I started feeling like the cat's dinner the drunk trod on after it'd been puked up the night before. I told her where I'd been and who with; she sneered. I told her again, and this time explained why, only leaving out the nitty gritty particulars she didn't like need to know. She had a pretty good idea, anyway, you can bet on it.

'So you see,' I says, 'I have to go to Brazil with this bloke the Tank's hired to take care of some bizniss over there. It's a responsibility, and extra money and all that, but I dunno...'

The words are hardly out of my jagger before Vicky's contempt does a lightning Harry Potter evanesco spell and, hello, in its place is a big Cheshire-Cat grin of like gloppy joy. Wait, is that right? Joy? Yes, that's what it is, all right.

Well, brother, just fancy that. Talk about go-getting.

Then she shrugged and told me not to worry, after all it was a job like any other job and this was only for the time being anyway, just till I had enough to start a firm of my own, then instead of doing I'd be the one sitting back giving all the orders and counting the money. (And at this last word her warble gushes all like orgasmic, brother.) But I tell her I'm not sure about this one, that I'm considering just flat out refusing to go, no matter what McBride says, and to be honest I've even been having thoughts of quitting the firm altogether. Serious thoughts.

And then of course it comes, just like I'd expected: the little cobra-shake of the bonce, the soft mothersome whisper, the let's-be-practical-about-this cool, the oh-so-wise words of down-to-bizniss advice:

'But sweetheart,' she honeys. 'You can't. You're mad if you leave now. I mean, what's Mr McBride going to do if you quit on him now? He won't just sit back and let you go, will he? And then what? What about our plans? Anyway, where are you going to find something better?'

'I don't know, Vic. Maybe I could like take a course in something. Bizniss-related.'

She makes a noise like someone unblocking a bunged-up drain.

For a second, in my like wild despair, I even think of asking her to marry me, brother, to use that as an excuse to get off the assignment. But I can't, I just can't. I'm not ready for that kind of seachange, not nearly. I'm too young, for a start, and then the thought of being shackled to Vicky for life... I don't know. I'm not that desperate.

I remember looking at her then, real up-close microscope scrutiny like, taking each bit of her phiz separate — the pink downy ears that stuck out when her yogi was pulled back like it was now, the nose that was a bit too lumpy at the tip, the tiny kiddy teeth set too wide apart in her chewing-gums, the odd zit-spot round her pouty jagger, shiny red with a yellow eye, and last night's smudged mascara, you know — and I tried, I really tried, to see her as ugly, brother, cos this money-grab overdrive and like marvin ambition didn't half put a stink on things, I mean a Big Stink, it was absolutely the worst thing about her, like a hunger she couldn't control, a big bad case of the gimme-gimme.

So I tried to explain the situation, pointing out the risks, to make her understand my fears, but you know it all turned sour in my throat.

She'd got her hands on my head now, working the hair.

'Come on, sweetheart. I honestly don't know why you're acting like this. It's a chance for promotion, right? Give the bloody orders instead of taking them for a change. And more money. Maybe enough for that house we talked about. I mean, it's what you've always wanted, ain't it? And you're good at what you do. I mean, it's not like you was going to war, is it now?'

My bonce sinks down between my knees.

'I suppose not,' I mumble. 'But it can get bloody hairy on these jobs.'

The hands slide down to my neck, then my shoulders.

'Look at me. You'll be fine. You're a businessman, Dodger, you're not going to get involved in any of the nasty stuff, are you? You just go along and make sure things run smoothly. And when you get back, we can go on a trip of our own, just you and me.' Smiling again, she wobbles her funbags in my face. 'You, me, and your two friends here, tweedledum and tweedledee.'

Well, what can you do, eh? I mean, give an inch you might as well give a fucking mile, know what I mean?

Anyway, she's right. I'm a bloody professional, I am.

PART TWO

There is a road in the hearts of all of us, hidden and sel-
dom travelled, which leads to an unkown, secret place.
Chief Standing Bear of the Oglala Sioux (1868-1939)

13

SIDEKICK RIDING SHOTGUN

S o there I am a week later, sat on the aisle seat of the Boeing 777-200, flight BA 249, feeling low as a worm's tits and twice as shrivelled with my gob hanging open like a dead guppy still not really believing this is bloody happening to me. I mean, a trip to Rio sounds nice enough if you're going for jollies, but what I was wondering as I waited there staring out the window was what the hell was I expected to do on a pigging contract job with mondo bizarro Chief Sitting Bill Kane, flipping hold his pipe and rattle for him while he lopped Captain America's head off with a ruddy tomahawk, was that it?

Oh, and you know what? The yampy bastard wasn't even there.

Picture it, brother: Nearly time for take-off. I glance at the empty seat beside me and check my watch for like the thirtieth time in five minutes. A kid of about four in the seat in front pokes his face in the gap, sticks his tongue out and gives me the finger when his mum isn't looking. Cute. Through the plastic square of the window Heathrow is looking grey and depressed, a lot like me, but I don't see no more buses bringing any passengers. And like some divvy git I keep repeating to myself: Where in Gog's bloody name is he? We'll be taking off in a moment. Why hasn't he come? Just thinking about what the Tank's going to say is giving me the bloody giddywillies, cos he don't care: it's your job it's your bloody responsibility, so it's you got to pay the price. I spit out another bit of nail and look down at my red raw fingertips. Soon I won't have any nails bloody left to chew and I'll have to start on the furniture.

Some fuss over luggage starts up a couple of seats in front of me. Some Brazilians I seen back at the airport in the long slow check-in queue with fridge-sized suitcases arguing over the excess baggage charge are now having difficulty fitting their equally collossal packed-to-bursting hand luggage into the tiny overhead compartments provided by Mr Boeing and co. The loud Brazilians are not taking kindly to being told the bags can't go between their feet under the seats. The trolley dolly responsible for my stretch of the aisle, with more paint on her mug than a 70s porn star and reeking of the strong French perfume these flight birds get at half price, starts shoving and punching the Brazilians' bags into the tight little spaces with a sort of contained fury that's a sight to behold, squeezing and pushing till they all bloody well fit in, then starts telling people off left right and centre in that politely rude way they have, pushing seatbacks up and checking numbers on boarding passes, huffing and rolling her eyes to make sure she lets everyone on the plane know she's not the sort who's going to be taking any sort of shit from anybody. When she's done and brushes past I ask her how much longer before take-off but she just like huffs again and pretends not to hear, the solid bitch, and clops away down the aisle in her heels wriggling her chubby arse in everyone's face.

There's coloured lights winking and bells pinging like mad as people try to call her back for it might be blankets or a glass of water or another set of earphones or just to find out what the little button's for. There's a few crackles from the speakers like someone's going to make an announcement but it never comes.

The little hand on my watch creeps round and round and still no bloody sign of Kane.

Then I catch sight of the attendant coming back, showing one last passenger along the aisle to his seat, and for a second I think 'finally', but only for a second, cos then I realise it's not him. I'm still watching them come towards me, and look up when they stop beside me and she helps this bloke fit his bag into the overhead compartment above my seat, but it still takes me a good fifteen seconds to tune in to the fact that *it is* him, brother, cos he looks so totally different from when I seen him last. He's got a 1940s haircut and he's shaved clean, exposing a comicbook hero chin. He's wearing a pair of old-fashioned-turned-trendy-again thick-framed designer glasses like architects wear and he's got one of those fake suntans look a bit orangey round the edges. Close up he smells like a bleeding beauty parlour and I see there's gel or mousse or wax or something on his yogi plastered on right thick like it was cement. He's kitted out in a natty grey suit of dittoes with a black shirt open at the collar makes him appear the Italian or it might be the Spanish biznissman like, all mucho snazzy and GQ so even the attendant is smiling at him and being like real polite for a change.

I tuck my legs in and he slips in beside me, not glancing in my direction or acknowledging me in any way, thanking the attendant only. When she moves off I tap my watch conspicuous-like, turn to him and say:

'Fashionably late? Cut it a bit close there, didn't you?'

He just slides his lamps slowly towards me, without actually turning his bonce.

'How's your nose?' he says in his quiet plummy voice.

Well, what a piece of fucking work, eh brother?

***

And we take off. I bloody hate this part. A couple of gut-rumbles on and we're into thick white cloud, nothing visible below anymore, and the aircraft levels out.

While the screens play a slicked-up pantomime of the safety instructions for us normal passengers mad Kane keeps up this like whispered mumbling to himself with his lamps shut like he's praying. Asking Willie Wonka Wanker Plonka to hold the plane up in the sky, I'm guessing.

We say practically nothing to each other the entire flight. I'd already noticed back that night in Wales how he was prone to these bizarre long stretches of like complete silence and total immobility, like one of them alligators you see in the zoo it might be. He does this frozen reptile thing for a about an hour, brother, then starts reading some bloody book about would-you-believe-it South American amphibians with glossy colour photographs, but even then his movements are kept down to a minimum. I just ignore him and play a daft shooting game on my even newer brand new iPhone for a bit. Then, after a quick meal of grey paper sangwidges and yellow plastic pudding, I curl up as best I can to take a nap.

I wake up with him poking my shoulder.

'I brought this for you,' says he.

I unglue my eyelids.

'What?'

'Here.'

He hands me a little blue-and-white paperback, small and thick. I look down and squint at the title. It's the 'New Pocketsize Edition' of the 'Harlequin Language Series Portuguese Phrasebook and Dictionary', complete with 'Pronunciation Guide'. On a yellow stripe placed diagonally across the bottom righthand corner it claims in bold ketchup lettering that it is 'Ideal for Travellers'. Oh goody-goody.

'You should get some practice in before we land,' he says.

'Yeah,' I say, 'good idea,' sounding like I mean it. 'And what about you?'

'I can get by on my Spanish.'

I do a slow nod. 'Right, right...'

And as I say this, brother, I'm thinking how his eyes look fucking weird behind those designer lenses.

***

A bit later on we get talking a bit, nothing serious, stuff like football and what's Brazilian food like, when, without really thinking, I ask:

'What was Iraq like?'

He zaps razors at me.

'I don't speak of that war. Behind all the lies about liberating a people, building a nation and bestowing democracy was a very true greed and a real inefficiency that left over 100,000 civilians dead and a country in ruins. All in all, a shameful, criminal disaster. I still get nightmares. But apart from that I loved every minute. And that's all there is to know.'

He looks away then, and clams up for the rest of the trip.

Jee-zus.

14

HORLICKS

Eight hours, three Soviet greige uniform conveyor belt meals, two crapshite films and a lot of queuing for the khazi and bloody jiffling and squirming in my seat later, our captain's velveteen voice proudly announces that we are at last approaching Rio de Janeiro, adding as a like bonus to this welcome bit of news a lot of unasked-for factoids regarding our current speed and altitude — as if anyone gave a flying fuck — such as the expected time of our arrival, the temperature both in degrees Celsius and Fahrenheit, the airport's full name, details of the arrival procedure, and one or two other things I completely forget, all repeated in two or is it three different languages.

There's a quick riff of pings and the passenger instructions for landing light up on our screens. I look outside over Kane's shoulder and past the bouffant candyfloss hairdo of the Brazilian beast in the window-seat next to him (it may be my nose what's broken, brother, but it's her what's spent the entire flight snoring like a bloody waterhog in heat), expecting to catch a glimpse of the scenery I seen in the glossy travel brochures back in London: a shimmering blue ocean, little V-shaped wakes of tiny sailboats glinting far far below, maybe, a long curved beach, white sands packed tight with tanned curvy tot wearing nothing but dental floss, and of course the famous knob-shaped hills, especially the one with the huge white Christ doing his Pilates exercises on top.

But there's none of this, brother, zip, nix, nada, not through my bloody window there ain't. What I zap instead is a dull smudge of shit-brown and scrubby green ground reminds me of the wasteland round the Ms back home, all flat and boring as blisters, with no one about anywhere, the only sign of life being like some micro grebby grotty-looking buildings scattered about, and then some as it might be lakes with water the colour of last week's coagulated tea.

Hang on, I'm thinking, where's the tropical paradise we was promised? I've been swindled.

My eardrums get started on the pop-goes-the-weasel routine, which means the cabin pressure's changing, which means we're going down. About bloody time, too. I go into my breath-holding seat-clutching performance for the landing, but not before clocking how Kane has his lamps shut and is doing the crazy mumbly whispering trick again, so I guess perhaps I was right about it being like some sort of Indian prayer.

It's answered, too, thank Gog, cos we arrive in one piece.

***

Coming out of the plane it's like stepping into a plastic bag in a wet sauna at noon on a hot day in June, brother, it's that warm and airless and muggy. No sun, mind you, which is another bloody let-down (I'm so radged you'd think I'd packed me bloody bucket and spade), but close as clingfilm and instantly I start lathering from every gaping bloody pore, sweat dripping off my chin, soaking my armpits. I'm sweating in places I never even knew I had, brother. My rigging's sagging and sticking to my skin and even my underkeks are glued to my nutmegs, they're that hot and oily.

As we board the bus taking us across the airfield to the arrival lounge I check Kane to see how he's taking it. And guess what. Not so much as a drop on him, not anywhere. I mean, not even his architect glasses is steamed up. I'm telling you, brother, this geezer's not of this bleeding world. I wouldn't be surprised if he glows in the dark.

The luggage takes bloody eons to come onto the carousel. Then a monster queue through customs and passport control.

But finally we're out. Ah. Brazil. Wow.

Getting a taxi is easy enough, but one deek at the gringos — especially the super smooth orange-skinned biznissman here beside me — and the grinning drivers all get the urge to like wildly overcharge. Well let them, I say. It's the Tank's bloody money and I'm going to let it run like ruddy rainwater through my fingers. Teach the fat turd a lesson.

Throughout the taxi ride we stick to the shtum routine we kept on the flight. Suits me. Our driver's a bloody cliché: thinks he's Ayrton Senna, swerving and weaving the cab at near a hundred miles per hour round bends and va-voom over pavements and between other motors like it was an ambulance and he was like rushing us not to our hotel but to bloody hospital. I check out Rio whizzing past. Bursting bright colours that actually hurt my lamps a bit at first, yet oddly everything strangely grainy like in a film shot in poor lighting conditions. Then I remember the kewl new Ray-Bans I bought for the trip and slip them on. They make everything go a sort of washed out Wimbledon green. The radio's pumping out electronic soul samba full blast and I'm like getting right into it. It's La Vida Loca, brother, and then some. Suddenly we plunge into a major jam and the vicious driver has no choice but to tread on the brakes. The heat's bloody volcanic now, even the glass on the windows is sweating (but not Kane). Ayrton Senna gets impatient, bouncing in his seat to the rhythm of the music, drumming his prongs on the wheel, honking and swearing in Portuguese with his bonce hanging out the window. But it's no use, there's just too much damn traffic. And noise, brother, such noise like you never heard.

Throughout all this Kane's gone alligator again. I don't even think he's breathing, brother, he's that still.

Well, when we arrive the Hotel Saraiva's all right, nothing spectacular, midrange gaff, white front, not big, not small, but clean, pretty bird at reception, nice smile and a perky pair of tits, and at least the view from my bedroom window is more bloody like it: couple of roads away between the buildings there's a glimpse of Copacabana beach, just. Kane's buggered off to his room, so after a change of togs and a bite I decide to go for a stroll along the seafront, a right milky bar in my muscle-vest and kneebangers. The sun's come out on the wide warm bright avenue with the wavy black-n-white crazy paving, and everywhere there's people, barefoot or in flipflops, drinking the local swillage and coconut water and polychrome fruit cocktails at the hut-shaped beachside kiosk bars, playing foot-volleyball on the hot sand, riding bikes, jogging, having what's known in the girlie mags as a Good Time. I manage to order a can of icy Brahma and head down with it to the water's edge. The sea looks a bit on the rough side here, with huge crashing waves that eat up at least two bathers while I watch. There's cheap hawkers moving up and down the beach relentlessly flogging everything from sun cream to football shirts, bullying tourists into parting with their hard-earned, and a couple give me a hard time till I tell them to fuck off in international sign language. But you can't be sour long in a place like this, brother, cos you are after all being treated to the sight of the Brazilian gals in their thread-thin thongs. They make Shakira look like Worzel Gummidge on a bad-hair day, it's totally mad, I mean with like just a sideways look or a shake of their shanks some of these birds can send a charge of a thousand-plus volts right zap through your crown jewels that'll curl your netherhairs to a dry bloody crisp, they're that fit and tidy, and when I think back in like contrast to flab drab Fiona the sloppy farmer's daughter I swear I don't know whether to larf, barf or bloody cry. Even Vicky looks a bit lettucy by comparison, brother, no joke.

But I've been away almost an hour and there's slavework to be done. I return to the hotel and take the lift up to our floor. Kane's room is down the other end of the corridor from mine. After a slow cool shower and a quick sam-up I grab the envelope I have for him and go knock on his door.

He's a long time answering it.

'Yes?'

'It's me.'

The door swings open.

He's standing there in his striped boxer thunderbags and a bead necklace and nothing else, panting like he's just been running, and there's definitely sweat coming out of him now. He's human, all right. Behind him the room's a mirror image of my own and even the crappy sunset paintings just very simple like variations of the ones I got, only his are all hanging crooked.

'Can I come in?'

He steps aside for me. I take a couple of strides past him and hear a sound like a cross between a grunt, a moan and a snuffle coming from the part of the bedroom hidden by the projection of the wall. I poke my head round to see what's making it and what I clock makes me sick to my bloody newingtons, brother, cos there, up against the far albert, is a tiny middle-aged feller in a shapeless crumpled suit and ugly tie, only I'm staring not at his phiz but at his toeshells cos he's bloody hanging upsidedown, ain't he, strung up by a rope round his plates slung over a hammock hook. I mean, *what?*

I step nearer. He looks like puke warmed up, half-dead and totally terrified. His gropers are tied behind his back and the old vein-gravy's running rivers from his puffed-up hooter that's on sideways and from one of his ears (the other one still has the twisted leg of a pair of cracked specs hanging from it). There's more claret oozing from his smashed swollen trap in a mess all over his dial and dripping into his blinking lamps and blotched all down his shirtfront like a world map and dribbling onto the nice tiled hotel floor in a big sticky puddle of deep dark red gore. And you know right away all these ultra-horrorlogical visions of me lying knee-deep in cockroaches in a jam-packed Brazilian prison start to like popcorn in the brainpan, crackle crackle, a British billion to the bloody second. Christ all-fucking-mighty, I'm thinking, not two sodding hours in the place and already Chief Sitting Bill here's gone and lost the bloody plot. Yeah, this should land us in a right fucking horlicks and no mistake. And I am instantly overwhelmed by the unshakable impression that huge uncontrollable forces are conspiring against me, brother, dragging me relentlessly towards disaster. I think of Vicky with a dull pang of anger and like self-reproach mixed in with a good helping of regret.

'Who the fuck's that?' I gasp once I've got my warble back. 'What the bloody hell's going on?'

Kane gives me the hard mental eye a moment before speaking.

'I was hoping *you*—' he points his prong at me, then turns it on himself '— could tell *me*.'

15

SMURF

The little geezer's groaning and burbling something pitiful, gof mof muf, trying to like communicate and I bend down near him to see if I can grok what the hell he's warbling on about.

'I tell him,' he's saying, 'I tell him...'

But it's too much effort. He lets out a long breath and I watch ickle gummy pink bubbles of spit and blood come up between his pulped lips then pop.

'What did you tell who?' I ask, encouraging him to go on.

'I tell him—' he starts again. His lamps dart a nasty deek at Kane and he comes to life a bit. 'A million times I tell him. Mr McBride he send me. But this animal he no understand.'

'Who did you say you were?'

'My name it is Pinto, Augusto Soares Pinto.'

'I caught him prowling around outside,' says Kane, taking a couple of steps towards us.

Seeing this, Pinto starts to struggle and squirm like a landed fish.

'No, please, get him away.'

I dig around in the little guy's pockets and bring out his wallet and documents and a black notebook and pencil, checking through each item carefully.

'I think we better let him down now,' I say to Kane, trying to inject as much calm into my voice as possible.

'Why?' asks Kane.

'Because he's telling the truth.'

I put the geezer's papers back in his pockets. Kane watches me, narrowing his lamps.

'Explain,' he says.

'Listen, I know for a fact that Frank always has what he calls outside monitors on the payroll wherever he has operations going, someone outside that no one knows about to like keep an eye on things and make sure he's informed if anything goes out of skew. I've never met any of these people, I mean that's the point, innit, but I've seen their names sometimes on paper. This geezer's name checks. It's him what gave us the dirt on the Captain, about the human trafficking and all the rest.'

But Kane's shaking his bonce.

'Why would McBride not tell us if he was sending someone out here to meet us?'

'Well I don't bloody know, do I? Perhaps you should ask Frank that next time you speak to him.'

'I will.'

'Look, I know how the Tank works, OK? It's all about security and safety nets and thinking ahead. On a need-to-know basis, like they say. No one else knew we were coming to this hotel. Anyway, who in their right mind would send this—' I point to little Pinto over my shoulder, '—to sort anyone out?'

This has got Kane thinking, seems like. I don't wait for him to finish drawing his conclusions and grab hold of Pinto's legs to unhook him. Kane doesn't help, but then again he doesn't do anything to stop me neither.

*　*　*

Minutes later I've got Mr Pinto sitting the right way up in the comfy armchair and I've just about managed to staunch the haemorrhaging with a snotter out of his jacket and a couple of the hotel's towels. I straighten his smashed gigs on his nose for him and make him down a stiff one from the minibar, and soon he's looking more or less human again, but you can tell he's still scared glocky, but then who wouldn't be, eh brother, under the circumstances? Every time Kane just blinks the little feller flinches like he's been slapped round the earhole.

'It's OK,' I say, handing him another wad of toilet paper to bung up his leaky nosewells. 'I'm really very sorry this happened. I'll have a word with Mr McBride to make sure you get a little something extra in your next pay packet to like make up for it.'

I pour him another glass and study his face. Tricky one, this. Beady black itty lamps like you see on a hamster when it wants to bite. Mingled right in with the little sod's fear I can detect a sort of slow-burning indignation giving off heat every time he glances at either of us. Now a swivel-eyed feller like this ain't going to get his revenge up front, brother, never, simply not his style. On the other hand, these slippery sly ones are a bunch of right bloody snakes in the grass and it's obvious that he's not just going to let this go either. One way or another he'll try to spike us for this. I can tell Kane notices this too and he's thinking the eggzak same thing and it starts to worry me.

We're all three of us silent for a while, each alone with his private thoughts, just maybe giving each other the eye now and then, sizing up the situation some, proper The Good, the Bad and the Ugly (and no prizes for guessing who's who here). Then with a shrug Pinto sticks his prong in his jagger like it was a lollipop and stirs it about having a feel-around.

'My tooth it is loose,' he mumbles.

Kane goes to sit crosslegged on the bed and says:

'You're lucky it's not your bloody head. A man can never tell when his head might suddenly come loose.'

At this we both like look down at Pinto's head together as it were automatically. He's completely bald on top and the skin's looking a bit red and raw still smudged with blood, so with a glance back at Kane I crack nervously:

'Scalped him, did you?'

Kane pouts like he's about to smile and scrunches up his lamps. 'You know,' he says, 'you've just given me an idea.'

I turn back to Pinto. He looks like he's just swallowed his own testicles.

'So what can you tell us?' I ask him.

Pinto swigs at his vodka that's full of wispy blood and phlegm now and tilts his head back to stop any more blood from dripping into the glass.

'I said to you,' he says, 'Mr McBride he pay me to watch closely the activity of Mr Tobzcyk. Everyday I check his movements and write down places, dates and times in my notebook. Four days ago Mr McBride he say to me two colleagues they will come here to Rio de Janeiro and I must go to meet them here in this hotel. This is what I do. But—'

He's going to start earaching again but I stop him in time.

'How long have you been in the service of Mr McBride?'

'Nine, maybe ten months. I come here from São Paulo in February. Why?'

'And you've been keeping an eye on Tobczyk all the time since then?'

'Yes.'

'OK, and what did you find?'

Pinto reaches into his breast pocket and brings out the black notebook I seen before, which he consults with a deep frown. He's a bony little runt, with a long nose and a weak chin, and while he's reading he hunches up drawing in his narrow shoulders and keeping the pages close like they might be a poker hand he wants to make sure no one else can get a snook at. We wait while he goes over his notes on Captain America. After a bit he starts unreeling the information in this bloody weird flat robot voice like he was a tape recording announcing arrival and departure times at a railway station, ruddy comical, every word like stressed the same and without no feeling in it whatsoever.

He gives us first Tobczyk's address (which of course I already know) and describes the big flashy drum in tremendous detail, from the size of the pool to the games room to the shape of the double bed (oval, if you must know), a proper gangster's mansion in the old style. Now you may find this strange, but unlike back home, being conspicuous with your moolar ain't necessarily a bad thing in Brazil, quite the contrary, in fact, flaunting wealth, no matter how you come by it, is one sure way of assuring indulgence and even favour from everyone who's anyone, including — or, I should say, especially — the authorities, who are all bent as a bloody bendy-bus on a button roundabout.

While he's talking, Pinto's squinting proper bag of nails, lamps pointing everywhere at once and somehow managing to look straight at me without for a second leaving off Kane still camped on the bed. Kane looks like he's not even listening, puffing away at this pipe he's sparked up — not the gaudy Indian wossit he called I think it was a chanupa that I had to smoke back in Wales, but a normal standard briar like the sort granddad smoked.

'But then he moved out of the house. Everything go, cars everything. I ask and find out he has sold the house.'

'When was this?'

'Three and a half weeks ago.'

The date coincides with the day of the ambush, all right.

'And who did he sell it to?'

Pinto goes on to give me details about the bloke who purchased Captain America's gaff, the bloke's wife's name, their kids', and even the names of their bloody dogs.

'You Brazilian?' I ask, interrupting Pinto in the middle of a sentence.

He sneers indignant-like and the robot voice vanishes instanter.

'No,' says he. 'I am Portuguese.'

He says this very proud and like it should have been obvious to anyone just from glancing at him, he being such a fine specimen of Lusitanian manhood and all.

I ask you.

'Well, of course you are,' I says. 'Now, did you notice anything different about Tobczyk's movements before he moved out? I mean was there any change to his routine, or anyone you hadn't seen before coming to the house or talking to him?'

Pinto munches over this for a second or two, then shrugs and shakes his bonce.

'No. He changes time he goes out always, but the places he goes are usually the same: the tennis club, restaurants — he likes especially the Chinese food — accountant office, lawyer's office. The people as well. Sometimes maybe a new group come to his house or has dinner with him somewhere, but this just seemed normal. As well he usually travels with a great frequency, Manaus, São Paulo, and outside Brazil to Paraguay, Colombia, Bolivia, Peru...'

'How do you know where he goes by plane?'

The tone goes indignant again. 'A stupid question, if I may say. I have contacts, of course. That is what I am paid to do, and I am very good at my job. Information is power, not force. And it is such professionalism that makes good business, not—' Another meaningful sneak at Kane.

I nod. 'Right, right. We get your point.'

A spell of quiet, then:

'What were his habits at night?'

It's the first time Kane's shown any like interest and we both stare at him a moment.

'He went out two, three nights every week,' Pinto says in a thorny warble. 'Parties, nightclubs maybe.'

Kane swings his long pegs out over the side of the bed and stands up. Pinto loses about three inches all round, like washing that's shrunk in the tumble drier.

'Did he go on his own? Did he have friends? A girlfriend?'

Pinto shakes his nut. 'No girlfriend. Sometimes girls, professional girls.' His voice has gone tinny and his left eye starts doing something downright uncanny, brother, he's that shook up: it keeps veering off like to one side away from his nose independently of the other, then jumping back. It's pitiful to watch, but sort of funny at the same time, if you know what I mean. 'As for friends,' he says, unable to disguise a rising tremble in his songbox. 'I don't know. He sometimes had lunch with one judge or the colonel of the military police, but it was business. The only person he had meeted more frequently before was Camacho. He was always very careful to hide this, but I know they went to many parties together, private shows, nightclubs. They were good friends.'

Now in case you don't know, brother, this Camacho, full name Tessoro Ramon Camacho, aka 'El Pitufo', is a Colombian drug kingpin with major operations throughout Latin America. He had got sloppy a few months before and got himself arrested by joint task forces and the Brazilian feds — plus a little help from their friends the United States' Drug Enforcement Agency — just as he was leaving his luxury flat on the intersection of Rua Hilário de Gouveia and Avenida Atlantida on Copacabana beach, not three streets from our hotel. And no bloody wonder, neither, seeing the bust had come the same week that a defence cooperation agreement was signed between Brasilia and Washington. The pressure was on and no mistake, and to this stick had been added the US State Department's golden carrot: US $5 million for information leading to Camacho's arrest. With that much wonga waving under their noses, brother, even the Brazilian police had no choice but to enforce the law for once.

But then surprise surprise, just four days after his arrest Camacho goes belly-up during a prison riot. Stabbed to death. No one was charged with the murder, though, and the whole thing was swept under the carpet. But then who's complaining, eh? Know what I mean?

Now as far as I know, Camacho had worked independently from other Colombian barons, using his connections with former members of the United Self-Defense Forces of Colombia, known as AUC, to like grease the lines for transportation of thousands upon thousands of Ks of topgrade cocaine to Europe, the United States and even West Africa from various points along the Brazilian coast. Of course a lot of our own charlie had originally come from him via Captain America. Since Camacho's arrest, however, obtaining the goods had cost Captain America considerably more effort and risk, and no doubt it was this added stress factor that had made him greedy for a bigger cut, and started him thinking what he should never have thought, I mean not even in his like wildest daydreams with the fairies: of taking out the Tank. I'm guessing he was not only thoroughly pissed off at having all the extra hard graft and hassle of finding new reliable suppliers, possibly even having to sniff out Camacho's own Colombian contacts, a notoriously difficult lot to deal with at the best of times — and all this for the same percentages from us he was getting before — but he was also extra worry-jittery and losing beauty sleep over all the attention the feds and the DEA were giving the dope bizniss in his area. Camacho's arrest must've rattled him no end. Of course he also knew there was no way he could cut the Tank out of the deal and branch off on his own for more money without like serious consequences. And I do mean serious. It was the Tank's set up and that's how it was going to stay. Unless, of course, dot dot dot. You got it, brother. So Tobczyk hires the Ivans to go after the Tank. He made his choice. The wrong one, as it happens.

Pinto's still listing Captain America's secret meets with 'El Pitufo' Camacho, complete with dates and times. Listening intently now, Kane takes a long pull on his pipe and starts stroking his chin like he might be Sherlock bloody Holmes on a 'three-pipe problem, Watson', squinting down at the little bashed-up Portuguese rat with a keen glint flying sparks in his lamps.

'What about this sexual slavery business, the child prostitution?'

Pinto blinks sideways at him.

'He have different places for this, apartments, old houses. He take new girls, very young, to keep inside.' He makes a twisting motion with his wrist and says, 'Lock up. Some work for him, some he sell. To the clubs.'

'Where? Where are these houses?'

'Outside the city is more usual. But always he change. I only know one now. It is here, in Campo Grande, a good neighbourhood. A big house.'

'I want the address.'

Pinto taps his noteboook. 'It is here.'

'I also want the names of every judge and the police colonel Tobczyk was in contact with,' says he.

Pinto gives his notebook a little waggle. 'I tell you. Everything is here.'

'Good,' says Kane, and quick as a blink snatches the notebook from Pinto's hand. The little geezer winces like he's had his hair pulled out by the roots but decides to play it safe for the time being, choking down the cry of like righteous anger flapping around in his wattle dying to get out.

Kane then turns to me.

'Now. Shall I kill him, or will you?'

16

LITTLE TURTLE

Pinto's right eye is doing the weird side-flick thing again, but apart from this he's so utterly fucking stunned he can't move or make a sound.

I'm pretty surprised myself, come to that.

'Are you out of your bloody mind?'

'It's got to be done,' says Kane, totally cool and unruffled like it's only a tooth has to be pulled out we're talking about here.

'What the fuck are you saying? Do the Tank's man? Even for you, Kane, that's taking crazy a bridge too far. The Tank'll go fucking spare. And he'll blame me too for not stopping you. He'll have our bollocks for golf balls and he won't rest till we're both fucking belly-up and turned to bird feed.'

'You're wrong. It was McBride who asked me to put this piece of dirt out of its misery.'

Now it's my turn to like lose my voice for a bit, brother, cos this is just too fucking much. When I find it again, I just mutter:

'You can't be serious.'

But Kane's lamps is fixed dead on me, and there's not a trace of anything resembling a human emotion on his dial at all, and somehow I know this is all for bloody real.

'Fuck this,' I say finally. 'And fuck the Tank. I can't fucking believe it. I mean, doesn't anyone tell me anything any more? D'you mean you knew all along who this geezer was?'

'Yes.'

'Why didn't you bloody say so, then?'

'I was curious to see your reaction.'

'You were what? Oh my giddy aunt, you're madder nor they said you was. Fucking cunting hell, what am I even doing here?'

He's zapping me, Kane, like he's trying to decide something.

'From now on,' he says, 'I'm going to call you Keyan.'

'You what?'

'Little Turtle, because your instinct is to hide your head at the sight of the enemy.'

I turn to Pinto to see if he's hearing what I'm hearing. With a string of snot and blood dangling from one nostril he's looking from one to the other of us while we speak like it might be a tennis game in hell he is watching and he has a firebrand up his arse maybe and a pitchfork through his lychees but can't get up or scream or do anything but sit there and watch us decide his fate. I mean what *can* he be thinking at this point?

'Look, let's just give it a rest with this Native American lark for a bit,' I says. I bob my bonce at Pinto. 'Tell me about him, what did you marmalise him for? And what's this malarkey about the Tank ordering you to top him?'

'Like the scorpion, he hides his sting in his tail.'

I got my gropers on my bonce by this stage, tugging out chunks of hair.

'Look, I just don't get it. Just tell me in plain sodding English why the Tank told you to get rid of him. That's all I'm asking.'

Kane takes his pipe out of his jagger very professorial and waves it about while he explains.

'Think about it,' he says. 'McBride hires Pinto here to spy on Tobczyk. Why? So he can be warned if anyone's planning anything against him. Does Pinto do his job? No. He's useless. And he's a risk to us now, too. He wants to see us hurt and is working out how much he can get for what he knows. The moment he leaves this place he's going with this information to the highest bidder — probably Tobczyk himself. Why feel guilty about taking this dust-being's life?'

If he's trying to make me feel better about this he's not succeeding, brother. I remember it's only like a week ago he was calling me a 'dust-being' as well. I go on:

'Who says I'm feeling guilty? It's not me slotting him, is it? Scared, yes, scared of becoming an accessory to murder. In case you didn't know, whosoever shall aid, abet, counsel, or procure the commission of any indictable offence shall be liable to be tried, indicted, and punished as a principal offender. I'm paid to know stuff like that, and to give counsel. Well I'm giving it now: stop being so bloody crazy. Killing this geezer is the wrong thing to do, Kane, especially under the present circumstances, here, now, in this hotel room.'

'It's the right thing to do, Little Turtle.'

'Of course it bloody ain't. And stop calling me Little Turtle.'

'A new name for a new life. But that's enough talking. It's time.'

As if an alarm has gone off and woken him out of a trance, Pinto suddenly leaps to life out of his chair like a bloody jack-in-the-box and scrambles across the room trying to reach the door, giving off a hideous screech like it might be a nail scraping a blackboard, proper goosebumper. I don't even react, it's all so quick, but Kane's on him before you can say Britney Spears, real velociraptor, forcing Pinto down on the floor with his marylebone and twisting the little bastard's arms across his back in a knot (look familiar?) and pulling his head back to meet it.

Me, I have to sit down, brother, this is just too fucking crazy.

'Look, you can't do him in here,' I say in a weak-like warble. 'I mean, how're you going to do it? And then how're you going to get rid of the body afterwards? People'll hear, probably have done already, people next door or someone, what with him screeching blue bloody murder that way like a rusty fucking violin. Soon we'll have bizzies swarming all over the fucking gaff, and then what? You going to do them all in too?'

'Turn on the radio,' says Kane.

I stare. 'Look, mate, just stop and think about this a moment. I mean let's not be too hasty and go and do something we'll all regret afterwards.'

'Turn it on.'

He doesn't shout, brother, but it's a proper threat and no mistake. I see a layer of ice hardening fast across his lamps. What can I do? I go and turn the blaster on.

'Louder,' says he.

I twist the knob up all the way. The racket is proper rock concert, what with drums banging and bass thudding and Pinto screeching for his life. Then I see Kane like do a quick jerk with his arms, and the screeching stops dead like the sound's been chopped off with an axe.

'OK, you can turn it off, now.'

17

THE BIG CRUNCH

I can't bloody Adam and Eve it, brother. An hour ago I was almost happz, out on the randy zapping the fit bronzed birds on the beach, real kid-in-a-sweet-shop like, with a can of chill swill in my fist and still a few dregs of like hope in my harse, hope that all this would work itself out somehow without taking any bits off me, all in all as kotch as I was ever going to be on this bloody nightmare trip. But now... Fuuuuck. I mean really: foxtrot uniform charlie bloody kilo. The illusions are all gone. My stillborn hopes line up before my lamps, withered and black like a row of sundried raisins, the wasted opportunities I can never get back. I wish I could rub Vicky's face in it now, brother, shove it right in and churn it around, cos deep down in my gut now I want nothing more than a quiet corner to curl up in and like fade slowly away.

My gropers are shaking. I keep to my side of the room away from Kane and dead Pinto. 'And now what?' I ask. 'You going to flush him down the bloody toilet?'

He gives a chuckle. 'Do you have any idea how much trouble that would be? For a start, cutting him into small enough pieces would take hours, not to mention the mess.'

'I was being sarcastic!'

'Sarcasm does not suit you, Little Turtle.'

'No, nor does thirty years in fucking prison.'

'Nobody heard us, nobody saw us. Who knew he was coming here? No one. It was all arranged before. The hotel staff think he's on the second floor.'

'And why should they think that?'

'Because that's where he'd booked a room.'

'You mean he was—'

He's chuckling again. 'You're too slow, Little Turtle.'

'Listen, mate, someone's bound to miss him sooner or later. They'll come looking for him.'

'No, he won't be missed by anybody. Anyway, none of the people he associated with would dare go to the police. His flat's also been taken care of. Other than that, he had no family or close relatives, nobody here in Brazil. Our meeting was a secret only he, McBride and I knew about.'

'But the hotel. They'll—'

'For fuck's sake. He was staying just the one night. The bill was paid in advance. He had nothing in his room. That was the arrangement. I planned the whole thing with McBride four days ago. They'll assume Pinto has left the hotel, and nothing more will be said about it.'

Well, at least he knows his job, I'm thinking. I look down at the limp package lying there in the middle of the floor with its arms reaching out for something that ain't there. The bonce especially gives me the giddywillies, brother, hanging off the neck at like at an impossible angle, a proper screamer job.

'Christ,' I says. 'Poor bastard.'

Kane's bonce spins towards me, scorn like arrowing out from his crazed lamps.

'Who are you trying to fool? This creature—' he points at Pinto '—was wakan-sica, an enemy. In a war that's what you do, you kill the enemy. And don't kid yourself, you're just as responsible for his death as I am. No one forced you into this business. This is the life you chose for yourself. The poison you sell kills hundreds of people, directly and indirectly, destroys entire families. So what are you going to say? Killing him was wrong? It was inhuman? It's the most human thing there is. Let me tell you something: the homicidal impulse, rightly applied, is the key to all evolution.'

I look at him, brother, but I don't say nothing. What is there to say? Anyway, I thought evolution had like gone out with the arrival of modern technology. I mean, what's Wayne Rooney, then?

'Understand this, Little Turtle. I'm a hunter. My life is simple: no friends, no attachments, no distractions. These are the sacrifices I've made. And the reason is simple: I don't hunt animals. I hunt people. — Have you ever stopped to consider the comparative merits of different life-forms? No, of course you haven't. Well, let me tell you, then. We're part of a much wider constituency than most people imagine. Human beings are not at the top of the pyramid. In fact there is no pyramid. And if there were, we'd be right there at the bloody bottom.' — He glares at me here like I was a dog turd he'd just trodden on, brother. — 'Especially the so-called civilized peoples, your glorious teched-up, fed-up, drugged-up, fucked-up mobile-dependent, twitter-abusing consumer fucking society. From a global perspective, a germ does less harm to the world than a civilized human being. We're a plague. Fifty years ago, there were three billion of us. There are now over seven billion of us. Think about it. Another thirty years or so and there'll be ten billion. Building and buying and eating and producing waste. And there's no room for anything else. It's all dying out there. So that's right, spreading a little death among our sorry species is a good thing, if you can see the big picture. In my very small way, I'm just helping nature to redress the balance.'

Blimey, I'm thinking. Lighten up, mate, you're killing the mood.

***

For about ten minutes after this I don't move. Believe it or not Kane starts doing like a little dance round the body now, whooping and chanting, but not loud like he did on that hill in Wales, just keeping it like under his breath for obvious reasons. Having, I imagine, given like proper thanks to Wanker Plonka for such a neat little kill, he turns to me and very matter-of-fact tells me to go out and buy two extra large rucksacks of the sort 'favoured by German hikers' (his words), a packet of large bin liners, preferably black, a large office stapler and three rolls of heavy duty packing tape.

It takes me about an hour to find everything. When I'm back with all the stuff he says:

'Now sit down and wait while I break him up.'

While you what? Eh? Did I hear right? Christ. I feel a cold sharp claw clutch at my nutmegs, brother, no joke, and the clutching turns to like violent squeezing when I see Kane means this in like a literal sense. Squinting and measuring carefully with his prongs, he chooses very precise spots on Pinto's body, on the limbs, ribs and back, and goes to work on them with these very sudden deft jerks, karate chops and weird wrestling holds, breaking the bones one by one, all very methodical, bish-bash-bosh. The sound alone, sort of like the noise you might make crunching down on an icecube, only many times amplified if you can imagine it, is enough to make you want to gnaw your bloody knuckles raw, brother, real doomsday, and maybe shove your bonce like under a pile of extra-thick pillows.

While he's doing this cracking and crunching, Kane turns to me to explain:

'It's important to make sure there's no bleeding. Did you know, Little Turtle, that bones are about eight times stronger than concrete? It's very difficult to break them, as you can see.

The pelvis and the femur are the hardest. We won't bother with those. The average bone requires about 160 psi to break — that's pounds per square inch. It's all down to strength, preparation and technique. If you took an x-ray of my hand—' he holds it up a second '—you would see that the bones are much larger and denser than average. The medical term for this is osteoclerosis. In my case it's the result of years of hard and painful training. Of course you also have to learn where to apply force. A combination of power, speed and accuracy, that's the secret. Like this...' *Crack.* 'Of course not everyone's bones are the same. Now take this little fellow. I would say he was in his mid-fifties. He was short, with a small bone structure, and he never took any exercise. A heavy smoker, obviously. Taken all together, that means his bones are relatively weak and brittle. Coffee and alcohol also tend to decrease the amount of calcium the body absorbs, and I bet he drank too much of both. See here. I can–' *crack* '–break his lumbar vertebrae–' *crunch, crack* '–with no more effort than it would take to break, say, a thick broomstick...'

Gog all-ruddy-mighty. That's quintessential Chief Sitting Bill Kane for you, brother, all yamp and no play.

Well, just when I think the worst is like over and the bones all broken, Kane begins to fold the body up as if it might be a collapsible chair or one of them Brompton folding bikes, tucking the arms neatly into the folds of the legs all in like knots and pressing the wobbly bonce all the way down onto the chest, worse than any contortionist ever, brother, and like morbidly fascinating yet nauseating at the same time to see. While he's bending and folding he sticks each part down with the heavy duty tape, wrapping it all nice and tight. The whole thing then gets stuffed into three bin liners, one inside the other, and Kane tapes that up on the outside as well.

When he's done, Pinto's mortal remains look like a big packet waiting for delivery – which in a sense is eggzakly what they are.

We lift him into one of the rucksacks. Into the other rucksack Kane shoves a couple of pillows and three sheets off the bed.

'Now, Little Turtle' he says. 'Go out and buy two tickets on the largest boat doing a tour of Guanabara Bay and the Cagarras Islands. And on the way back buy yourself a sharp penknife.'

18

DOUGLAS HURD

Imagine tension, brother, the high-voltage variety, nerves being scraped with a cheese grater, with every fibre raw and ruddy and bloody and your innards turned to goo and then some. Now times the feeling by ten. You got it. The fear sits in the pit of my stomach like a heavy maggoty meatball lump, festering and deadly toxic.

But, well, I think, trying to like look on the bright side, at least it's not me carrying the 130-pound rucksack holding Pinto's mangled knotted remains, thank Gog: if we get caught I'll say fuck blimey, I knew nothing about it, never seen this man before, who is he, I've only got some pillows and sheets, officer. Yeah, that's right, cos you know being caught with this bit of dead cargo will get you put away for life and no two ways about it.

So we're herded onto the schooner with the other passengers, all giggling and pointing and taking snaps and shit, and I'm doing my best to act your typical gringo tourist, gaudy dickie on me back and a daft grin like frozen stiff across my rosies, but the panic kicks in good and proper when I realise there's a would-you-believe-it film crew coming on board with us. They're shooting a documentary for Brazilian TV, we're told. Too fucking true.

So I'm jumping around inside my skin like a wild cat in a bag; the old guts start to do the Harlem shuffle in quicktime and I'm that close to cacking my keks when I hear Kane whisper close beside me:

'This is a stroke of luck, Little Turtle. Attention'll be focused on the camera. Away from us.'

Luck? Yeah, right. Keep calm and carry on.

Next we have to remove the rucksacks to put on the lifejackets, obligatory for all passengers. The grin begins to show like major cracks and my rigging's drenched through with nerve-lather. We lean the bags against the side of the boat, Kane making sure his is secure wedged against his pegs. And here we go, anchors aweigh. The boat sails out into the Bay. Hooray. Only someone's forgot to put in the stabiliser, brother, cos we're not half bloody rocking. I grip the rails. The guide on the mike points out the Sugar Loaf mountain and a few other sites of historical interest as we pass. Me, I'm just having a hard time breathing and there's a thick black taste in the back of my songbox like coal tar. The horizon won't sit still. The scenery, I hear everyone around me squeal in like orgasms of aesthetic joy, is really fucking beautiful, but I don't get to see any of it, do I, cos next minute I am just too bloody busy yacking up over the side. The sea's cross-channel choppy and now the sodding boat's wambling with these like slow heavy heaves that carry my guts up into my throat then all the way down into my fucking socks.

Kane pats me on the back and says it's great my getting the pukes like this, absolutely perfect, very good, Little Turtle, because you see it's keeping the film crew from like pointing their camera at us. Ruh-really? I want to snap back with something suitably caustic-like but can't even get my fucking nut up to speak. I hold my belly and think: sod this all to bloody hell, what the Tank's paying me is not worth the fucking pain, mate, not by a long bloody shot.

We arrive at the Cagarras, originally called Shit Islands cos the rocks are all washed white with guano. I've puked my insides out hollow by this stage and am quavering like a fucking epileptic on a bouncy castle, but at least the sick feeling's about 80 per cent gone. The boat drops anchor for passengers to enjoy a 30-minute swim. Only a handful stay behind, including the film crew, but they are all concentrated on the starboard side where the islands are and the passengers are splashing about like a bunch of bollock-brains in the water. Sneaky as stealth we carry the rucksacks over to the port side near the stern, hidden from view of the others, and Kane lifts his onto the edge of the taffrail. When no one is watching, he signals me to cut open the bottom of the rucksack. I do, and the Pinto packet slides down, out and overboard with a muffled plop like it might be a Douglas Hurd hitting the toilet bowl, then sinks into the opaque lemonade-coloured waters. I look down. Bubble bubble... gone. Not a trace. Talk about a burial at sea, brother. Kane quickly staples the slit and fills the empty rucksack with a sheet and one of the pillows from mine. The deed it is done. No one's seen us, no one's heard. We're clear. Gog be praised.

Kool as a pint and chuffed as fucking nuts, Kane turns to me smiling as we troll back to the other side of the boat:

'You know, Little Turtle, we really must do this again sometime.'

Yeah, right. Another day, another dollar.

19

SOOPAH-KANE

But he's not diddly-done yet, brother, not by a long bloody shot. Right away we grab a taxi to the address in the Campo Grande neighbourhood, a big two-storey drum painted yolk-yellow hidden behind high brick walls with all-round state-of-the-game eletrick wire fencing on top and a tall black metal gate with two security CCTV cameras keeping a watchful eye.

'Don't tell me you're actually thinking of trying to get inside,' I says.

'I am,' he says.

'Place is a fucking fortress,' I says, nodding at it.

'It's just a house,' he says.

'Oh yeah?' And just how do you expect to get past that?' I'm nodding at the gate now. 'Anyway, they've probably got a whole fucking army in there.'

But he just steps up to the gate and presses the button on the intercom. A garbled voice crackles through. Kane mumbles something in bad Portuguese and the voice says something back. Then nothing happens. Kane walks back to where I'm standing.

'Well,' he says. 'That didn't work.'

I roll my lamps. 'Oh, my sainted bollocks.'

'Wait here,' he says, and gallops off down the street.

Great. I go and sit on a low wall in front of a parking lot on the corner and wait. Then I wait some more.

A snooze later he comes back with this fit young bird in tow. She can't be more than eighteen. Tight jeans, white T-shirt, long dark hair down her back like an oil-slick. I get up but when he sees me he waves at me to stay put, so I sit back down.

He and the girl stop a few yards away from the main gate and he says something to her, explaining and pointing back at the house over his shoulder. She don't look too sure. So he then takes a wad of ready from his pocket, plucks out three crisp notes and hands them to her. She shoves the money in the back pocket of her jeans (and barely manages it, brother, they're wrapped so tight) and shimmies up to the gate. She presses the button on the intercom and the voice comes on again, squawking and creeching. She says something in her sweet warble, but this time the voice doesn't answer back. Two seconds later there's a faint buzz and the gate starts to slide open.

Well, that was easy, I think.

The next moment a tonk muscled-up heavy ballooned big from too many steroids is standing there with his huge Schwarzenegger arms crossed over his bulging pecs, staring down at the girl like he wants to bloody eat her. He grunts out something, barely moving his lips he's so hard and tough, jutting out his Cro-Magnon chin. She hesitates, takes a step back. He says it again.

Well I'm watching them so I don't even see where he comes from, brother, all I know is one second Kane's not there and the next he is, proper the Flash, but the Flash on speed and with a turbine engine up his arse, possessed: zwoooomsh. Mr Muscle barely has time to unfold his arms before Kane bashes his nose up into his skull with the heel of his hand. Christ that must hurt, I think. Instantly a glug-load of blood like Ribena on tap spurts out of Mr Muscle's face. He flops to his marylebones and doesn't get up. Seeing this the girl Usain-Bolts it out of there screaming hairy murder and now Kane shouts to me:

'Get in here, Dodger!'

I run past the girl going the other way and we exchange fleeting looks. In that split-second my lamps say to her: *Yeah, I know just how you feel.*

I reach the house and the old Fear is already frothing up out of my socks and through my legs straightening the little hairs out stiff and then up into my liver like Coke out of a bottle what's been shaken, brother, and in my ears there's like the scream of heavy distorted eletrick guitars chugging and screeching gory punk pandemonium, at full concert pitch, waaaaaaa. At the same time it's also bizarrely dreamy though, cos it's just too much kraziness all happening at once, distress information overload, so that it hasn't had time like to properly reach the right command centres in my brain. When I reach Kane he's just putting the last finishing touches on Mr Muscle, who's well out-of-it in Never-Never Land by this time, bonce bouncing back and forth on his limp neck like a broken Barbie doll. Kane leaves him then and pushes the gate closed.

'Won't she call the plod?' I ask, stepping over the bloodied mess.

'Are you joking?' he says, not looking back. 'She's more terrified of them than she is of me. She's got her money, she won't do anything. Now come on.'

No alarms, no shouting, no heavy clop-clop of feet running towards us: everything's quiet as cotton wads now. I'm numb with shock but somehow satisfied, like a kid panicking on a roller coaster. We commando up the driveway, one either side, still not seeing or hearing anything, and climb up the front steps of the house to a broad like veranda, all flowery blue tiles and large potted plants at the corners and hanging from the ceiling and hammocks and arched windows with frilly scrollwork round the edges, real Hollywood colonial Latino like an old Zorro movie. The next instant I hear this hoarse croak like someone scraping a bit of wood with a shovel and freeze. Something moves at the other end of the veranda. It's a hoary old geezer shuffling towards us in his flip-flops, shlep shlep shlep. He must be at least a hundred, bent and shrivelled like a burnt sausage, skin like cured elephant hide and body very small and skinny so the work togs he has on hang off him in like loose droopy folds everywhere with his shoulder-bones poking sharp out through the flimsy fabric and the hems on his strides all frayed and black and like shiny with so much floor-grime from dragging behind him and being stepped on, they're that bloody big on him. He stops in mid-shuffle when he zaps us (and I see how the whites of his lamps are not white at all, brother, but the colour of strong Yorkshire tea, a tawny copper), sort of startled at first, but then more confused than scared really, and gives out with another diddy croak.

'Oarrr...'

Kool as anything Kane steps up to the prunified pigmy and in a warble of like steely authority says something in the way of as it might be an order and points into the house. The old geezer croaks a third time and shuffles off the way he come, shlep shlep, crooking a finger at us to follow him. He hasn't seen Mr Muscle lying in a coma next to the gate, thank Gog, hidden behind the hedges lining the driveway, and I'm guessing he thinks we're like customers come to sample the goods.

Inside the house it's very cool with more fancy tiles and the ceiling very high and two big chopper fans on a slow spin. There's lots of plastic furniture and big ugly paintings in screaming colours and more flowers in tall glass vases and diddy ornaments perched on every available surface all in ultra bad taste. This huge living room (called that but, I suspect, not much living ever actually gone on in it, if you know what I mean) branches off into a dining room on the right and, at the end straight in front, a long, wide corridor. The old geezer makes sure we're still following and takes the corridor but doesn't stop at any of the doors. He creeps straight through instead and opens a door at the far end gives out onto an inner like patio. This makes me mucho uneasy again as I'm thinking if we're caught here we'll be rat-trapped, brother, no way out but that bloody tiny corridor where we wouldn't stand a fucking chance.

Finally the pigmy like shuffles to a stop at the gate to a fenced-off back area and we zap through the wire a group of about a dozen bungalows arranged in two straight rows. The old man looks up at Kane then at me and the leather breaks out into a million more creases. It's a smile, brother, almost all gum apart from two long tusks the same colour as his eyes. He points to the bolt on the gate and the huge padlock and says something to Kane sounds like the old shovel scraping the bit of dry wood again.

Then I see her, a girl, goodlooking, can't be older than fourteen or fifteen, in tiny red shorts and a white bra, coming out of one of the bungalows near the front carrying a bundle of clothes in a plastic laundry basket. She stops when she zaps us, a flash of eyes black as petrol, but only for a second, then in the orangy late pee-em light she walks across the central aisle separating the two rows of bungalows and goes in another bungalow direckly across from hers, like a vision.

Well. So there it is. All true.

After the girl's gone the pigmy then turns to us smiling again, but it only hangs there about half a second this toofless grin cos Kane well he just thumps it right out of existence. The punch catches the old sod on the side of the bonce and you can see his lamps like judder for a second inside their sockets as it might be a cartoon cat getting smashed with an iron weight with little stars flashing and bubbles popping and fairy birds tweeting. The poor wrinkled pigmy sparks out collapsing all at once like a house of cards and lands with a puff of dust, splat, his face kissing the dirt, but hard.

'Bloody hell,' I says in like a shouted whisper, 'what did you go and hit that old sod for? You've bloody killed him!'

And he has too, brother, good and proper.

Kane zaps me hard over his shoulder.

'Don't you think this old bastard knew what was going on here? Why let him live? He'd only have let them know we're coming.'

Even if there'd been time to do it, brother, I wouldn't have argued with him. So I just says:

'How we going to get this bloody gate open, then?' I point up, right and left, at the CCTV cameras perched on top of the fence either side of the gate zapping us. 'And smile,' I says. 'You're on TV.'

Kane goes through the old man's clobber but finds nothing like a key anywhere. He then checks the padlock, feeling its weight and thickness.

I scan the area. Still no movement in the house or bungalows, everything dead quiet.

'Wait here,' he says. 'I'm going to look back in the house.'

'I'm not fucking waiting here on my own,' I says.

He stops me with his hand flat against my chest.

'Wait here,' he says again.

So I go and stand behind a scrawny tree a little way off while he goes back inside. The tree's much too tiny to hide me, but it's better than waiting out in the open within reach of the cameras, ain't it?

He's not gone ten minutes.

'Here,' he says, jangling a big bunch of keys hanging from his prong. 'Found them on the big security guard.' He starts trying the keys on the padlock. 'Looks like the rest of the house is empty. But we better hurry before anyone else gets back.'

He gives the fourth key a turn and the padlock pops open.

***

There's sixteen girls in all, brother, all about the same age as the first one I saw. The first bungalow we open is the one I saw her go into, just a small box room with three rusty washing machines, wonky shelves full of soap and washing powder cartons and fabric softener, a large sink at one end and two long benches to wait on. She's there with one other, a chubby bird with fat brown thighs, and they both look terrified out of their skins when we come through the door. The fat one takes a big gulp of air and immediately starts boo-hoo-hooing, her round brown shoulders heaving and her fat wobbling. The other one, the one I seen outside, just stares at us, her black lamps like glassy with panic now, but says nothing and doesn't even move or blink.

Kane goes and talks to her, very gentle, explaining why we're here, I'm guessing, but it's a while before she understands. It's obvious she doesn't believe or trust either of us an inch. I look at her and from the way she's still staring I'm guessing she's thinking it's a game of some sort being played on them, a game with some cruel like twist at the end. She stares but she doesn't look either of us in the eye. But she talks to the fat one anyway, helps her get up, and together they follow Kane and me out of this first bungalow to the next.

The next one is like a shabby hotel room: two little beds, a lopsided wardrobe, two chairs, and a poky bathroom. The other bungalows are all eggzakly the same inside. Some of the girls have taped like pictures cut out of magazines on the walls, but somehow this makes the rooms look even sadder, brother, especially as most of the pictures are of like little houses or puppies or maybe flowers. They all smell the same too, the rooms, a like mix of sweaty seat-cushions and baby shampoo.

Kane rounds them up and makes them pack quickly what little clobber they got then herds them out of the bungalows fast towards the open gate. When they see the old geezer lying cold in the dirt with his lamps half-open showing slivers of white some of them

start crying but not with fright now but with like the dawning reali-
sation that this is for real, no game, they're getting out at last.

Problem is, brother, we soon find none of these girls really
has anywhere to get out to, not even after Kane gives money for
bus fares and the like, no home nor family to return to, some of
them having been sold to the Cap by their own bloody parents in
the first bloody place.

Makes you think, don't it? I mean, it really piles up, don't it,
brother? All the shit in this world. You'd think the stink by now
would be strong enough to have made it all the way up to heaven
or wherever it is old Gog and his sidekick angels are supposed to
be like looking out for us here below and worrying about us. But
that's just it, innit? That's why for me there was never no Gog nor
Heaven nor bright Nirvana nor fairy-light Spirit World to con-
sole, brother, cos I was then what you might call a hard-nosed
iron-arsed pig-headed non-believer, as doubting a Thomas as
they bloody come, and did not care a gnat's fart for all this lofty
talk of the Beyond and the Afterlife and the Soul and whatnot the
religions like make their fat living out of, no, not me. And here, I
thought, looking at these sad girls so severely shat-upon so early in
life, was proof, hard and as it might be incontro-bloody-vertible.

Kane was looking at them, too, a very like weird expression
on his clock, cos I'm guessing he was also remembering his dead
daughter, seeing a little of her in them. But that, I suppose, was
Kane's true like genius, if you can call it that, cos he could see,
brother, he could see it all, the whole like sense of it, the beauty,
even in the midst of all the dirt and desolation (and Gog knows
he saw enough of that, more than anybody, believe me), through
that world of pain he saw a sort of deliverance.

Well, we got them all out pronto, but in the end it was to the
copshop they had to go, brother, no other choice, especially as
they were all pissing themselves now thinking there'd be black hell
to pay for escaping. And for all we knew they were probably right.

They went on their own, of course, we couldn't be seen with them nor have nothing to do with it. I watched them walk away down the street, scabby-kneed and huddled close, hurrying along, no older than skoolgirls. To see them like that it was hard to imagine anyone wanting to do the dirty on one of them. But we all know there are, brother, and plenty. And you know thinking about it now I reckon they weren't much better off there in the lap of the law than they had been back in their bungalow prisons either, those kids, for who knew what these bent bizzies had in store for them, eh, some dirty scheme no better than Captain America's the moment our backs were turned, I wouldn't be surprised, sold right back into the great grinding maw of the billion-dollar sex industry.

And you know what? Next day it's not even in the news.

What a world.

20

TURTLE ISLAND

asp. My exhaustion finally catches up with me. I'm back in my room at the Saraiva, nanxed to the nines, reeling from jet-lag, sunstroke, shock, seasickness, tension, panic, hurt bones, and a whole bunch of other nasties all thrown at me at once in the space of a few hours. Enough to do anyone in, brother. I don't even shower or undress and plonk back on the bed already like sparking out even before I hit the mattress.

Straight into the zeds, a deep dive, and woolly oblivion for a bit, all very nice and still, then from the other end of a long dark tunnel comes a noise. Can't make out what it is, but it's downright disturbing, pulling me back. I try to shut it out but it won't go away. Keeps getting closer, louder.

I'm finally forced to open my lamps.

Smeg! Someone's at the door.

'Go away,' I groan.

The knocking steps up a beat and to it is added the voice of a Dalek.

'Open the door, Little Turtle.'

Fuck's sake!

'Piss off. I'm asleep.'

'You can't sleep now. We've got work to do.'

'I'm sure you can handle it all by yourself.'

'Come downstairs and have some dinner. You'll feel better after you've had something to eat.'

'Fuck dinner. I'm not hungry. I just want to bloody sleep.'

'You can sleep later.'

'What's wrong with you? Don't you ever let up?'

'Never. Now open this door.'

I give in, brother. I get up and unlock the door.

He's standing there holding two envelopes. I recognise one of them. What with all the killing and bone-crunching and body-dumping and mangling and slave liberating to worry about, it had slipped clean from my mind.

'You left this in my room,' says he.

'Yeah, it's for you. A file I put together on Clay Tobzcyk before we left England: smudges old and recent, what bit of bio there is, numbers, addresses, contacts, whatever I could lay my hands on. It might add a bit to whatever's in Pinto's notebook. Now can I go back to bed, please?'

'I've got something for you, too,' he says.

He hands me the other envelope. I take it but don't open it.

'Thanks. Nighty-night, then.'

'Turning a visitor away from your door brings great misfortune, Little Turtle.'

Jesus James Christ, what have I done to deserve this?

He trundles in and plots himself down crosslegged on the end of my bed. I sit propped up with my back against a pillow.

'Listen, could you please stop calling me that. You may think it's funny, but even a good joke loses its flavour after a while, and this one wasn't even funny to begin with.'

He sits very still, staring at me. I'm starting to get uneasy when he says:

'The name I have given you is not a joke, Little Turtle. It is a name for a brave, for a warrior, a full person and not a half person.'

'Well,' I says, 'to me it just sounds like you're taking the mick.'

He shakes his bonce. 'Why do you say that? Do you think the turtle is not a strong animal, not proud? The turtle is wise, and hears many things, and its shell is a shield, so no arrows can go through it. That is why Keya is the guardian of life and a spirit of healing. It brings powerful medicine that can destroy bad spirits that live in the water. It is the symbol of long life, dedication, and steadfastness. You do not see this?'

It's a laugh the way his lingo changes when he's off on one of these Hollywood Indian speeches, brother, all stiff and with no contractions. Still crosslegged, he raises his bonce, lamps closed, very serious, and in this ultra-solemn-like warble says:

'There was another world before this one, you know. But the people of that world lost their way, and turned to evil. So, displeased, Wakan Tanka set out to make a new world. He sang many songs to bring rain, which poured stronger with each song.' (Here he mimics the rain and sings a few notes.) 'And as he sang the fourth song, the earth split apart and water gushed up through the many cracks, causing a great flood. By the time the rain stopped, all of the people and nearly all of the animals had drowned. Only Kangi, the crow, had survived.'

'And what in Gog's name does that have to do with anything?' I ask.

'Pay attention, and you may understand. Kangi then pleaded with Wakan Tanka to make him a new place to rest. So Wakan Tanka decided the time had come to make his new world. From his huge pipe bag, which contained all types of animals and birds, Wakan Tanka selected four animals known for their ability to remain under water for a long time. He sent each of them in turn to retrieve mud from beneath the floodwaters so that he could make the land. First it was the turn of the loon to dive deep into the dark waters, but it couldn't reach the bottom.'

'Loon? You mean as in—'

'Then the otter,' he says, cutting me off, 'tried as well, but even with its strong webbed feet it could not swim down far enough. Next, the beaver used its large flat tail to propel itself deep under the water, but it too brought back nothing. So finally Wakan Tanka took the fourth animal from his pipe bag and asked it to bring back some mud to make the land. This last animal was the turtle.'

'Ah,' I says, 'and the good old turtle saves the day, right?'

'Yes,' he says, smiling. 'The turtle managed to stay underwater for so long that at first everyone was sure it had drowned. But then, with a huge splash, it broke the water's surface and swam back. Its feet and claws and the cracks between its shell were filled with mud. Singing, Wakan Tanka shaped the mud in his hands and spread it on the water, making an island that was just big enough for himself and the crow. Then he used two long eagle wing feathers to spread the mud wider and wider until it completely covered the waters.

'But now Wakan Tanka thought the land had become too dry, and began to cry. His tears became oceans, streams, and lakes. At last he was pleased with the result. He named the new land Turtle Island, in honour of the turtle who had provided the mud from which it had been formed. And he then took more animals from his great pipe bag and scattered them across the earth. Finally, from red, white, black, and yellow clay he made men and women. Wakan Tanka gave the people his sacred pipe and told them to live by it. He warned them about the fate of the people who had come before them. He promised all would be well if all living things learned to live in harmony. But the world would be destroyed again if they made it bad and ugly.'

21

GASPER

Wuuaah... By the time he was done telling this yarn I was nine-tenths asleep, brother, totally wrecked, yawning like mad and reeling with hot tears running like Wakan Tanka's ruddy floodwaters from my stinging bloodshot lamps. So, seeing my lights like about to go out, he right away began tapping the unopened envelope that was still tight in his groper, and said in this very changed, bizniss-like warble:

'Now tell me, Little Turtle, does Clay Tobzcyk know you well?'

I rubbed my lamps and tried to keep them open.

'How d'you mean?'

'Have you met face to face?'

'Yeah, course we have.'

'Would you recognise one another in the street?'

'Yeah, probably.'

'Then we need to give you a bit of a makeover, my lad.'

I came to at this, believe me. 'A what-over?' I says, lamps popping. 'Now there's a bloody morale raiser for you.'

'Don't worry,' he said, starting to grin. 'It's good for a brave to put on war paint before a battle.'

He opened the envelope and went through the stuff very meticulous-like, then dug out his pipe and lit up again. For a long while he just smoked and stared at nothing. Then he put the pipe away and looked back at me.

'What sort of man is Tobzcyk? What makes him tick? Is it greed? Vanity? Is he the sort who's always seeking the approval of people around him? Is he extroverted?'

'I've absolutely no fucking idea.'

'Physical peculiarities?'

'Yeah. All of him. He's one huge fucking peculiarity, from top to bloody toe.'

'You'll have to do better than that.'

'Well, I don't fucking know, do I? He's quite tall, beefy, skin creased and leathery from too much sun. And he's got this funny warble — voice, that is — sort of hoarse and high-pitched, like someone running their nails down a blackboard.'

'What sort of music does he listen to? What kind of food does he eat? How does he dress?'

'What d'you want to know all that for? You going to top the bastard or write a bloody book about him?'

'Have you ever been on a hunt, Little Turtle?'

'My name ain't Little Turtle.'

'Before stalking game and reading a trail the first thing a hunter must learn is to take time to know his prey. He must study its habits, he must know its ways. Every creature is different.'

'All right. I've no bloody idea what sort of music he listens to or what food he likes. As for dress, I remember he seemed to go in for shellsuits. More Jimmy Savile than Saville Row, if you know what I mean.'

'Did he prefer any colour over others?'

'Gog almighty, I only met him four or five times.'

'Enough to tell me what I need to know. Now think, Little Turtle.'

I shrugged and let out a long breath.

'I remember him wearing something sort of wine-coloured, you know, what-d'ye-call-it, burgundy.'

'Jewellery?'

'Fuck's sake. I don't know.'

'Earrings? Piercings? Neck chains? Bracelets?'

'No, I don't think so.'

'When you met him, what time of year was it?'

'Christ, let me think. July, I think, was the last time.'

'Was he wearing his tracksuit?'

'Yeah, I think.'

'So long sleeves?'

'Yes.'

'And round his neck? Did he have anything round his neck?'

'Wait a sec, now that you mention it, he did. A scarf-thing, it was, silky, sort of like a Boy Scout necker.'

'Was the weather warm?'

'Yeah, a scorcher. I remember cos Derek had these like sweat rings under his armpits we kept prodding him about.'

'The other times you met Tobzcyk, was he wearing a neckerchief as well?'

'Yeah, that's right. I suppose he thought it made him look young and trendy. That and the wristbands.'

'Tell me about those.'

'You know, just ordinary wristbands, like tennis players wear. He always had these like coloured ones. That's why I noticed the Brazilian goodluck charm. It was strapped round the tennis wristband and looked a bit odd. But then they all looked bloody naff, really. I'll say one thing, he's no fucking taste at all, Captain America, not in clothes, not in nothing.'

Kane pulled out one of the smudges from the file I'd given him.

'Look at this picture.'

'It's Tobczyk.'

'You don't say. Look at his neck.'

'No necker-thing.'

'Yes. And?'

'And what?'

'On his neck there, a dark ring like a rash or a mark left by chafing.'

'Yeah, so?'

Kane sucked in air deep and let it out again slowly like I'd seen him do a few times before when he was impatient.

'Does he eat a lot?' he asked after a bit. 'Is he fat?'

'He's a bit blown-out, yeah. I have no idea how much he eats.'

'How did he behave in McBride's presence?'

I had to munch over this one a bit.

'Let me see. Quite chumly, most of the time, like a couple of old skool friends gloating over all the mischief they get up to.'

'Was there any rivalry between the two?'

'Yeah, a bit, I suppose. Captain America was always champing at the bit some, complaining and whining about this or that. Money, as likely as not.'

'Did McBride treat him as a subordinate?'

'Frank treats everyone as a bloody subordinate all the bloody time.'

'How did Tobzcyk feel about this?'

'He'd learnt to live with it, I suppose, I don't know.'

'And what was Tobzcyk's behaviour towards you and the others in the group?'

'We hardly exchanged two words. He tended to ignore us.'

'Why do you think this was?'

'Cos he's an arrogant bloody bastard, that's why.'

'What was he like with his own people?'

'A fucking prima donna bloody slave-driver scurf. Frinstance, last time he come over he clouted one of the Brazilian lads he brought with him in front of everyone and called him a fucking 'douchebag asshole' just cos the poor sod hadn't got him the make of fags he wanted.'

Kane nodded a few times, ruminating-like. I straightened up and crossed my arms over my marylebones.

'OK, I've told you everything I know. Now you tell me something: how's any of this going to help you find him?'

'No, no, Little Turtle, it's not going to help me find him.' He cocks his bonce. 'It's going to help you find him.'

I should've seen it coming, brother. I showed him my teeth.

'Hilarious. All right, then, how's it going to do that?'

'I'll show you.'

He got up, trolled over to the phone on the bedside table, lifted the receiver off the cradle and chewed out a garble of Porto-Spanish into it.

'There,' he said, replacing the receiver.

* * *

True to nature, Kane offers no explanation, and I know better by this stage than to bother asking for one. I watch him out of the corner of my lamp while he goes through the contents of the envelope on his lap.

At one point, without looking up, he says, 'Aren't you going to open yours?' like it was a Christmas present or something.

I slide my prong under the flap, stick my groper in and pull out a British passport, a UK driving license, an international driving license, an International Press Association card and two UK Press Card Authority passes. They all have my smudge on them, but the name under each is Clifford Fuchs. On one UK press card it says I am a photographer affiliated to BPPA, the British Press Photographers' Association. The other says I am a member of the NUJ, or National Union of Journalists.

'Clifford Fuchs? Who the fuck is Clifford Fuchs?'

'You are. And it's pronounced 'fewsh'.'

'But I don't feel like a Clifford Fuchs.'

'It's a good name. Very convincing.'

There's no getting away from it this time, brother, I have to ask.

'OK, Kane, I give in. Please tell me, what the hell is all this paperwork in aid of, anyway?'

But before he can answer there's a knock on the door.

I open it and one of the young blokes from reception hands me a photo album and a stack of fliers. He says something to me in Portuguese so I shake my bonce at him and manage to look almost as confused as I'm feeling.

'Me no understand,' I explain in my best Tarzan. 'You make mistake.'

He gives me a little wink, grins and vanishes.

I turn to Kane.

'And what the fuck's all this now?'

'Bring them over here,' he says, patting the bed. 'I asked for them.'

I sit down beside him. Opening the album on his lap, he starts flicking through the pages. It's a sort of menu, brother, but the dishes on it are not food. On every page are gummed big glossy snaps of professional birds in their b-day gear, bent every which way over up under sideways and down with their legs open wider than a church door on a Sunday morning, and each with her own flashy calling card in Day-Glo colours stating name, contact number and a list of like specialities. My brain's into meltdown already but when Kane stops at the pages with the kinky arse-spanking BDSM gals with cat-o-nine-tails and kitted out in black leather and studded boots and starts copying telephone numbers onto the back of the envelope it's bloody nuclear fission.

'I never figured you for a perv, Kane. You Scouse Indians go in for that kinky stuff, do you? But what about all the work that couldn't wait?'

'This isn't for me.'

'What?'

'It's for you.'

I do a huge fly-catcher and give him the old let-me-out-of-here zap.

'This,' he says, pointing to one of the fliers, 'is where we're going to find the information we need.'

I'm halfway to the door already so I have to read the flier upsidedown. In swishy mock-oriental letters is written 'Kinbaku Garden' across a picture of two Japanese girls trussed up tighter than a shorthorn's balls in a pigmy's jockstrap.

'I don't get it.'

'I know one or two things about El Pitufo that you won't find in his police records. His Ni was weak. He had phobias. He was terrified of heights. Wouldn't go above the second floor in a building if he could avoid it. He was also highly allergic. Shrimps, dust, bee stings. That sort of information can come in very handy in my work, Little Turtle. Lastly, and most importantly for us, he was a masochist.'

I screw up my lamps at this.

'You're wrong there, mate. From what I've heard Camacho was the eggzak opposite.'

'Yeah, sure, but that was business. I'm talking about his private life. He was into Japanese bondage.'

Kane explains how Camacho spent a small fortune organising private performances by what are known as 'rope masters', usually blokes doing it to women but sometimes women doing to blokes or other women, too, which is what he particularly liked to watch. Now it turns out this Japanese bondage lark is a highly specialised bizniss, involving complex techniques, so it isn't easy to find skilled practitioners outside Japan, and as it happens in Rio there's really only one place to go if you're into this sort of twisted kink: The Kinbaku Garden.

'OK,' I says. 'And what's any of this have to do with Tobczyk?'

'Camacho and Tobczyk weren't just partners in business. They shared a secret passion.'

'What, you mean Captain America is into this bondage shit as well?'

'Naturally.'

'What do you mean, 'naturally'? How do you know?'

'You told me, Little Turtle.'

'Me? What? When?'

'Just now. Let's say you confirmed my suspicions. It's clear from Pinto's notebook that the two men met far more often than was warranted by any business deals they had going on. I know Camacho wasn't gay. He was something of a homophobe, in fact. So what shared interest might draw these two together? I smoked and Wohpe carried my prayer to Wakan Tanka, so after a while everything became clear. Tobzcyk always wore a scarf and wristbands to hide burnmarks left by ropes.'

'I don't fucking believe it.'

'But there was one important difference between the two men. Camacho just liked to watch, but Tobczyk, well... It's called asphyxiophilia, or erotic asphyxiation.'

'He was a gasper?'

This is a crazy stunt and no mistake, brother. These people get off by strangling themselves to within a gnat's tadger of snuffing it and say it's like nothing on earth, sheer bliss better than any dope and twice as addictive. I heard a girl talk about it once. By compressing the carotid arteries on the sides of your neck you cut off the supply of oxygen-carrying blood to the brain, and if it's done right you can even get like mild hallucinations. But the real trick is to cum while in this state, that's where the big kicks is for these nutters. Of course it's also bloody dangerous and dicing with death every time cos the teeniest little mistake can take you out and put you to bed with a bloody shovel six foot under before you even like know what's happening. It's a mad fucking world, brother. I mean you couldn't make this stuff up, not if you tried.

'If I understood this correctly,' I says, 'having marks like that on his neck means Tobzcyk is into the extreme stuff big time, right?'

'It looks likes it, doesn't it?'

'And it being such a dangerous lark he'll need like a real expert to cater to his needs without too much risk.'

'Probably.'

'But like you said, there can't be very many of those around.'

'Your thinking is remarkably clear today, Little Turtle. Somewhere out there is the one person who Tobczyk relies on for his fix, the one person who can take him right to the edge then ease off just at the right moment without killing him.'

'Tobczyk wasn't queer either as far as I know, so I'm guessing this is a woman we're talking about.'

'I am pleased with you, Little Turtle. And if, as I suspect, she's a Japanese bondage expert, that narrows it down even further, you see, because there aren't many women rope masters any-where, not even in Japan.'

We sit zapping each other for a spell.

'How come you know all this?' I ask after a bit.

'I read.'

Yeah, a right bag of tricks you are, Kane.

I then say kind of thoughtful-like:

'Captain America, eh? And the all-powerful Camacho. Who would've believed it?'

'The signs are there for those who can read them.'

I stare down at the picture on the flier, still like digesting it all. And I'm thinking: just wait till I tell the Tank. He'll fucking split.

'You speak Spanish, right?' I ask after a bit. 'I'm curious, Kane. What does 'El Pitufo' mean?'

'It means Smurf.'

'Eh?'

'Little blue cartoon creatures.'

Honestly. They don't make them like they used to, do they brother?

'And what did you ask all those questions about the colour of Captain America's clothes for?'

'To help you create an accurate mental picture of him. I knew you'd probably noticed things about him at the time which didn't seem worth remembering, but you never know what details might be important. And as you can see, I was right.'

I stare at nothing for a few seconds, gobsmacked, mulling over all I've heard in like amazed silence.

Then the pip drops.

'Just hang on one fucking moment! If you think I'm going to some bloody sadie-n-masie fucking pornpalace to pass myself off as some daft seat-sniffing perv and get myself strung up just to get the dope on Captain America's whereabouts, you're even fucking crazier than I know you are.'

22

TIGHTROPE

Well, brother, it's either the Japanese rope trick or piss off to a dozy little town called Vitoria in the neighbouring state of Espirito Santo (this last name, it turns out, actually means Holy Ghost, which seems sort of appropriate, don't you think) to buy us some barkers. I ask Kane why can't we just get them here in Rio, there probably being like shitloads of places we could get tooled up easy for the right amount of wonga, but of course he says no, absolutely not, nix nix, we can't run the risk of word getting to Captain America about this, however tiny the probability of this happening, people here are all blabbers, love to talk, and we don't want to set off any alarms, not no way. So he's got this set-up with some geezer in Vitoria instead, a runner who gets the goods straight from Ciudad del Leste in Paraguay. How, Gog knows.

Vitoria? Paraguay? Now I put it to you, brother: does this make any bloody sense? Course it fucking don't.

So it's Kane himself going – I mean no fucking way am I driving three hundred miles and crossing a state border with a trunk full of war, mate, not even here in wild vida loca Brazil. But he says it's a cinch. As for the quality of the hardware, he says you can't get better anywhere else. Apparently gun laws in Paraguay are so lax no one's even bothered to write them down, and they sell thousands of weapons every day to Brazilians and other tourists right under the cozzers' noses, or more likely with their help, so it's big bizniss all round, and that means they can offer really top-grade stuff at fantastically low rates. Kane says you can get a new 9mm for as little as a monkey (that's £500 to you, brother), plus another tenner to have the goods delivered across the Brazilian border and another fifty to go from there proper room-service-like to any place you want in the country, cleared all the way. Not only that, the range of choice is mahusive, with no questions asked and no hassle from nobody.

No bloody wonder gun crime here is what it is.

Now there's still one last chance left that I may not have to go through with any of this playacting crap, brother, cos I know Captain America runs a legit imports and exports bizniss here in Rio for his cover, and I've got the address and contact numbers right there in the file, so what I do next is try all those, but all I get is 'Mr Tobczyk's away on sick leave and we don't know when he'll be back. Would you like to leave a message?' No, I bloodywell wouldn't.

So that's it, then. Smeg.

For dinner Kane goes out and brings us some sangwidges and passion fruice cos he says I'm not going out again without my makeover.

'I'm fine as I am, mate. Really.'

'If he's still in Rio, there's always a chance we might run into Tobczyk or one of his boys, and if one of them should recognise you we lose the element of surprise. I don't want that to happen under any circumstance. Never leave anything to chance if you have a choice, Little Turtle.'

'Remind me to ask the Tank for a rise when I get back.'

* * *

My makeover consists basically of a poncey haircut, a fake moustache and beard (not one of the kiddy ones, brother, the proper kind make-up people use in like films, ultra realistic) and a pair of neeky steel-rimmed specs.

'I don't look much like my snaps in them documents.'

'That's okay. Everyone's entitled to some change. Anyway, if they don't know you that well and haven't seen you for a while and aren't expecting to run into you here, Tobczyk and his men wouldn't recognize you now even if you walked up to them and trod on their bloody toes.'

I zap myself in the brown-specked mirror and like cringe. There I am, brother, a poncified git in granny gigs with a bushy minge round my trap and shredded yogi sticking up from my bonce looks like it was cut with a set of blunt secondhand gag dentures. As the new politicos like to say when they want to sound wiv it, a right fucking omnishambles. And as if this wasn't enough, I am now well and truly on my way to having some yampy bird tie like ropes round my nutmegs and half-strangle me on the say-so of a nutter thinks he's a fucking Indian. How's that for a larf?

Clifford Fuchs, photo-fucking-journalist? Little Turtle? Ker-rist.

You know, on the plane over I read my horoscope in the paper they handed out. It said to take it easy and trust my instincts this week. Well, brother, right now my instincts are telling me to get the fuck out of here, live-o, before it's too late.

***

The reason for the fake name and mockuments is only made clear to me next ay-em over breakfarts (and they don't half do a handsome nosh-up here, I can tell you, even have the snazzy little zigzag edges on the fruit). This is just before Kane leaves for Holy Ghost-land, and if like me you was thinking I was going to have a bit of a day off you was dead bloody wrong, brother, cos he hands me a couple of what he calls 'scouting parties' for today that aren't going to be easy to pull off, not nearly, never mind pleasant.

Come evening, I am to pay the aforementioned Kinbaku Garden a visit and, employing all my natural wit and Charlie Charm, enquire discreet-like if there's any one of the ladies in the establishment might as it were indulge me in a little perversion that's not on the regular menu, if you know what I mean, requiring specialised like training and skill in the strangling arts.

'Set up a meeting with this woman if you find her, then quietly leave without drawing attention to yourself. Do you understand?'

'What's there not to understand?'

But first the hard part. This morning, using my fake photographer's ID and press cards, I am to arrange an interview with one Fernando Tavares Lima, he being none other than the bloody colonel in the Rio state military police department, the PMERJ, that was named by Pinto in his notebook as the bent cozzer he spotted talking to Tobczyk on and off over a period of like several months. Now, some time during the night (I tell you, brother, the creepy sod don't sleep, don't eat, he's not fucking human), Kane has somehow also learnt that it was this bloke ordered the raid on the favela what led to information that helped turn up enough incriminating evidence against El Pitufo to get him put away.

'But I don't get that at all,' I says. 'If this bent cozzer was in with Captain America, why the fuck would he go after Camacho?'

'Because of the World Cup in 2014.'

'Eh? Have I missed something?'

'I suspect his hand was forced.'

I wait, but he seems to think this is quite enough clarification. Well it takes a bit of doing, but eventually I get it out of him, brother. It's like this. First you got to understand that the Brazilian Federal Government is putting a lot of pressure on the local plod to cut down crime and clean up the favelas in time for the World Cup. So this has got Lima on a tightrope, what with his crooked connections pulling him down one way and the threat of ending up in prison himself on corruption charges weighing him down on the other. So he has to arrest Camacho. Now it's no bloody coincidence Camacho died just four days after his arrest, neither. The official inquest concluded he'd been killed by prisoners of a rival gang during a riot, but you just know those prisoners didn't kill him for the fun of it. Looks like Colonel Lima knew El Pitufo wouldn't keep his trap shut for long if he didn't get a deal, which Lima knew he couldn't give, so Lima decided to get rid of the drug baron before he started to bubble and make things sticky for all his old pals in uniform.

'Then he's probably after Captain America as well,' I say.

'Lima is under close scrutiny, so he can't be happy knowing Tobzcyk is still out there with so much evidence against him.'

'Maybe he'll find Tobczyk and save us the trouble.'

'That's not going to happen.'

'Why not? He did for El Pitufo.'

'Hunting down Tobczyk is my job, Little Turtle. No one else can have it.'

'What difference does it make who bloody tops him? He'll be dead, won't he?'

'You know fuck-all of the ways of war. How you die is more important than how you live.'

'Sure it is. Anyway, just what eggzakly do you hope to learn by interviewing this Lima joker?'

'Two things. First, with Camacho dead, Tobzcyk had to find new contacts in order to keep his business afloat. The favelas would have been the obvious place to go first. Despite the recent raids, many of the old traffic routes were still in operation. The way things work in the favela follows the hydra principle: cut off one head, and two grow in its place. So some time between Camacho's arrest and his own hasty departure, Tobzcyk established contact with these new suppliers. And that means they probably know how we can reach him. I want Colonel Lima to tell me who they are and where I can find them.'

'And why the fuck would he do that?'

'He doesn't have to know he's telling me.'

'OK, and what's the other reason?'

'Remember what I told you before: a hunter always studies his prey.'

The cube of papaya I'm about to pop in my gob slides off the end of my fork and rolls under the table. But I don't care, I'm too busy zapping Kane with my bloody jaw hanging open, cos I ged-dit now.

'You've got to be fucking kidding me.'

23

FORKED TONGUE

'Bleeding bloody Gog almighty, we haven't been here a day and you've already seen two bloody geezers off, scrunched one up into a ball no less, and now you're saying you're going after a bloody military police colonel. I mean, I thought we were here for Captain America.'

'Three.'

'Eh?'

'Three geezers. Don't forget the security guard.'

My lamps do a slow spin then fix on him again. He goes on munching away at his toast, as poker-faced as ever. I throw my fork down.

'That's my whole bloody point!'

I try, brother, but no matter how much I argue the case against such out-to-bloody-lunch lunacy, Kane's not budging an inch. He's going to do this colonel mush and that's that. What's more, if I interfere at all or get in his way, he says, he'll make bloody sure I regret it.

Well, fancy that.

'Don't you think it's a bit daft sending me to talk to him first?'

'Not in the least.'

Is it me, or is it just the fucking world spinning? I mean, just for starters, brother, in case you hadn't noticed, it's a fact established beyond any doubt that I don't speak a fucking word of bloody Portuguese, but this doesn't seem to strike Kane as what you might call a problem at all.

'Do you still have the phrasebook I gave you?'

'You should do stand-up comedy, you should.'

'I am sure you'll find someone there with enough English to act as interpreter. It's a perfect set-up, really, because this way Lima will feel he is more in control. He can't be happy with the idea of an interview.'

'Then why is he doing it?'

'Because he hasn't any choice.'

'What d'you mean, he hasn't any choice?'

'The last thing Lima wants right now is for a couple of journalists to come nosing around asking him a lot of questions about him and his wormeaten battalion, but whether he likes it or not, the world's eyes are turned to Rio as it prepares to host the World Cup and the Olympic Games, and the state police needs all the good publicity it can get, especially abroad, because everyone is worried about the violence and lack of security. Of course Lima's superiors will jump at any opportunity of showing themselves in a favourable light in the foreign press.'

Right. Plain as buggery.

'We'll promise them, in writing if we have to, the final word on the article, anything they want to change they can change, text, pictures, anything. We'll say we just want a chance to tell the folks back home about what great heroes they are and what an important job they're doing decriminalising the favelas to make Rio safe again.'

'And how the fuck am I going to make them believe all that?'

It's Kane's turn to roll his lamps.

'By *lying* to them, Little Turtle, by *lying* to them.'

'Nice. Did you think that one up all by yourself? And what bloody rag are we supposed to work for, then?'

'We'll say we're freelancers. I have ready a made-up portfolio that should make their eyes pop.'

'I don't even have a bloody camera.'

'Yes, you do. It's upstairs in my room.'

I got to hand it to him, brother, he fucking thinks of everything, the gafty bastard.

'You're not half sussed for a Scouse Indian, I'll tell you that.'

'They're expecting you at ten. You don't have to say much. Let them get a good look at you, and perhaps pretend to make preparations for the photo shoot. Take a few light readings, that'll look convincing. Tell them we'd like to do the interview the day after tomorrow, if that's convenient, say around two in the afternoon.'

I pause a second to like organise in my nut all the things I think are wrong with this glocky mad fucking plan of his.

'And when you've got what you need out of this Lima geezer, you're just going to kill him, is that it?'

'Yes.'

'And it hasn't occurred to you that topping a fucking colonel in the Rio military police may just be a tad difficult, even for you, not to mention the fact that it'll most likely bring the entire bloody force down on us like a ton of fucking TNT?'

He leans across the table and his voice drops an octave or four.

'I'll say this for the last time. I am going to make damn sure Colonel Lima doesn't make it to the end of the week. Is that understood? I have pledged this, and smoked on it. So don't let's say any more about it.'

***

So after breakfarts we go up to his room and he gives me the camera he's bought, a really snappy looking Nikon D3s professional DSLR, plus a case full of compartments stuffed with all sorts of like expensive lenses and cables and hi-tech knick-knacks and shite, then he hands me a bit of paper with Colonel Lima's military police unit's address on it in big block letters, and, just like that, tells me to be on my way.

'But, but...'

'There's a bigger power in the world than ours, one that shapes our being and everything around us. Find your way back to the centre, Little Turtle. Trust in Wakan Tanka. I'll see you in one or two days, depending on how it goes.'

24

MAYFAIR

In the cab I'm shitting bricks, brother, big ones, with sharp pointy edges. I mean it's one thing dealing with crooks back home, I'm used to that and it's my job, but it's quite another to troll in to a copshop in a strange country whose lingo you don't speak and try to pull a fast one on a bent copper on his own turf.

It's a short drive. I pay the man and get out.

I am now standing before a long, eight-foot white albert with a blue gate in the middle, through which can be seen a sundrenched parking area full of corralled cozzer jars, some of them in a right fucking state, full of dents and scrapes and even like bullet holes; dozens of people hanging about among the litter twiddling their fiddlies like they're waiting for something that never comes; and a big box-shaped three-storey building, painted white and blue, with bars in the windows and dirt everywhere else. A young plod in a sweaty uniform meets me at the gate and shakes my hand in broken English. He is Captain Gonçalves. Spread across his rosies is one of them broad, honest grins people give you when they've got something to hide. I give him back one that's eggzakly the same.

'This way, please, follow me. I take you to Colonel Lima.'

Sounds easy, don't it? But inside I first have to get my documents inspected by a clone of Captain Gonçalves sitting behind a snot-and-cardboard desk as banged-up as everything else in the place, with bent legs and peeling corners. Looking little-boy innocent, I play it cool while he's going through my fake papers, though I can't say I'm feeling too confident. This Gonçalves number two is an odd bastard. First off he starts by leaning so far forward across his desktop that for a second I think he's going to lick something off it, and you know what, he does lick something, only it's his prong which he uses to turn the pages on the passport very deliberate-like, reading through it as it might be a really good yarn with thrills, spills and hills of posh-n-bex, burying his pointy neb right in, taking time especially over my smudge, comparing my phiz to it with one roving eyeball while the other stays clamped to the photograph, and all the while he's humming to himself and nodding a bit to like leave me in no doubt he knows what he's doing. I mean you can tell he's concentrating hard cos his eyebushes is jammed tight together and he's got his tongue out a yard across his chin, but it's also clear he don't know sherbet from shit, brother. Skyscrapers of paper and like mountains of police crap leave hardly no room for his elbows while he's putting on this make-believe for my benefit. A phone beside him is going mad clanging nonstop at the top of its voice but he ignores it. Everything has the Rio state military police emblem stamped on it, even the bloody phone, and I bet he has one tattooed across his arse in all.

Finally he looks up at me, hands me back my documents, then starts grinning and shaking his bonce for some reason that I can't make out.

Oh, fuck, I'm thinking, and where's that Captain Gonçalves bloody vanished to?

I turn back to the faulty clone.

'OK?' I ask.

Pointing and gesturing, he makes me sign my name on a form I can't read.

'OK, sir,' says the original Gonçalves, suddenly materialising beside me out of thin air. 'Please to come this way.'

And I'm like Flynn, brother, so hold on to your plums cos here I bloody go: through a glass door, along a corridor, up some steps, down some steps, along a short dirty passage, down another corridor, through more doors, proper little maze this gaff, over hill over dale, till we come out into a hallway done up like a doctor's waiting room, with framed certificates and snaps on the albert and naff red plastic seats lined up on one side and a potted plastic plant on the other.

'Please sit,' says Gonçalves. 'Wait one moment.'

I do as I'm told and he goosesteps through a door marked 'Cel. F. T. Lima' after giving it a smart-like military rap with his knuckles. He goes in, and doesn't bloody come out again.

I sit there. Every now and then a cozzer comes in through one of the doors, takes a gander at me, and goes out again. Flies and some other insects I've never seen before do the same. I take the camera out of the bag and try to look professional holding it thisaways and thataways with my lamp clamped to the viewfinder and not just looking at the little screen behind while I wait. Is anyone watching? A rectangle of light has somehow forced its way through the inch of grot on the itty window at the end of the hallway and when I tire of arsing about with the Nikon I start to observe this as it creeps across the floor towards my foot, but however hard I look I can never catch it actually moving, if you know what I mean. A telly's on in one of the rooms somewhere, a bloke preaching his guts out screeching 'Jay-zoos' all the time in a crybaby warble with like canned religious music swelling in the background and great cheers. A fat middle-aged tart carrying a wooden tray appears and tries to sell me something looks like grade-Z fried dumplings dripping yellow car oil. I shake my bonce at her and she goes and knocks on Lima's door and is let in. I hear larfter from inside. And I'm thinking: have they really fallen for those fake papers? Any minute now they'll come for me with cuffs.

Nothing happens. The tart (she's a dog this one, brother, fur, fat and all) comes out and tries me again. I tell her to piss off in English and she grins. Her teeth are all crooked and she's wearing extra strong kingsize braces to punish them. She goes out and I scratch my arse and twiddle my fiddlies for an age or three. I count the hairs on the back of my groper. Still nothing happens.

In all they make me wait two fucking hours, brother, the skanky cunts, longer even, long enough for my nervousness to like peak and slump at least a hundred bloody times before finally turning into pure plain gut-acid resentment, till I'm thinking fuck you, you plod bastards, I hope ol' Chief Sitting Bill does the lot of you in, gives you all the full fucking deal proper doomsday gory and right painful-like.

When the door finally opens Gonçalves stands there waving me in without a word of like anything resembling an explanation let alone an apology. But I'm totally poker as I follow him into the room, brother, cos I may not know much but I bloody know my bizniss.

The room's bright and dusty. There's grey filing cabinets on one side, Brazilian and Rio state flags on woodworm-eaten poles on the other, and a sunbleached likeness of Pope John Paul II gracing the stained albert. Sat in a swivel chair behind a pock-marked desk is a bloke looks like a cross between Gomez of the Addams Family and a Mexican bandit in a spaghetti western, only he's geared up in a starched-stiff blue uniform with three stars stuck in his collar and a bunch of medals and coloured ribbons and badges like it might be a bag of liquorice allsorts spilled down all over his bloody shirtfront. His chin forgot to stop when it reached his neck so it just keeps going down into his collar in a single block, and what with the thick droopy moustache and a look in his lamps like he's just licked piss off a nettle the vibe he gives off is one of watch-yourself menace, brother, a proper little hornet's nest and no fucking mistake. I return the look: well, fuck you too, mate. But first impressions can be wrong and often as not are, and the next moment his scowl breaks out into an unexpected yard-wide smile of as it were welcome, showing lots of wrinkles down the sides though he can't be much over forty and a row of big square sharp white even teeth like it might be an advert for bloody toothpaste. Ultrabrite. His lamps, snot-green and with long thick black-enamelled lashes, have gone all twinkly now, and as he sticks out his paw for me to shake he says:

'I me sorry. I no speak English.'

The voice is deep but somehow a bit unsteady, like he's gargling with marbles.

I return the smile.

'And I don't speak Portuguese.'

He says something to the captain while nodding at me.

'The Colonel he want to know where will appear this—' He searches around in his nut for a word. 'This report.'

I put on my plummiest accent for this next bit.

'Mayfair. A big London magazine. Famous. Very popular. Very good. Nice pictures. You'll love 'em.'

Gonçalves translates. The Colonel seems pleased. The ceiling fan is on and uncombs his yogi some so he combs it back with his groper. He then picks up a paper knife and plays with it while he asks Gonçalves something else.

'The Colonel ask how much is—' He screws up his lamps looking for another word. 'How you say, payment.'

Well, fuck me, brother. These Brazilian bizzies don't fuck about, do they?

***

Sorted. All over in twenty minutes and easy as pissing in a pond. The interview's set for the day after tomorrow in the pee-em; I've promised the Colonel an article bursting with nothing but cheers and gush for him and his team of superplods, and two grand in his pocket into the bloody bargain.

Talk of crooked, brother, I mean blimey, there's just not enough to go round these days, is there?

But in my line of bizniss you learn very quickly to look out for anything goes too easy.

25

FULL THROTTLE

Early darkmans. I get out of the cab and troll across the pavement. On the outside the gaff looks just like any ordinary club: a big black box with the name stuck up across the front in jazzy bright letters, a double-door entrance guarded by an ape in a tight black suit and not a bloody window in sight.

The inside's more unexpected, a bit like one of them old samurai flicks, you know, all light wood, ricepaper and raffia-work in very tame bleached-out colours, with screens and prints on the alberts showing curly waves and snowy peaks and whatnot and bamboo plants and straw tatami mats on the floor where punters sit crosslegged drinking like tea and sake off tiny breakfarts trays.

In the middle is a low wooden stage, sticking out so the punters can sit round three sides of it and see whatever there is to see like real up-close.

I have to leave my shells at the entrance. A pretty little Brazilian mulatto bit in a blue kimono and heavy geisha make-up moves along with those hopalong babysteps and shows me to a vacant floormat about halfway to the stage.

There's only two empty places left now that I can see, so I'm guessing the gaff's popular. Who would've thort.

Nothing happens for a few minutes and I'm thinking, well here's a waste of time for you, if you like. Then the black curtain at the back of the stage parts. This very pasty bird comes on holding two tar-black candles. With the houselights dimmed low a spot comes on her giving the effeck of as it might be a scene happening by moonlight, very nice and atmospheric-like. The music turns to heavy drums mixed with these woody clacks and thwacks. Then a solid-looking Japanese geezer in a black kimono and red headband appears behind the woman with coils of rope hanging loose on his forearms. His arms look rock-hard and there's veins on them as thick as the ropes. He plonks the ropes down on the floor beside the bird and takes a bow, then begins to undo the bird's kimono. The punters clap like there's no tomorrow and in no time she's in the nip. The drums pick up the pace a bit as he starts to tie her arms with these lightning fast and smooth moves so the rope looks almost like it might be strands of oil or syrup, flowing and golden, and I have to say I am a little impressed by this, I mean Kane wasn't joking when he said it was like skilled labour, brother. Next he starts on her legs which he ties folded back (and this sort of brings fresh to mind images of dead Pinto), then he does her jagger and goes round that a couple of times so it's gagged good and proper and uses another rope on her chesticles (they being on the small side) till they're squeezed flat in the middle like it might be tubes of toothpaste. But is she bothered? I doubt it: from the oh-maybe-I'll-go-back-to-sleep expression on her dial she might as well be watching the telly or doing the bloody crosswords.

Now he ties a good thick roll of rope with lots of complicated ins and outs between her legs and round her arse between the cheeks up and down quick as you like, pulling tighter and tighter till she's well harnessed and going purple at the edges. And then comes the part everyone's been like dying for, brother, cos they all start goggling and ogling and panting and gasping, these punters, almost like it was them on that stage trussed up and not the zombified bird at all: the bloke slings the ropes round this pulley wossit hanging down from the ceiling, knotting the ends round different points on the girl with Ferrari speed, then gives them a few smart tugs and begins lifting her off the floor (it's a wonder her bloody shoulder joints don't pop out), up over the stage till she's sort of level with his bonce.

Sure enough there's stifled cries from her now, and they get louder when the bloke gets out a leather whip and lays into her with it real doomsday, dealing out these right nasty lashes all over, but especially on her slot machine and her little clenched arse which goes bright pink first then salmon red. A sight, brother, and one I could've done without.

And the show's over. The punters are ecstatic in their like appreciation of the great master's art. The master lets the girl down and unties her. She's in tears. Pain, joy, gratitude, hate? Who the fuck knows? Who cares? Everyone seems to think this is wunnerful, really triffic.

Right. Enough of this shite. I cop a zap at my Jaegre-LeCoultre. Time to get a bloody move on, Dodger.

I try to make my mulatto geisha twig that I want to know if any of her mates can parley English. She comes back after a minute with another geisha in tow. This one's even prettier, with a diddy turned-up nose, big sparkling lamps and a smile that makes you want to knob her right there and then in front of everyone right on the floor cowboy style.

'Can I help you?' she says, bending down towards me. If she only knew.

'Yeah. I was, like, wondering if any of you girls — I mean, do any of you like ever take part in the show, if you know what I mean.'

I'm having a bit of an um-ah here, brother. I mean do I feel like a square peg in a round hole, or do I?

'You like the performance?'

'Yeah. Very different, ain't it?'

'Oh, excuse me one moment.'

She hops off to attend to another customer and I have to wait a couple of minutes before she's free again.

'So, can I get you anything?'

'No, I don't want to order anything, thanks, I just wanted to know a bit more about these shows you put on here. I mean, I've never seen anything like it before.'

'Kinbaku is traditional in Japan, a very old culture of erotic art. It means "tight binding". The bakushis must study for many years to be masters. The bondage expresses the pleasure in ultimate control, to become the slave of your lover.'

She says this like she's said it a great many times before, a bit stiff and reeling it off like it might be lines out of a script.

'Right. And what about the girls?'

'They are the models. Artist models, you know.'

'But can like any girl become a model?'

'Yes, any.'

'Have you ever tried?'

A quick smile. 'Yes, of course.'

'And don't any like women ever get to do the tying part? I mean, you know, have the man as the model?'

'Few times. There are some women bakushi.'

'Ba-what?'

'The masters of the rope, the name is called bakushi in Japanese, or nawashi.'

'Is that what they are.'

'Excuse me.'

She's off again, a bit longer this time. When she gets back I figure I have to just get to the bloody point or I will miss my chance.

'What if I wanted to have it done? On me, I mean. You know, have a girl tie me up.'

She shrugs. 'Yes, it's OK.'

'Who could I get someone to do it? Is there anybody here, a girl I mean, who does it private?'

'Carla.'

'Carla? Is she here?'

'No, sorry. She is travelling.'

'When does she get back?'

'I don't know. She has many private customers.'

'How can I get in touch with her?'

'I'll give you her card. Wait.'

She waddles off and comes back with a little black bizniss card with wispy Japanese writing across the top in grey and *'Kinbaku: Arte de Amarração Erótica'* in block capitals at the bottom. In the middle is a name, Carla Nakamura, and a phone number and e-mail address underneath.

'Your sake is finished. One more?'

'Yes, OK. One more.'

Now I'm so chuffed at my easy success with this that I start thinking hang on, Dodger, ease off on the bile a bit, mate, perhaps you are on a lucky streak for a change, everything running so smooth here and at the copshop earlier. Why always so wary-chary?

But brother, I couldn't be more mistaken.

'Mr Clifford?'

A paw on my shoulder makes me spin my neck so fast the little tubes in it twang like guitar strings. They're out of tune, in all.

'I am surprise,' says the bloke on the end of the paw.

It's that sweaty cozzer Gonçalves, only he's not sweaty now but done up in his going-out gear, spick as you like.

'What a coincidence,' I say, knowing full well there's no such bloody thing. Lucky streak my arse. These cunts had me followed.

'You like this bad sexy things?' he asks, sounding like Borat.

'Who wouldn't?'

'I think is very sick.'

'Oh yeah, very sick.'

'May I join you?'

'Make yourself at home, mate.'

He plots down beside me. Three punters down, the pretty geisha is giving us the zap. She knows what he is and is starting to wonder about me.

'Mr Clifford, you are happy about your accord with Colonel Lima, yes?'

'Very.'

'Good, good. So we must to be honest, Mr Clifford, we must speak only truth each to another. Secrets is a bad, bad thing if we have accord, no? You don't agree?'

'OK. What about it?'

'Mr Clifford, because you come here? Because to this place?'

Now I'm figuring this has nothing to do with Captain America but with Camacho. The Kinbaku was his favourite playground, after all. These daft plods must think we're after a story on him, curious about the fishy execution in prison, maybe trying to dig up the dirt on the Colonel and blow the lid on the tin of worms that is the state police's connection with the drug trade in Rio. But how do I play it, brother? What, or how much, do I tell Gonçalves?

'It's got nothing to do with Camacho, if that's what you're thinking.'

His bonce swings down slowly to one side and he's narrowing his lamps at me and pouting his lips like he's been watching too many Bruce Willis films.

'We are friends, no?'

'What's that supposed to mean?'

'Friends help one to the other, Mr Clifford. You help me, I help you. Everybody happy.'

'If you're happy, I'm happy.'

But something's still not right cos his bonce is shaking from side to side and the diehard pout has turned into a leery oily smile.

'No, no, no, my friend. I am sad.'

He goes on zapping me for a bit, the smile getting smaller and smaller till there's nothing left but a hard stare. Then he gets up and leaves. At the door another bloke who's been waiting at the wings all along joins him and they go out together.

Shit.

Shit, shit, shit.

26

BULLSEYE

finish up my sake while I grind over nice and piecemeal everything Gonçalves's just said, only it's really the bits that didn't get
said that are the problem, if you know what I mean.

So much for making an exit without drawing attention to
myself. Kane's going to have a bloody cow.

There's another performance getting like ready to come on
so I pay my bill quickly and head for the door. Outside I take
a quick lookround to see if my chum Mr Plod is still lurking in
the shadows, but there's too many people about and I don't see
nothing suspicious. I womble off to one side to look for a taxi to
take me back to the hotel. There's plenty passing up and down but
it being such a busy night they're all taken so I have to go to the
corner where there's a busier main road. I've still got my lamps
like peeled for anyone might be following but as I'm expecting
this to be in a motor I fail to clock a couple of roughies trickle out
of a dark doorway mouselike behind me and very quickly take up
positions back and front, blocking my path.

Of course I've no doubt what this is, brother, not for an
instant. They're like pretending to be muggers but I can smell
plod a mile off, and these two have the ronk all over them and
no mistake.

The one in front's got his groper under his shirt like it's a
barker tucked in his strides and the one at the back grabs my
arm.

'Gonçalves not joining us?' I say, making sure I pronounce the name loud and clear.

'*Cala essa boca, filho da puta.*'

I don't know what the words mean but you can bet your lychees I get the drift all right. I shake my bonce and try the chumly approach, giving a smile. It's not working. The front one zaps his mate over my shoulder and gives this micro nod, a sort of tictac or signal with his lamps it is, and instanter I get clonked on the back of the bonce hard enough to drop me on one marylebone and there's the old familiar feeling like an electric shock shooting through my insides real doomsday. My bonce is down and I've hardly had time to like register what's happening when the cunt in front sees his chance and chooses an angle, kneeing me spot on target right in the jagger. This sends me back-flipping and I land like a wet sandbag hard and heavy on the pavement, splat. I don't go out but it's as near it as fuck, rolling about in this fairy twilight zone, moaning and in my mindfog trying to swear at these scrote bastards I can no longer see properly cos the world's all blurred up and bottled in bloody malt vinegar. I'm tasting blood: my trap's gone spongy and my nosewells is going proper spigot spout, gargling thick blood back into my throat. Suddenly my rigging's being yanked sideways and the stitching torn by a groper digging deep in my jacket pockets taking all it can as fast as it can, snatch snatch snatch.

One, two, and they're gone.

I lie there moaning, not moving. The stink of the pavement all gritty and grimy against the side of my bonce is making me sick but I can't make it to my feet. I have to wait till things stop spinning a bit, brother, I've got the giddywillies so bad. I've been stoved like this a few times before and I know it's like a mistake to try to get up and wander off cos chances are you'll fall straight back down again and risk cracking your skull-bone open against some hard edge so the damage is like twice as bad.

I got my lamps open now and can see there's people passing and giving me the wide-eye lying there but the moment they zap the damage and the puddle of gore they like turn away and move off quick-sticks not wishing to get involved in anything messy, all except this girl with a kind round dial who kneels down and asks me in soft Portuguese something like 'Are you OK'. She has a couple of chums with her, another girl and a boy, but they stand back at first. She helps me up, this kind one, and gets out her moby to call an ambulance but I say no, I'm all right, thanks, I just want to get back to my hotel like. With true sisterly instinct she argues with me over this for a bit and her mates join in now not afraid anymore but given we don't grok half of what each other is saying and the fact that I'm really all right only a bit stunned and the bleeding's stopped except for my hooter (always the same, brother, I should have it replaced with a new one made of rubber), they eventually help me get a cab and explain the situation to the driver.

In the back seat moving through traffic I try to make sense of what's happened and go through what's left of my pockets to check what's missing. It's not just the ready they've taken, brother, but all the fake Clifford Fuchs documents as well, press cards, passport, the bloody lot. And what that means is Lima and Gonçalves not only want to frighten the nosy gringo journalist off this story, they also want him trapped in the country where they can keep an eye on him long enough to figure out what's the goods he's got on them and maybe even shut him up if they have to. Yeah, I'm thinking, Kane's take on Camacho's death was on the button and no mistake.

And then I remember: they've also taken the bondage bird's card. Bollocks.

I actually consider going back for another, but the thought only lasts like a millionth of a nanosecond cos fuck it, I'm too done in. If he likes Kane can bloody well come and get the fucking card himself.

At the Saraiva I ask the driver to wait while I go and fetch some ready for the fare. The receptionists all do fly-catchers when I troll in and start asking me what happened. I ask for my key and tell them nothing, the nosy sods.

I come down and pay the driver.

Back upstairs I wash up and pass out.

***

When I open my lamps again I'm feeling like fifty shades of shit — all of the runny variety. It's the ay-em and the sun's going like a fucking blowtorch through the curtains I forgot to close last night and so bloody nuclear bright that looking at it shining there on the albert feels like having nine-inch nails driven through my eyeballs and into my brain inside all the bloody way in, proper screamer.

I shut the curtains and crawl to the khazi.

Though hidden a bit by the fake beard I can see my jagger's puffed up real horror-film, making me look an extra from the Planet of the Apes. But the way I look is not half as bad as the pain I feel when I try to actually move my lips. A quick inspection in the mirror reveals a big ugly gash on the inside of the bottom lip. I check my choppers with a prong. They all feel a bit numb and loose, but that's quite norman and only to be expected like, given the wallop they received, just thank Gog nothing's broken nor chipped even cos I fucking hate going to the dennis.

I wash off the dry blood and do a quick spring clean. I'm bloody marvin but all I can manage in this state is liquid through a straw, so I order up swill and coffee.

I'm on my back again when Kane arrives banging on my door a couple of hours later. I open it and the moment he zaps me the eyebrows shoot up.

'What happened to you?'

I tell him.

'They took everything?'

'Yeah.'

'But the interview's on?'

'Yeah, I suppose.'

'And did you manage to get anything at the Kinbaku Garden?'

'Yeah. I had a bizniss card with the bird's name but that got taken too.' It's very painful for me to speak, brother, and the words come out all wobbly and mangled. 'And before you ask, no, I don't remember' comes out sounding like 'an feefoh you ass, wo, I wo wewemba.'

Kane's smiling.

'Pack up, Little Turtle. We're moving.'

27

DREAM-CATCHER

Kane's got this blue Toyota pick-up parked outside looks older nor he is, all dirty, scratched and banged-up, and in it we drive round to a furnished first-floor flat he's rented on short-lease in a quieter part of town somewhere away from the bright tourist spots, seedy-like and not near the beach at all. And when the fuck did he get this done, I ask. But he's in gator mode not saying nothing. I ask him is this our new home and is he going to carry me over the threshold. Not a blink.

The gaff's small, a shoebox livingroom, couple of bedrooms not big enough to open your arms in, a bathroom full of cockroaches and a kitchen looks it was made for the gnome people of Squatland, it's so fucking tiny. Few tins and packets of food here and there on the tiny shelves. His clobber's already here too, bags in one of the bedrooms and a large holdall and a couple of long boxes in the living room. The artillery, I'm guessing. I notice he's also got this odd-looking thingamajig hanging over his bed just like the one I seen back in his tent in Wales, a sort of midget-sized hoola-hoop with like fishnetting strung across it and four long feathers stuck on the bottom.

'What's that?' I ask.

'A dream-catcher.'

'Come again?'

'You see, the web is a perfect circle. It'll catch your good ideas, and the bad ones will fall through the hole in the center. We hang dream-catchers over our beds to sift our dreams and visions, separating the good forces from the bad. The good is captured in the web of life, but the evil in our dreams drops through the hole and is no longer a part of our lives. They help shape our destiny.'

I give a huge yawn. 'My destiny definitely needs shaping,' I says. Then I take my stuff into the room I'm going to be sleeping in. He goes into the kitchen and says:

'Would you like a house-warming glass of milk, Little Turtle?'

'I'd like it better if you called me Dodger.'

'Yes, but that isn't your name. That name is the half man's name, bad wakan.'

'That's what you say.'

'Why do you fight it? Don't you want to become a human being, a full human being? You must throw off your old skin if you want to grow, like the snake, because it has become too small for you. Little Turtle is your true name now, even if you don't know it. And maybe one day you may even have a sacred name, and a spirit name.'

I uh-huh a couple of times and like stroke the chin for a bit. Then I ask:

'Like you, you mean?'

He nods.

'So your name's not William Kane?'

He shrugs. 'Tell me, Little Turtle, the hair and nails you cut, are they still you after you throw them away?'

My turn to shrug. 'Fuck knows. Never gave it much thought, to be honest. But if you're not William Kane, who are you now, then?'

'I told you,' he says. 'Otaktay.'

'And that means...?'

'Kills-Many.'

I shake the bonce at this one, brother, I really do. 'Me,' I says, 'I could never make sense of refined humour.'

'Do you know what you're doing with your life, Little Turtle? Like all people, you have great power, but it's buried deep inside you.'

'Power?' I says, going for the joky approach. 'Money is power, mate.'

He just stares at me. Hard. Starts giving me the wibbly-wobblies, it does. So I change the subject, like pronto.

'And what's all this about milk, anyway?' I says, injecting lots of chum into it. 'I mean, what's wrong with a nice bottle of cold beer?'

'I don't drink alcohol.'

I'm all smiles. 'My mother told me never trust a man who doesn't drink.'

'You should listen to her.'

'Oh I did, I did...'

'Did?'

'Yeah. She's dead now, bless her.'

He goes sort of quiet for a bit, then asks:

'And your father?'

'Never knew him. Left before I was born.'

He kind of leans back in his chair, sighing like, then tilts the whole chair back on its hind legs and hooks his thumbs into his front pockets, zapping at me down the length of his nose.

'You know,' he says, 'my father left us as well. My mother, my sister and me. I was about, oh, four or five... He was never around much anyway, so it didn't really make very much difference. I hardly remember him at all... And Mum, well—' He clicks his tongue against the roof of his mouth. 'She was a very hard-working woman. You know, always busy with something, jobs, money, problems... Always complaining. God, how she liked to bitch at life. She worked bloody hard. And she *was* hard, you know, a very hard, prickly woman. But I think it was all just so she could turn round to us and complain about what an awful lot she had on her hands, what with all the washing and cleaning and cooking and looking after us, ungrateful little wretches that we were, my sister and me. Cursing her luck and her life: that was her one true pleasure.' He gives a sad sort of chuckle. 'I dream of her sometimes. Not very often, just occasionally. She's always wearing her old apron, long and white and full of soup-stains, and she reaches out, stretching her arms out for me, but I just tell her, "You're not my mother any more. You're dead. And I'm not your son. He's dead, too."'

I look at him. 'Your dream-catcher doesn't catch those, then?' I ask.

He gives a half-smile. 'No,' he says, then looks away and returns to his silence, thinking, thinking...

He's diving deep, I can tell, going back. Well, who would've thort, eh? I mean I never expected him to start talking like this, brother, about himself and his childhood and the like, all intimate, especially not to yours truly. A bit of humanity seeping through the armour, it would seem...

28

PHYLLOBATES TERRIBILIS

W e sit in this silence for a long spell, thinking and remembering, me as well now, about Mum and my own childhood and all that, mucho like nostalgic and mushy, then after a few minutes of this I sort of look up casual like and I notice he's got this big glass box in his room, a terrarium I think it's called, filled with dirt and pebbles and bigger rocks and plants and shit and sitting there in the middle of it all is this diddy yellow kermit, the colour so bright it looks artificial-like and painted on.

'What the hell's that?' I ask.

He snaps out of it too and sort of looks round. 'A beauty, isn't he?' he says, seeing what it is I'm pointing at. 'I call him Kola.' He explains that this means 'friend' in the Sioux Lakota language, brother. 'I picked him up on the way down from Vitoria. He's from Colombia originally.'

Gog, I'm thinking, what next?

***

Well, I have my moo-juice with florncakes and then really let my hair down and trough down a couple of cream crackers. After our cordon-bleu celebratory banquet Kane gives me a peek at what's in the holdall. A Heckler & Koch PSG1 sniper rifle, a Beretta 92FS, a couple of Brazilian Taurus PT92 stainless chrome semis and a weird-looking stocky FN P90 carbine uses small caliber high velocity cartridges.

'You could start a revolution,' I says.

'There are many kinds of revolution, and they come in different sizes, too.'

'Do they, now?'

'There are some hunting knives in my room, as well. Do you like knives, Little Turtle?'

'Only to spread butter with, mate.'

He goes out again soon after that not saying a word and as I'm still feeling a bit off and still like nanxed I go to my room for a bit more John and Yoko bed-peace just lying there half-asleep till he gets back. But apart from the kingsize cockroaches (I'm not joking, brother, I found one sniffing about in my shoe was as big as a bloody lobster), there's a community of about a million skeeters living in this flat – I mean it's *their* fucking flat, and to prove it they don't stop biting and whining in my ear for a second so come night-time I'm itchier than a bear's arse on an anthill and can't really nod off all the way like into the deeper zeds.

So I'm awake most of the darkmans and at one point during the wees I hear Kane come in but don't get up right away. Two forty-three, it says on the Jaegre-LeCoultre. I cock an ear to listen. He's in the khazi and the tap's running and then the shower. I wait till he comes out but he goes straight to his room.

I get up to have a glass of water and go for a slash.

It's when I'm washing my gropers I notice it: red droplets and like pink trickles on the side of the basin.

Uh-oh. I know what that is.

***

Morning. I don't much feel like getting out of bed but I do. It's late. There's the jumbo cockroach in my shoe again and I chase it about the room but it's too fast for me and squeezes between a crack in the plaster.

Breakfarts is florncakes and dry wholemeal crackers again. Kane's still not saying nothing, but I ask anyway:

'So, where did you go last night?'

He doesn't look up and just keeps munching away at his flakes. 'How's your mouth this morning?' he asks.

'I saw the blood in the washbasin.'

But Kane's pretending I haven't said anything. After a bit he raises his lamps and zaps me straight on.

'Did you feel any mosquitoes?'

'You're not going to tell me, then?'

'Did you know, Little Turtle, of all the humans who have ever died, at least half were killed by mosquitoes. That's about 45 billion people.'

'OK, mate, suit yourself.'

***

For the rest of the morning I sit around twiddling my fiddlies and playing silly games on my iPhone while he takes care of his kermit Kola. He's feeding it like dead beetles and ants from a tin and spraying it with mineral water. A bit later he goes into the kitchen and boils a pan of water. (Is he going to cook the ruddy thing?) Then he puts on these thick gloves and takes the frog out of the terrarium wossit and puts it in a metal sieve which he holds over the pan with the steam still coming off it thick. (He is!) Well it must be pretty hot and Kola gets frisky trying to squirm and jump away but Kane holds it down. What the fuck, I'm thinking. This goes on for a couple of minutes. Then he takes the frog still alive and in the sieve back to his room and with this flat metal spoon starts like scraping its back. I can't see what but there must be something coming off the frog cos Kane keeps transferring the spoon to a small glass vial or is it phial like something out of a kiddie chemistry set he then seals up tight with a rubber stopper.

I play the divvy git again and yes, ask him what he's doing. I might as well have asked the bloody frog. Well, you can only try, can't you brother?

For lunch we go down to a baker's across the street where they serve oily rice, beans, cat meat and last week's salad. It's cheap and tastes it too. By the time we're done there it's almost time for the interview with Lima.

Back in the flat Kane goes all nurse on my jagger and it's not looking nearly so bad now. I get my camera and the rest of the gear together and he's got this digital voice recorder and note-book and pencils and stuff.

***

We take the Toyota. Again, Kane driving. He knows the way. We park outside the copshop gates and a different uniform lets us in. Where's that cunt Gonçalves? We go through the check-in routine again with the dozy tongue-artist going over Kane's papers but when it's my turn of course Kane has to go into a shitload of pseudo-Portuguese explaining what happened and why I haven't reported the mugging yet (they're saying I should have a document from the police saying my passport was nicked) and please hurry up, Colonel Lima's expecting us and so on. My only contribution to all this is to keep repeating that cunt Gonçalves's name and pulling faces and shrugging as though to say 'where is he?' and 'why isn't he here?'

But we get through eventually, brother, and are led through the ratmaze to Lima's office, but this time round there's hardly no waiting, just enough time for Kane to excuse himself and nip to the khazi and back.

Lima's as chumly as before, shaking hands and flashing the big white smile all round, but there's no fucking mistaking the zap he gives me as I sit down. He knows all about the other night, brother.

Kane asks Lima something and he nods, so Kane turns to me and says:

'OK, Cliff. The Colonel's says feel free to take all the snaps you want while we conduct the interview. I'll just set up my recorder here...' He plonks the digital recorder down on the desk close to Lima, who pouts down at it as it might be a nasty cockroach eyeing his lunch. 'Good. So we can start.'

Kane asks Lima a short question and Lima starts stroking his moustache and frowning and making with the wrinkles before answering. I cross to one corner of the room and point the camera at him and take a few snaps. When he sees this he raises his groper in front of his dial and grumbles something to Kane.

'He says he's not comfortable answering questions while his picture's being taken, after all, so perhaps we can leave the pictures till after we've done the interview, Cliff.'

I sit down again.

Lima chews over Kane's question a bit more. Then he starts talking and his lamps go instantly shifty. I haven't a clue what he's chunnering on about but Kane's nod-nodding away and making diddy scribbles in his black notebook just like the real thing. There's a knock on the door and the same bulldozer I seen before selling dumplings sticks her bonce round the edge, but this time Lima just waves her off. He then gets up and talks to the cozzer outside and I think he's saying something like he don't want no more interruptions.

He comes back in and sits down. The smile's back in place. There. All cosy now. Where were we?

Kane picks up the recorder and plays back the first question. The sound's a bit rough so he takes a tiny mike out of his pocket, plugs it in and asks Lima to clip it to his lapel. Lima takes the mike but then pulls back his groper with a jerk like the thing's bitten him. He looks down at it then at his thumb, where a pearl of blood is forming. He sucks it, says something to Kane, who shakes his bonce, then picks the thing up again, only this time with great care, holding it by the edges.

Right. It's on his lapel now. OK? All set.

Kane begins to ask another question but this time before he can finish Lima launches into a long speech, full of deep warbles, chest-thumpings and extravagant hand gestures.

Kane takes more notes, and I'm thinking: what the fuck does he need to take notes for when he's got the recorder?

We're into the third or fourth question, brother, and Lima's really letting himself go on this one, grinning ear to ear and show-ing with his gropers and stuff like pens and a stapler and a glass paperweight on his desk to represent like cars and cozzers and houses and things who did what where and how on some raid, when suddenly his songbox gives this odd kind of out-of-tune sigh and he stops in mid-sentence, zapping us with a look as it might be of surprise. Christ, I think, the fucking pip's dropped, he's on to us. But – and I'm not yeasting here — as I look his dial goes from a natural copper tan to a pasty lemon-curd, changing proper special FX right before my lamps, and then he starts like clawing at his heaver and gasping and drooling over his desk and opening his jagger again wide to like shout for help. But before anything comes out of it Kane's round the desk and on him live-o, shoving the notebook tubed-up right down his throat so he can't make a sound.

By this stage Lima's lamps is Cinemascope wide, popping with sheer terror like I seen once on this horse freaking at a fire-work display. Then he's gagging for air and the lamps start rolling back into his bonce, brother, real doomsday; he's going limp all over sagging to one side on his swivel chair like he's no bones left in him, but Kane holds him up and, gripping him hard by the shoulders, whispers something in his ear, first like he's making a statement and then like he's asking a question. Lima burbles and starts shaking and I swear, there ain't a drop of blood left in his rosies, brother, they're totally fucking porridge grey. Kane takes the notebook out of Lima's gob now and asks him again, whispering in his ear more urgent-like, only this time he holds up the diddy vial or phial I seen back at the flat with the scrapings off Kola the kermit's back, saying something about it to the Colonel like he's a teacher explaining a difficult problem to a thick student. Lima gurgles out something impossible to twig, chokes, drools a bit more, swallows, then manages another word or two, but very hoarse. Kane listens, encouraging him. When he's heard all what he wants to hear he takes the stopper out of the vial or phial and lets these three or four drops roll out of it onto Lima's tongue. He then stuffs the notebook back in the Colonel's jagger till it's halfway down his gullet and stands back when the juddering and shuddering routine starts up again. Lima shakes off one final jerk and stiffens, and I see the light sort of go out in his lamps like it was a bulb someone's switched off. This time he keels over not sideways but forwards, splat, his dial going down hard right on top of the paperweight and stapler with a nasty wet crunch, if you know the sort of noise I mean, brother. He doesn't move after that.

I don't fucking move neither. I mean, what in fuck's name was all that about?

There's total silence for a second. Kane leans forward, lifts Lima's bonce just enough to slide the notebook out of his jagger, then lets it drop back. Thud. He waits another second, checks Lima's pulse, neck and wrists both, then rushes suddenly to the door and starts shouting and making a lot of fuss like the place was on fire.

The guard rushes in, takes a zap at Lima, has a quick feel, goes green, stutters, pulls out his barker, waves it at us, then starts asking angry questions and giving sharp orders, not really knowing what the fuck else to do. Kane, acting like he's totally gobsmacked by all this, starts on what I'm guessing is a much revised and cleaned-up version of what's just happened. The guard's listening but his barker's still raised and pointed at our bonces. As for me, I am so numb it's almost like it ain't me sat there at all, brother, almost like I was watching all this from the outside, a staged scene, myself included, in a film as it might be. Proper out-of-body-experience, it was.

More people start pouring in, mobys out and everyone phoning at the same time, some arguing, then some time later a doctor shows up and examines the Colonel's remains.

We're taken away to another room for questioning. They lock the door on the way out. My camera's confiscated, but there's only that one snap of Lima holding his groper up in it, so I don't see what they're holding on to it for. They keep us there five hours, brother, and not even a bloody glass of water they give us, let alone any explanation. Kane's the only one enjoying himself, the crazy sod. Of course eventually it's all made clear, which means to say one moment we're being treated like a couple of fucking war criminals, then the next all these people — cozzers, doctors, suits — are suddenly crowding round us, darting and buzzing worse nor the fucking skeeters at the flat, nodding and smiling, offering us iced water and cigarettes and chewing gum now, some trying on a halfarsed sort of Portu-English to express their arse-felt apologies for the misunderstanding — you know how it is, everyone was caught by surprise, what were we to think, it was all so sudden and unexpected-like, what can anyone do in these situations, no doubt it's the same in your country, a healthy feller like Colonel Lima, who liked to keep fit, so hale and hearty, so young for his age, still in the prime of life and with so much still to look forward to, being taken out so sudden like that, so unexpectedly, who would've thort...

And what did they say killed him, brother?

A massive coronary.

Yeah. And you know what else? In all this time, Gonçalves never showed his face. Turns out he hadn't come to work that ay-em, wasn't answering his phone, no one knew where the fuck he was or what had happened to him.

Well, fancy that. Perhaps coincidences do exist, after all.

What do you think?

29

MICROWAVE

Now you know as well as I do what seen Lima off was no fucking coronary, massive nor otherwise, and that whatever Kane scraped off that bloody kermit's back was what done it, only I'm not getting nothing out of him tonight, not no way, brother.

It's late darkmans by the time we get back to the flat but I'm like whirring full fucking pelt still and not the least bit nanxed, what with all the zeds I been catching and the kick-in-the-nuts jolt I got from watching Lima snuff it and the warm chuffed-like feeling comes over me when I realise that cunt Gonçalves has somehow somewhere someway gone belly-up and kingdom-come too, courtesy of Chief Sitting Bill the Angel of Death. But how it's all been done, brother, well there's a question I wouldn't mind answered for a change. I mean I got a few theories knocking about the bonce, but none of them unshakable and one hundred per cent convincing-like, know what I mean?

Kane was in gator mode before we left the copshop and now he's shut up in his room, chanting his Scouse Indian prayers right waily-like and proper ceremonial, hey-a-hey-a-hey-a. He's stomping about like a herd of buffalo in there and this time he's even got the diddy rattle out. His way of saying thank you, no doubt, thank you Wanker Plonka for helping me take out them wakan-sica cunts so neat and smooth, ta very much, I. O. U. 1.

I fidget about for a couple of hours, scavenge what scraps of grub I can in the kitchen (we never had dinner and didn't have time to do any shopping; the baker's shut and there's nothing to eat but moo-juice, crackers and a couple of nanas look like Kane shat them), give up, and go to my room to begin my nightlong battle with the bloodsucking skeeters.

* * *

Like last night, I wake up in the wee wee hours, hot, sweaty and itching all over, hearing Kane bustling about. It's true, brother, he don't fucking sleep, ever. But before I can get up to see what he's doing the front door clicks shut.

The crazy bastard's gone out again. What is he, a fucking vampire or what?

* * *

Next ay-em I'm up early but he's not back yet, so after a quick splish-splash and a chas and dave I go down to the baker's on my own for breakfarts. I stuff my guts and also buy fresh French rolls, cake and instant coffee to take back to the flat.

When I come in he's there, crosslegged on the floor, dismantling the guns into their component parts. All except the Beretta.

'I hope you're rested. We're going out in half an hour.'

'Where?'

He goes on taking the shooters apart and arranging them in patterns on the floor and says without looking up:

'First get the camera. We're going to take some nice pictures.'

It's pictures of the guns he means, brother, but why, Gog only knows. This done, he goes into his room and comes out holding a plastic bag.

'Here,' he says, handing it to me. 'Your fake passport and press cards. I don't think we'll need them any more, but keep them with you just in case.'

Draw your own conclusions, brother. I've drawn mine.

***

In the car I ask about Kola and he says:

'Kola's a poison dart frog. The Choco Embera Indians in Colombia's rainforest use it to hunt for food. The poison is extremely potent. One frog has enough to kill around twenty humans. And the best thing is it's virtually undetectable.'

'How come they said Lima had a coronary?'

'The toxin shuts down the nervous system, which leads to heart failure and fibrillation. The symptoms are classic cardiac arrest: chest pains, vomiting, hypotension, atrio-ventricular block. But the poison itself is so rare there are no readily available lab tests for it.'

At the traffic lights a kid in dirty thunderbags with a dummy stuck in his blackened jagger knocks on my window and shows me the palm of his groper. I wind the window down and give him the change left over from breakfarts. Poor little sod can't be more than six.

'But how did you get this stuff into Lima in the first place?'

'A jagged edge on the microphone. The same principle as the dart. Zap: straight into the bloodstream.'

'Bloody hell, I could've touched that thing by mistake.'

'Yeah, you could have.'

'Tell you what though, it's better than what you did to Pinto. Cleaner too. And you don't even have to worry about getting rid of the package after. I'm surprised more people don't use it.'

'Well it's very hard to obtain. Not the frog, I mean, but the poison. The frog you can buy as a pet anywhere. The problem is if it doesn't eat the insects it gets in its natural habitat it becomes non-poisonous. In other words, useless. But Kola's fresh from the jungle.'

'And Gonçalves, you going to tell me what happened to him?'

'Oh, I went for a more traditional approach there, something nice and old-fashioned.. But enough chatting, Little Turtle. We better park down here. Bob Marley said he'd meet us at the bottom of the steps at ten.'

'Who?'

I look where he's pointing, brother, and fuck me if it ain't the entrance to one of the favelas. There's a flight of steps broad at the bottom and narrowing as it climbs up into a passageway at the top no wider than a doorway. Blink and you miss it.

'We going in there?'

Kane nods.

'There he is. Come on.'

***

Now I have to say, I'm seriously considering walking away from this. It's not so much the favela itself, though of course like everyone else I've heard some are downright hairy bloody holes, but what's really frying my fat here is what Kane may have cooking in his damaged brainpan to do once we're up there. I mean, if he tries any of his Indian warrior brave shit in this fucking powder keg no fucking way we're coming back down on our feet. Know what I'm saying, brother?

'Is there anything else you're planning here and not telling me about till it hits me in the face? I mean if you're going to top anyone up there tell me now cos I'm fucking not going.'

'Don't be ridiculous. It's like a bloody fortress up there, held by a very well equipped army. Last year they shot down a police helicopter using a stinger surface-to-air missile with an infrared homing system. We'd never make it out of there alive.'

'Well, as long as we're clear on that point.'

We get out of the car and saunter to where this Bob Marley bloke's slouching against a lamppost. He's a lanky nineteen-year-old

Jimi Hendrix lookalike, is Bob Marley, complete with pubic hair moustache and hooded eyelids, so why the fuck they call him Bob Marley Gog knows. He's wearing the usual surfer shorts, T-shirt and flipflops with about his own weight again of bling dangling from his neck and wrists. Kane says something to him while nodding at me like he's doing the introductions.

Bob Marley gives me a long bored zap, scratches his nutmegs and starts up the steps. We follow him. The steps are so steep I'm red and breathing through my jagger by the time we reach the top. There's two motorbikes and a skinny bloke waiting for us there.

I get on the back of one bike with Bob Marley and Kane gets on the back of the other one with the bones.

We zigzag fast up the narrow uneven streets, winding and with sudden like bends and out-of-level joins, always going uphill. The houses we pass aren't like the slum gaffs you imagine, bunged together any old way out of bits of cardboard, old doors and shit, but proper solid constructions, homes and shops and bars painted in bright kiddy playskool colours, only they're all squeezed together tight as a duck's arse and piled one on top of the other and at different angles so these tiny roads and narrow stone staircases run through everything like they might be diddy veins in a huge organism, and I'm telling you, brother, get lost in here and you'll never come out, no fucking chance. As if to mirror this from above, crisscrossing every-which-way against the sky are these great spiderwebs of wiring (the electrickery here is all stolen, and the dodgy DIY connections off the main grid proper fire hazards and no mistake) that make you feel even more trapped. There's litter and burst binbags and rubbish all over and open sewage running down the sides of the streets and the ronk's proper gut-turning in some places but no one seems to mind and there's rickety stalls set up everywhere selling food and doing a brisk bloody bizniss, too. Funny thing is this stink of stale piss and shit and dirty water gets right up in there in your nosewells along with this appetising like smell of frying onions and fresh coffee and roast chicken, and it's a bloody bizarre mixture that really says a lot about the place, if you know what I mean, what you might call a sort of metaphor. There's plenty of people coming and going wherever I look but they don't take much notice of us, I mean we get more attention from the flea-bitten half-starved bitsas who chase us for a bit but you can see have no energy at all being so thin and in this heat and even their bark's like real tired and feeble as it might be some old geezer clearing his lungs in the morning.

On the rooftops overlooking the entrance points are kids with fireworks. This is the favela's warning system: at the first sign of plod they let off these rockets to let everyone know the heat is on. These kids are at the bottom of the trafficking bizniss ladder. If they make it past their teens in one piece they hope to reach the top rung some day. Not so different from London, really.

The further up we get, going into the hub of the place as it were, the more we see these like squads of it might be four or five blokes, never fewer, all with barkers welded to their gropers, machineguns slung over their shoulders and grenades clipped to their belts, guarding the entrances.

We stop at this house looks no different from the others except it's painted red and black, has a huge parabolic on the roof and a balcony reaching out several feet over the street.

We're very professionally frisked going in by four tooled blokes at the door. Bob Marley leads us up an ugly red-and-black-tiled staircase (the colours I'm told are because of the football team, Flamengo) and onto the balcony where four blokes is sat in plastic sunloungers round an above-ground pool like a huge blue bathtub. A bloke with no voice is singing out of tune to a heavy factory beat over extra large speakers on the walls. There's a panoramic view of the beach far far below and a mile or two away to the right can be seen the luxury apartment buildings with flats going for as much as two million smacker, our money. Some of the windows is right in the line of fire, too.

The gaffer, a bloke goes by the name of '8', as in the number — *oito* in Portuguese — is a right bloody horrorball: face just a broad formless wob of flesh, like a bag of minced meat before it's cooked, with two dead piggy lamps buried deep and close together under a tiny bumpy forehead, skin on it like eroded breezeblock, and a set of huge crooked teeth look like they're trying to jump out of his jagger at you. It's a real thug's phiz: intuitive, stupid, cruel, ignorant, shrewd and vicious, yet somehow it still don't look half as crooked as Lima's did (now there was a face for the criminal face scientists, brother). Kane tells me he got his number moniker after killing eight rival gang members one night back when he was still making a name for himself. The deed also got a bit of repercussion notoriety-wise cos he apparently used something they call the 'microwave' system, which is basically you stick your client neck-deep into a stack of old tyres, pour kerosene on him, then set the whole thing alight.

Should get a larf out of the Tank when I tell him.

As we come off the steps these four geezers look up at us with the same dedpans you meet in the trade the world over, a sort of emotional chain mail, an expression that says 'you are nothing to me, you can't touch me, I'd as soon pop you in the canister as do bizniss with you'. I know it only too well. Two of them are smoking skunk zeppelins as thick as my bloody arm and there's a blanket of heavy smog over their bonces like a grey North Sea Particular.

Kane shakes 8's groper and then I do. He's been scoffing fries and it's pure bloody grease. The other three go on zapping us but make no effort to communicate otherwise. Kane and 8 exchange a few opening flourishes, both speaking very low and calm as they might be at a funeral. Bob Marley's standing behind 8's chair and there's two others standing one behind each of ours. Me, I'm just here as a prop, saying nothing and grokking less. Another mumbly question, another mumbly answer, but I can't make nut nor bolt of any of it, brother. Then 8 gives Bob Marley an instruction and he goes downstairs again and returns carrying a kilo package of familiar brick-like appearance, plonking it down between us on the table among the crisp crumbs, chicken bones and half-empty beer glasses.

Well, if it ain't old Uncle Charlie.

Kane and 8 mumble a bit more, then 8 takes hold of the package and makes a nick in it with a knife. With the tip he scoops up a couple of grams and holds it up for us to see. Bob Marley's ready with a glass tray and on that 8 cuts the charlie into three neat rows.

He offers it to me to try first. I hesitate and Kane takes the tray himself. Saying something to 8 he whips out a short gold straw from his pocket like he's the real-deal pro, does the first line, then hands the straw and tray back to me.

'Go on,' says he. 'They'll think it's suspicious if you don't.'

I snort my line. 8 takes the tray from me and snorts his. With a grin like a grenade wound he then looks up at us as if to say, 'what did I tell you?'

He's right, its proper pukka, grade-A chang, no doubt about it. Now I don't know how versed you are in the stuff, brother, but what a lot of people don't know, even like the hardarse users and abusers, is that street charlie you get anywhere in the world is never more than forty per cent pure these days, and often not even as much as five per cent. But even the jemmy stuff begins to look a bit dicey when you know what goes into the making of it, I mean I reckon if most people knew a bit about the actual process, which hasn't changed in like over a century, they'd do like I do and think thrice before taking it in any form or by any of the means available. Basically you get a bunch of coca leaves, leave them out to dry for a day, chop them up small, sprinkle them with powdered cement, soak them in petrol, press them, soak what you get from that in battery acid and add kerosene to the mixture to get your crude or freebase coke crystals, these are then dissolved in sulphuric acid to produce something about sixty per cent pure and very similar to crack. After that you have to use oxidising agents to convert this into salt cocaine to make it soluble in water, otherwise it'll float around inside you and give you a stroke or a heart attack – which is why you can't sniff or inject crack.

Not too appealing, is it? But it's a living, innit, so what can I say?

Well, 8's proud as a beanflicker with a hard-on over this stuff, proper beaming. Kane nods and grins back, then out of his backpack he takes out four neatly wrapped bricks of Brazilian ready, all in crisp clean-smelling new hundred-real notes. He hands the lot to 8, who doesn't touch it, ordering Bob Marley to take it instead. Bob Marley counts the whole thing out very thorough-like while we all twiddle our fiddlies and zap each other with nothing to say.

Out of the side of my jagger I whisper to Kane:

'How you going to find out where Captain America is?'

But 8 hears. He perks up at the sound of the name.

'Captain America?' he says, then adds something I don't understand. Kane answers, gives me a quick zap out of the corner of his lamp like he wants to jugulate me, and carries on the conversation like nothing's happened. I don't know what he says, but it seems the bomb's defused, 8's stuffing his guts and no one's looking tense.

The charlie goes into Kane's backpack. But we don't leave just yet. Kane looks at me again, but nodding like he wants everyone to see, and says something to 8, who bursts out larfing. Then 8 says something and they both have another nice giggle. Me, I just glance from one to the other like a git while they mug me up. Kane makes another crack and now 8's larfing twice as fucking hard, huge crooked ivories scraping away at the foul air like he was trying to bite a chunk out of it. Even the three cabbages by the pool are larfing now, fwaw fwaw fwaw.

Well fuck this, brother.

Wiping his tears, 8 calls Bob Marley and delivers another order. He's sounding definitely more chumly. Bob Marley leans over the side of the staircase and shouts to someone downstairs, relaying the order. Kane and 8 pick up their friendly natter, of which it seems I am the main subject or butt, cos every now and then one of them looks at me, says something to the other, and then everyone falls about larfing again.

A dumpy girl with a tight dress and about a ton of lippy spread across her kisser brings us all cold beers and fried chicken drumsticks to nibble on. Everyone's having a larf now and even Kane's taking swigs at his glass and munching away getting grease all over his prongs and jagger.

And I'm thinking: Drinking booze? Snorting the happy powder? What happened to all that talk about their being 'wakan-sica' and all that crap? Fucking lunatic.

And what a great little beano this is, eh brother? Except it fucking ain't, of course. I mean what the fuck are we doing coming here in the first place anyway? And how's buying a K of charlie going to fucking help? Not eggzakly what you might call within budget protocols, is it? Don't forget, brother, it's me has to keep the bloody books on this trip, it's me has to keep the overheads down to a minimum, and it'll sure as shit be me having to explain to the Tank what we did with all his wonga. I mean this brick of charlie's cheap as chips by comparison with the prices we sell it at back home, sure, but it's still a nice chunk of change, innit, it's still lolly. And if there's one thing the Tank likes it's his pigging lolly, I can tell you.

Well the party goes on for another hour or so and at one point I can tell there's even talk of jumping in the pool for a cool-off, only nobody does, thank Gog, otherwise there's no telling when we'd be out of this fuckhole, but Captain America hasn't been mentioned again and I still haven't heard the name Tobczyk either and frankly the whole experience just seems like one huge fucking waste of time to me and no mistake.

Finally Kane gets up and 8 kind of half makes it out of his chair, the fat biffa, and the others swivel their curried lamps at us as if to say 'it's been lovely, do come again', then Bob Marley leads us downstairs and out out out.

And about bloody time too.

We take the bikes again and they plonk us down where they picked us up near the top of the steps at the entrance to the favela. But Kane still has one diddy trick up his Scouse Indian sleeve.

He gets off the bike and whispers confidential-like in Bob Marley's ear, who then turns to Mr Bones with something like wait here a bit, I'll be back in a sec, you know, words to that effeck.

We climb down the steps. In the Toyota Kane brings out the Nikon and shows Bob Marley the snaps we took of the guns laid out on the floor of our flat. They talk over these pictures a bit like they was entering into negotiations, if you know what I mean, then Bob Marley takes out his moby and makes a quick call.

'*Oito? Os cara têm uns berro do caralho aqui pra vendê, meu irmão.*'

8, I'm guessing.

He talks a bit then puts the phone away and nods. 'OK,' he says to Kane. He looks at me and repeats it: 'OK.'

3 0

GOOSED

Nobody says a word during the drive back to the flat. Kane's at the wheel staring straight ahead. Beside him in the passenger seat Bob Marley keeps chewing the hangnails off his prongs and looking down to inspect them. Sat in the back I wonder: is it a habit, or is he getting jittery?

Kane parks the Toyota in the garage. We take the lift up to the flat and unlock the front door. Bob Marley's being extra cautious here: he has his groper on the butt of a barker tucked in under his shirt and makes sure we go in first. We all go in and when he sees there's no set-up of any kind he begins to relax.

OK, so far so good, only I still have no bloody idea what this is all about, brother. What it looks like is Kane's trying to flog the hardware, doesn't it, but I know that can't be right.

Can it?

In the living room Bob Marley squats down next to Kane to inspect the goods. He assembles the Taurus semis like he could do it blindfold and nods his appreciation of the sniper rifle after Kane's put it together. But it's the FN P90's really got his mouth watering, brother, I don't think he's never seen one in the flesh before and let me tell you, it don't half look the bizniss. Kane shows him the high velocity cartridges and assembles the carbine for him to see how it's done. Bob Marley takes the gun and tests its weight in his gropers, drooling. Kane's talking now like he's spouting off the technical specs, caliber 5.7 x 28 mm SS190, weight 2.54

kilos empty and 3 kilos loaded with magazine with 50 rounds, length 500 mm, barrel length 263 mm, rate of fire 900 rounds per minute, magazine capacity 50 rounds, effective range 200 meters, while Bob Marley listens all sweaty and dewy-eyed and tries not to cum.

When it happens, it happens quick, of course. I mean, like I blink and when I open my lamps again a millionth of a second later Kane's spoon-hand is under Bob Marley's shirt pulling out his barker and his watch-hand is clamped round Bob Marley's throat squeezing and pushing him backwards at the same time. But he's a live little cunt is old Bob and once he's over his initial fright he puts up a bloody good leff-n-rite, catching Kane one in the ribs hard with his L-bow then kicking out and missing Kane's ear by a fraction. He's still holding the FN P90 in one groper and as he tries to swing that into Kane's dial I jump forward and grab his legs but one gets loose and he lands a kick on the side of my bonce with his heel that sends me fucking spinning, brother.

I land with my back against the table and the dirty plate I'd left on it falls on top of me then smashes on the floor. By this time Kane's on his feet and he's got Bob Marley's barker. Bob Marley tries to scramble backwards across the carpet but it's too late: Kane brings his foot down hard on his right marylebone, then jabs the muzzle of the barker against his skull. Bob Marley's whimpering now, sagging, and then he starts to roll but not cos he's trying to get away any more but in real doomsday pain like some football player down for the count after a bone-crunch slide-tackle.

'What in fuck's name is going on?' I ask.

Kane keeps his lamps on Bob Marley.

'Get the backpack, Dodger. Bring me the roll of duct tape inside it.'

'What are you doing? Why did you even bring that bastard here?'

'I said bring it.'

I get the roll of tape and hand it to him. Bob Marley's recovered enough to start shouting a whole lot of threats and nasty names we don't understand.

'Get his legs,' Kane says. 'And this time make sure you don't let go.'

I grab hold of Bob Marley's legs and he tries to roll about and kick free again but his right marylebone's too buggered so he settles for more swearing. Kane gives him a kidney punch and a kick in the head then with the same foot rolls him over on his stomach. The swearing turns to a sobby sort of pleading but it sounds fake. I'm still holding his ankles. Kane empties the barker and chucks it on the sofa, then sits on Bob Marley's back facing his bonce. He ties his arms behind him with the tape, then comes and does the ankles.

'Bring a chair,' he says.

We plonk Bob Marley on the chair and Kane wraps him tight to it with more tape. Bob Marley's so scared now he's blubbing real tears.

'OK, Kane. You've got him tied up. Now I'd like to know what we're doing. Just for a change.'

'I don't know about you, but I'm doing what I set out to do. I'm doing my job.'

'Let me be more specific. What I meant was what are we doing going to a fucking favela, buying a K of cocaine off the local drug lord, then bringing his man back to our flat and beating the shit out of him. And while we're on the subject, perhaps you can also tell me what happened to all that crap you was spouting about everyone being dust and everything we do being wakan? I mean, what was that you was doing up there in the favela then, eh?'

'Do you know how you hunt a bear, Little Turtle?'

'Gog's holy trousers! You're not starting that again?'

'You smear yourself with bear fat, you go into his lair, and you shoot an arrow into his open mouth. Either the arrow breaks through the thin layer of skull at the base and goes into his brain, or he chokes on his own blood. Either way, you have your kill. But you must cover yourself in his smell first.'

'You know what? You're full of bollocks.'

'I've got my bear. Now for the arrow.'

Kane digs into the backpack and brings out the brick of charlie.

'I bet you've never even clamped eyes on a bloody bear,' I says, 'unless it was at the bloody zoo.'

'Observe,' he says, and goes into the kitchen. He comes out a moment later with a spoon in one groper and my florncakes bowl in the other, only the bowl's filled to the brim with white powder.

'You've got to be joking.'

Bob Marley starts screaming. Kane trolls up to him, scoops up a great spoonful of charlie and rams it into his open jagger. Bob Marley chokes and splutters and spits as much of it out as he can, but Kane only fills another spoonful and feeds it to him again. He repeats this four or five times, about 500 nicker a go, London rates. Remember: this stuff's jemmy, barely cut. Even with prices falling like they has been (but only cos demand's so bloody high, brother), that's a lot of green going into this player's jagger and no mistake.

There's charlie all over Bob Marley now, on the carpet, on the walls, all over the bloody gaff. But Bob Marley's still breathing, yelling gibberish at us.

Kane tries a new approach. He presses Bob Marley's rosies in with one hand, forcing him to open wide, shoves the spoon in, then clamps one groper over his jagger and presses his nosewells shut with the other. Bob Marley tries to shake himself loose but is forced to swallow.

I don't know how long it is, brother, watching this shit time gets all warped and wobbly, all I know is one minute Bob Marley's gurgling this white foam and the next he's trembling and convulsing, lamps like fried eggs, breathing hard and sweating harder. He's swearing again now, only sometimes he has to stop cos he can't get enough air in his lungs, going suuuuuckk through his nosewells and gasping jagger all coated in white icing but like nothing's getting in. The convulsions are really jerking and twisting him about now, and then he starts spewing up only it's not just the froth and the white pasty goo but real Technicolor vomit, all gloopy and lumpy and humming to high bloody heaven. His twisted face is all empinkened and enpurpled now, like the skin on it was turned inside-out, brother, with all the diddy veins and like nerves and stringy muscles a-showing.

It's not like I want to help him or save him or anything, I just want it to stop so I don't have to go on watching. Weird thing is I just stand there gawping, sickened by it yet sort of hypnotised. You know how it is, brother, you want to look and you don't want to look.

I snap out of it when Kane says:

'That's what I think of your business, Dodger.'

Then he steps across the carpet till his hooter's about an inch away from mine and says:

'Wakan-sica.'

31

PARABELLUM

I t takes Bob Marley about an hour circling the drain before he finally goes down and like morgues it. By this time he's covered head to hoof in his own gromit and with his gob all skewed and his bent eyeholes his dial looks like something a spastic's drawn in yellow crayon.

We're both still sat there looking at him, me on the floor, Kane on the sofa. And total fucking silence. Outside too, like the whole world's gone dumb or dead. I mean I can even hear my bloody heartbeats it's so quiet.

Kane finally gets up and goes to the window.

'You know,' I says, 'I'm going to have to tell the Tank about this. I mean, it's just got totally out of hand now. You've gone too far, this time.'

Not a word out of Kane, he's sphynxing again.

'OK,' I says, still watching the back of his bonce. 'I know you're mad. But I also know you are out here to do Tobczyk, and you've made all these plans all along and taken all these like precautions so far to make sure we nab him. So what the fuck are you doing now, running around like Jack the fucking Ripper going after anyone crosses your path? It don't make sense.'

He turns round now.

'It makes perfect sense. To me.'

'Listen, if you're so keen on cleaning up the world taking out everyone is wakan-sica like you say, why don't you go work for the cozzers? Special branch or something? Put everyone away to your heart's content.'

'I could never do what I do working for the police. This has nothing to do with the law.'

'OK then, let me ask you another question. Why Bob Marley here? Why not that cunt 8? He's the one you should be after, ain't he? Why not top him? You was sitting right in front of him, not two bloody feet away. Why not do him, eh? Oh, hang on a sec, it couldn't be anything to do with the fact that he'd have you hanging by your balls quicker than you could let off a fart, could it? Or could it?'

'Self-sacrifice would have achieved nothing. But if you can't get to the beast, you can still hurt him, you can still cut off his tentacles.'

'You know what? Then why don't you just fucking kill me, brother? I mean I'm a fucking testicle, aren't I? Ain't that right? There's Frank the Tank the big ugly beast running the show and here's his stupid fucking testicle taking the shit and listening to this bollocks.'

Kane spins round all the way now and zaps me like he's seeing me for the first time, and brother, there's fucking knives shooting from his lamps.

'Don't give me any ideas, you little shit.'

And it's like a bloody bucket of iced piss over my bonce cos I realise he might just do it, too, the vicious cunt, and so the old gut-wrench funk is back with a vengeance like, similar to what I felt with him that first darkmans in his tent, getting like these micro daymare flashes of him cutting my cougher open or snapping my neck like he done Pinto's, proper screamer.

But I don't show it. You must never show anything dealing with these psychotracks, I'm thinking. They get one whiff of fear it's like a shark with blood: a fucking frenzy.

He's still got his lamps fixed on me real bloody flesh-crawling and intimidating-like, so I try to sort of steer the discussion towards more practical, immediate concerns, hoping to get him into what you might call a more rational, saner frame of mind, know what I mean, brother?

'Well, two things worry me just at present,' I say, making sure the songbox don't gurgle too much or come out too scratchy. 'First, now that he's belly-up, how is he going to help us find out where Tobczyk is?'

Kane goes on staring. I clear my cougher.

'And two, when 8 finds out, he might just get word to Captain America to let him know two crazy gringos showed up here, bought a K of charlie off him and topped one of his lads with it.'

Kane's dial loosens.

'For a start,' he says, 'you should know that the chances of someone like 8 ever broadcasting the fact that one of his own men has been killed right under his nose by two nonentities is minimal. It's even less likely to happen when he realises he won't even be able to say he's caught up with us and put a bullet through our heads.'

'You're saying he won't be coming after us?'

Kane turns to face the window again. I feel the muscles on my back and neck relax.

'He wouldn't know where to begin. He won't understand why this has happened, even after I tell him.'

'You're going to tell him?'

'Not to his face, unfortunately. I'm going to leave him a message.'

I ask you.

'OK, so let's say you do all this. How's that going to help find Captain America?'

'It's not.'

At this I just shrug and keep my jagger shut. No point needling him again, is there?

'And it doesn't have to,' he goes on. 'I already know where he is.'

'You what?'

'Before he died Lima told me 8 was Tobczyk's main new connection with the Colombian cartels. So I told 8 we were setting up a permanent office here in Rio for the regular shipment of large quantities of cocaine to Europe, and that we wanted him to be our supplier. He told me the recent clean-up operations in the favelas had made life difficult for foreign operators he knew had been working here before, so they had moved out of Rio to the Northeast. It seems the police there are even more inept and corrupt than they are here. He mentioned Recife specifically. It's one of the country's main international shipping centres and a new port complex, the largest in Latin America, is being built there. But security, it seems, is lax.'

'Yeah, so? Why does that automatically lead you to think that's where Tobczyk's holed up?'

'Because that's where Carla Nakamura has also been going every fortnight for the past three months.'

'Who?'

He rolls his lamps.

'How'd you ever get into this business? Our Japanese bondage expert.'

***

The sun's not even halfway down the sky yet but I feel I've been up at least a week, brother, I'm that coopered. We don't bother cleaning up the mess and just roll Bob Marley up in the carpet the way he is, puke, coke, slobber and all. Only the chair needs a bit of a snite with some detergent and a damp cloth. Still, the ronk in the flat's got me choking proper rollercoaster-ride on a full stomach and I have to like tie a pillowcase soaked in aftershave over my bracket to keep me from yacking up myself. You know how it is.

Kane wraps all the bin-liners we have round the rolled-up carpet and tapes it all up with the rest of the duct tape. He then tears out the back of my packet of florncakes and writes a few words on the blank cardboard side with a magic pen.

I watch him tape this to the outside of the package like it was an address label and ask:

'What's it say?'

'It's just telling 8 that I know where to find him.'

Oh, right, I think, but say nothing.

Kane then sticks the Beretta with a full round into a Serpa holster clipped to the back of his strides and hands me a Taurus. It's the first time I seen him actually carrying.

I shove the barker in my pocket. We haul the enormous parcel out of the flat, take it down in the service lift and chuck it in the Toyota.

And here we go. Kane drives through the city OAP-on-a-Sunday slow and extra careful not to break any like traffic laws might bring a warden nosing about the pick-up at this very wrong time. He's very quiet as usual, except at one point where he starts his old mumble-mumble routine praying to Wanker Plonka like he done in the plane coming over.

We're approaching the drop-off point: the same place I first saw Bob Marley not four hours ago. There's shitloads of people about but this doesn't seem to bother Kane one bit. He parks the motor and tells me to wait. So I wait. But there's definitely a sense of what you might call unease tingling through my nutmegs, cos what the fuck it is we're waiting for, Gog only knows.

Ten minutes in, Kane takes a quick zap round to make sure nobody's looking in our direction and with his arm stuck out the window pops off a thunderclap from the Beretta, *ka-pow!* I'm not expecting this and do a cartwheel backwards in my seat cracking my bonce on the ceiling. When I look up rubbing the old skull-bone everyone in the street is scattering every which way quick-sticks and crazy with panic, women screaming, kids crying, men yelping, real doomsday, and in two seconds flat all that remains is these like itty clouds of dust and the odd flipflop left behind in the scurry for cover, proper dedlurk it is and no one about to like eyewitness the dirty deed.

Kane turns to me and says:

'OK. Now.'

We drag the thing out live-o and just plonk it down on the pavement hidden from view by the car, jump back in, then Kane eases the Toyota out and very slowly reverses it to the end of the street. A couple of bonces start poking out here and there wondering what's going on and where the gunshot come from, but by this time we're U-turned and cruising, brother, gliding away like cherry sauce on a dollop of icecream.

Smoove.

PART THREE

You have noticed that everything an Indian does is in a circle, and that is because the power of the world always works in circles, and everything tries to be round... The sky is round, and I have heard that the earth is round like a ball, and so are all the stars. The wind, in its greatest power, whirls. Birds make their nest in circles, for theirs is the same religion as ours... Even the seasons form a great circle in their changing, and always come back again to where they were. The life of a man is a circle from childhood to childhood, and so it is in everything where power moves.

Black Elk, Holy Man of the Oglala Sioux (1863-1950)

32

HIGHWAY 101

Back at the flat I pack my stuff quicktime like some glocky Keystone Kop in one of them old silent speeded-up flicks. After a wash and scrub the old Toyota is retired in favour of another secondhand motor Kane's done a quick deal on, a white Hyundai Tucson with plenty of grunt and black windows which he gets the mechanic to tweak, only this being Brazil nothing simple can stay simple so it takes fucking centuries to get the paperwork on the car sorted, a million diddy documents need signing and registration charges and fees for this and fees for that need paying and endless fucking swamps of bureaucracy need wading through even after you've palm-oiled just about every fucking dodo working in the bloody vehicle registration office and state traffic department including the director, his wife, her lover and all their fucking family and friends (the bribe system in Brazil reaches from the lowliest traffic warden to the President of the Republic, you understand), so we have to wait (gut-grinding it is too, brother, not knowing who might be like coming after you) till they open again at eight the following ay-em to get the final transfer papers made out in the name of, yeah you've guessed it, Mr C. bloody Fuchs, esq.

All right, and then you ask well why not just bloody rent a car, right? Or even better, just twoc one off the bloody street? Well, that's what I said, brother. And you know what Kane's answer was?

'That would be stupid.'

Stupid? Why?

Fuck knows.

So there we are, going through this dawdle for no reason I can discern, and it's while we're waiting in yet another queue turtling at about an inch per hour that mad Kane buys a local paper and flicking through does a sort of double-take. What is it, I ask. He holds the paper up, and fuck me if splashed there all over the fucking crime page ain't a smudge of the rolled-up carpet with the body inside it like a bloody sausage roll. Below it a column of text a foot wide and a yard bloody long tells how the cozzers are investigating the 'mysterious gangland killing' of one João Gregorio dos Santos, aka Bob Marley, which they're saying may have been carried out by Colombian traffickers, a theory that's been put forward by experts after they discovered a note left on the package written not in Portuguese, as you'd expect, but in bloody Spanish. I mean, what?

I have to confess, brother, I sort of freak out a bit when I hear this.

'I told you,' I says to Kane. 'I fucking told you, didn't I? And now what? What are you going to do when they come after us? You going to wipe out the entire bloody Brazilian police force as well? Is that it? Is that your cunning cunting plan?'

But him, he's what you might call unruffled, brother, undisturbed, unbothered and downright in-bloody-scrutable. As always.

'Thunder doesn't always follow lightning.'

'Thunder what? What the fuck's that supposed to bloody mean?'

'It means that when thunder's too far off, you can't hear it, you only see the lightning. As far as the police are concerned, there's nothing linking us to this crime, we're too far removed. Only 8 knows, and he's not going to say anything, is he?'

'How do you know there's nothing to link us to this? How do you know no one saw the Toyota? Someone could easily have seen us dropping the packet and taken down our number plate.'

'That's highly unlikely. And even if they did, by the time the police have traced it back to us we'll have finished the job and be on our way back to England.'

'Oh, that's wunnerful, that is, really triffic. Just fucking lovely. You know, I'd never have taken you for an optimist. Not in a million fucking years.'

***

Well, there's nothing we can do now except mizzle out of here fast as we bloody can, brother, so that's eggzakly what we do. The hardware goes in a hidden compartment Kane opens up under the back seat and on top of that we load a lot of souvenir crap we buy on our way out, gaudy pictures, lumpy woodcarvings, plastic glow-in-the-dark Christs, a football and even a mini pavingstone done up in the Copacabana wavy pattern that's like a symbol of the place. To all appearances now we're just a couple of gringo tourists taking a road trip up the Brazilian coast. (And yeah, the fake fucking phiz-minge is in the bin at last, brother.)

Once we're out of the city limits and onto this federal motorway (something called the BR 101) that's taking us all the way to where we're going, the Tucson starts to eat up the road real nifty, brother, and it's like watching meat going through a mincer most of the time only we got to watch out for these bloody mahusive potholes dotted about everywhere like it was an obstacle course or something, some of these buggers big enough to bury a bloody horse. I mean it's not tarmac we're talking about here, brother, it's fucking shredded wheat.

I turn on the radio but most of it's crap or some wanker talking shit and anyway Kane prefers — you've guessed it — silence.

We drive real Thelma and Lousie road movie all the ay-em non-stop and part of the pee-em and I've got hunger pangs and I need a slash and the old windmill's pricklier than an itchy blanket but Kane says let's get some road behind us first and I must say this time I like have to agree, brother.

First stop we make is at about three-thirty in a place called something like Gory-Puree in the next state along, Holy Ghost-land that is, the same place where Kane bought the weaponry. It's a shithole, with the accent on the shit. There's an old church where we don't go and there's a petrol station where we refuel and a restaurant where we refill and a filthy khazi where we unload and nothing else.

While we're eating I ask:

'D'you think 8 might come after us now?'

Kane nods.

'Maybe.'

'And Tobczyk, how'll we know where he is once we get there?'

'I'll know,' he says.

'It would kill you to say you was wrong and I was right, wouldn't it?'

But he just scoops another forkful of rice-n-beans into his jagger and goes chew chew chew on it like he never heard.

* * *

With me at the wheel we drive on through the evening and into the night and reach another micro nowhere town, stop for the usual necessities, change places, then keep on till we're both coopered out and our lamps fuzzy and our eyelids weigh about a kilo each.

There's a rundown motel for truckers next to the petrol station and we get a couple of rooms there. The room's painted orange and smells of disinfectant and stale farts. There's stains on the bed linen and hairs on the soap. I shower and get into bed but then as sometimes happens when you're nanxed beyond a certain limit I can't sleep and my lamps just glue open in the dark like one of them nocturnal creatures you see in wildlife documentaries on the telly with it might be David Attenborough telling you all about what they eat and crap. I lie there thinking about all the shit I'm in and having like half-formed visions of all these sticky ends for myself, shot or stabbed maybe or imprisoned for life in some hell-pit here in Brazil with only cockroaches to eat, and so natch there's still no sign of the old zeds. I notice now there's like music wafting in with the breeze through the open window, not loud but I can hear every instrument very distinct, sounds like something very old as it might be an old sea shanty or folk song with a squeezebox and a skip-to beat and a very simple straight-forward melody you could whistle to. I listen to this music for a while and this funny feeling comes over me like a sadness or a longing I don't know which, and I think of my old mother dead and gone and will I like ever see her or hear her voice again when I go belly-up or is it really just all over like when we morgue it.

Now this is not like me, brother, I'm not a what-you-might-call morbid or sullen sort of bloke by nature, a mood hoover, not in the least, but then exhaustion and stress can do things to you sometimes, can't they, so I'm thinking OK enough of this marmite, Dodger, no point lying here all night like some glocky git filling your bonce with horror stories and thoughts of like death and the afterlife, get up and go out and maybe get a drink or a bite to eat, mate, why not.

So I do, brother, I get up and go outside.

The restaurant's an all-nighter so it's open but there's only about three people in there, lorry drivers on the red-eye stopped for a quick meal and a rest. You can hear the cicadas chirping in there. So I come out and follow the sound of the music and zap across the road a few yards up on a low hill a long squat building or house painted heaven-blue with a flat roof and lightbulbs hanging in strings out in front shining down on about a dozen punters drinking at these diddy tables and more lights through the open doorway showing more people jiggling about to the music I've been hearing.

When I troll in they all zap me like I was green and had three bonces or had just landed on a fucking flying saucer or something. I plonk myself down on the only available table and wet my L-bow on a puddle of swill left by the last customer. The paint on everything here is stained and flaking off, on the tables, the walls, the ceiling and even the women, and you can see parts of the older layers underneath showing different colours, orange maybe or green or white. The furniture's all made of tin or grimy plastic, and the chair I sit on has a crack keeps pinching the back of my leg. I order a *cerveja* (this much Portuguese I've learnt) and a waiter looks like he walked off a set for a film about the Black Death brings it to me and plonks it down on the table next to a jamjar glass with week-old lipstick on the rim. After a bit people get tired of staring at me and get back to their boozing, talking, flirting, dancing or whatever it was they was doing before I come in. I sip at my beer and enjoy watching the couples dance, twirling and rubbing up between each other's pegs and the birds wagging their arses like they was on fire.

Suddenly there's this girl next to me holding a cancer in one groper and flicking the thumb of the other as if to say 'do you have a light?'. I shake my bonce, point to my glass and wiggle my eyebushes suggestively. She gets the drift and sits down. She gives me an up-from-below zap like she's trying to guess how much wonga is in my wallet. The waiter brings another glass and I pour her some swill. She's twenty, twenty-one tops, pretty in a dumpy, plain, stale British Rail doughnut sort of way, with very smooth cinnamon skin on her shoulders and tits, a flat phiz, a broad mouth and these beautiful big black slanted eyes like a Brazilian

Indian. We don't twig what the other's saying at all first couple of tries but then I think I understand she's saying her name's Zoo-Lady. Well, that's a new one, eh brother? Makes you sort of wonder what she's got hidden up between her legs, if you know what I mean. Well, after she's had a couple of sips she starts shaking her shoulders wobbling her tits and what this is is she's asking me to dance. Well I don't like to dance not even under normal circumstances, brother, much less in this ruddy gaff to this music I've never heard before, make a right plank of myself, but then there's not much else I can do is there, given the fact that we don't understand a bloody dicky the other's saying not nohow. Know what I mean?

So there I am chuffing away like some window-licker at this fusion of the Highland fling, the hokey-cokey and the hula-bloody-hula, shaking my windmill and hugging this bird close, and the heat's like sunbathing in a bloody suit of armour, brother, proper solar storm, so five seconds in there's sweat pouring off me like it's on tap and I'm starting to worry it's getting on her, which of course it is. I kind of nod to her after a bit, pointing at my dripping clobber, and indicate by gesture and like facial expression that perhaps we could step outside for a bit, why don't we.

This we do. We sit on the steps looking out onto the motorway like it was a lakeside view and she takes my groper and starts talking away not worrying one jot that I don't understand a bit of it, but it doesn't matter really cos she's got this very like soothing warble, a real singer's songbox it is, and I'm loving just zapping her chest heave when she breathes and lips move and her lamps twinkle and seeing how white and perfect her dominoes look when she smiles, which is most of the time, though there's a couple missing at the back. I look at her and think of Vicky. Maybe she was right about this trip, maybe not. But any regrets I might have had about leaving her have long since soured and turned to resentment. Toxic, it is. I mean my last message to her was a fucking cry of despair in the wilderness, but she hasn't even tried to get in touch to ask if I'm OK. Yeah, and there's another piece of Dodger necrotised.

But though there's some hurt there from her unexplained silence (and don't think for a moment I've forgotten the greed greasing Vicky's lamps that last meeting at her place neither, egging me on to come on this hare-arsed, arse-brained wild arse chase for the prize at the end), there's a sort of relief too, brother, like I'd known all along deep down in my sub-subconscious that something was seriously wrong between us, the feelings too shallow at both ends, the sugar too cheap and tasting of fast food, the luvin too by-the-numbers, and now it's all just like stamped, official and confirmed.

Well. After a bit I start to talk too, telling Zoo-Lady all about Vicky and anything else like pops into my bonce such as who I am and where I was born and shit, and it's all a bit of a larf really but also it gives me this right proper warm sort of feeling in my gut, and for the moment I sort of forget Kane and Captain America and all the rest.

We kiss and talk and then I pay for the beers and we troll back to the motel. She's no meat-puppet pro but she's a right little scallywag all the same and no mistake. We sit on the bed and in a moment we're snogging away and I notice how mixed in with the beer and cigarette smoke she smells of soap and cheap sweet perfume, and then my sweaty clobber's off and her shirt's off and there's all the fondling and groping and you know the usual slap and tickle and all that so I'm about hot to trot but then at the gate she sort of backs off a bit and I pull a face asking her what's wrong but it takes me a while to tumble to the fact that she can't do nothing about it cos she's on the blob.

Bloody hell. Just my bloody luck, eh brother?

But you know what, it doesn't matter, I haven't felt this good in bloody yonks, so we talk a bit more and she gives me this oscar body massage and then we snog a bit more and talk a bit more and end up doing a nice Bombay roll complete with chin-splasher. Ah, toojoors l'amoor.

She was very thoughtful after, though, I remember, and when I asked what was wrong she made me twig she was like praying. I don't know who to or what for. Then she sang me a song, brother, I don't know what it was about, but very sweet it was, in a warble like cool clear running water splashing over you on a hot blistering day. I'd never heard nothing like it, and it sort of melted something inside me, very deep. It's hard to explain. Still singing she then led me to the bathroom and under the shower. She washed me like I was a baby, rubbing the soap very gentle like all over, from my neck to my toes and into every cranny, then at one point she rested her hand on my chest, the palm flat against it, feeling my heart beat, and you know for a moment I felt all the fear and hurt and anger and frustration wash away, I really did, gurgling down with the dirty water into the drain.

Back in bed we fell asleep together in a tight clinch, real husband-n-wife.

***

Before I've even had a chance to like reach the proper deep zeds that give your body the rest it needs that wanker Kane's banging on the door saying it's time to go. When he realises what I've been getting up to he's not what you would call happy. And what the fuck is it to him? I'm starting to think he could do with a bit of nookie himself, brother. It's probably been so long that his splooge has all like overflowed into his head and caused irreparable damage to the brain.

I bring Zoo-Lady into the restaurant for breakfarts with me and when we sit down with our fruit and rolls and eggs he says nothing for a long while. He's still in a hump with his honker buried in the morning paper. I ask him is there any news about Bob Marley in it and still get no change out of him. Finally he looks up not at me but at Zoo-Lady and says something to her in Portu-Spanish or whatever fucking language it is he's speaking. She smiles a bit, blinks at me and gives me a kiss on the cheek.

'What did you say to her?'

'I said you told me you thought you were in love with her.'

'Why did you say that?'

'Because, frankly, I think you're a fucking idiot who doesn't know his head from his arse.'

I put my fork down.

'So I'm the idiot, am I? I suppose it's my fault you killed that fucking chancer and now the plod's sniffing up our arse, is it?'

'The only thing the police know now which they didn't know yesterday is that Bob Marley worked for 8. It's his arse they're sniffing up, not ours. But of course that changes everything.'

He's not looking at me still. He offers to get Zoo-Lady another glass of watered-down squeeze. Before he can get up I say:

'Bloody hell I wish you'd just come out with stuff and not wait for me to ask you what the fuck you mean every time just so's you can come out with another one of your clever cryptic remarks like you had a ruddy fortune cookie factory in your bloody gut.'

He's standing looking down at me with the two empty glasses in his gropers.

'What that means is now that it's out in the open 8 will want to come after us to show everyone nobody kills one of his men and gets away with it, which is fine really because quite frankly there's nothing I'd like better than to take a few more of those sad bastards out of their misery, but this girl—' he nods at her, '—will almost certainly suffer because of your carelessness and stupidity.'

'What? What are you talking about?'

'You blurted out Tobczyk's nickname in front of 8 and he recognised it. It helped confirm my suspicions as to his present whereabouts, admittedly, but it was still a very stupid thing to do, even by your standards. If he's half as clever as I think he is he'll make the connection. And have you thought about what will happen if they pick up our trail? They're much better at it than the police, I can assure you. They'll threaten and bribe and kill, they'll make their way up the coast stopping anywhere we might have stopped at, and they'll find out who saw what and when. And when they get to this girl she'll talk, one way or another.'

'Bollocks, you're talking bollocks. If you hadn't killed Bob Marley in the first place nobody'd be coming after us. If anyone's to blame, it's you, you mad sod. And anyway, didn't you say yourself that by the time anyone finds out where we've gone we'll be home safe and sound?'

'I'm not talking about us, you bloody idiot. I'm talking about her!'

He points at Zoo-Lady, and she gives this diddy shudder. We're not shouting but she can tell something's not right.

'Bloody hell, don't you think you're exaggerating a bit?'

'I hope I am. But then again, there's always the possibility that I'm not, ain't there?'

'So what do you want to do?'

He sits down again and puts the glasses down very gently on the table.

'Well, as I see it, there's two ways to go here. Either we take her with us, or we kill her.'

I stare into his lamps to see if he means this or is just saying it to scare me.

'You're just saying that. You wouldn't do it. She's got nothing to do with any of this, she's completely innocent, doesn't even know what the fuck we're on about here. Even you, Kane, wouldn't do that.'

He picks up the glasses again.

'You're quite right, of course.'

***

We take her with us, but only into the next state, which is Bahia. She thought she was going on a holiday with us, I reckon, happz as anything, she was, larfing and talking. We took a turning off the motorway and drove about an hour to some dead itty toilet of a town identical to the one where I found her. I gave her money and Kane set her up in the only hotel they had, paid for a month-long stay in advance.

I promised to return. I think she understood. I wanted to take her home with me. It's like I'd found something I hadn't even known I was looking for, brother. The past was disappearing, and this weird new future was opening up in its place like one of them flowers you see blooming in speeded-up films, petals bursting open, growing in like two seconds.

She stood on the pavement outside the front entrance as we pulled away. I watched her from the back window, getting smaller and looking a bit pathetic standing there waving, but somehow I felt it was really me playing the giddy clown here, brother, watching her through the window with a sort of knot tightening in my cougher.

33

THE GHOST DANCE

The UVs get real doomsday the further north we go, proper stewing, so in Bahia Kane buys himself a cheap pair of plastic Gaddafi-fashion cheaters by the roadside and drives with them on and his shirt off. He don't want the air-conditioner on so it's also fucking dusty and I buy these orange-tinted swimming goggles and put them on instead of my Ray-Bans when I'm not driving. He's got bottles of mineral water on the seat and on his lap and every now and then shakes some out on his bonce and over his heaver and I do the same. It's one speed now brother: GO, stopping for nothing but the bare essentials: motion lotion, calls of nature and takeaway peckage. At one place I make the mistake of trying a bean-n-roadkill Frankenstein stew and spend the next twenty-four hours farting rotten eggs, dead animals and mustard gas. Deadly.

We're tonning it on the straight stretches and only have to slow down when approaching the road plod stops which are signposted well in advance anyway so there's no danger of getting caught there. They stop us a few times to go through the routine vehicle and driving licence check but the moment they zap us it all goes into slow motion, brother, two monkeysuits giving us the eye and circling the car inspecting the lights and the fire extinguisher to look at the expiry date, but all it is is they're expecting a little beer money from the rich gringos. Fine, take it you twistical corrupt plod scum and fuck off pronto back to whatever hole shat you out.

We take turns at the wheel and also switch between drinking water and strong coffee to keep us going. Kane's consented to a bit of radio and I've hit on a station plays this stuff's not quite samba but a strain of it with a hard pounding backbeat sounds like about a billion drums all going at once smash-out and it's not half good for getting a rhythm into your driving especially when you're really about to like zombie out.

At one point Kane veers off the road into a dirt track and parks behind some trees straddling a field. I think he just needs a piss but he opens up the back seat and digs out the Beretta and both Tauruses saying we better keep these with us just in case.

'Just in case what?'

'Just in case.'

He gives me a Taurus and keeps the other two barkers for himself. I must say I start feeling a speck goosy after this, the old paranoia creeping in it is, and get on the crow for any signs of like danger, zapping back over my shoulder every few minutes or in the rearview to see if a crew looks fishy or we're being tailed. But as you might expect I don't see nothing other than what's cooked up by my own noid brain.

We pass a couple of road accidents, one bad with a coach burnt black in a deep ditch lying on its side like some dead busosaurus, and both times I can see Kane has to like struggle with himself not to stop to try to help, this seeming to be a sort of recurring thing with him, but there's no time and there's nothing no one can do anyway, the traffic cozzers and fire brigade and ambulances having all done what they could already. So on we go, barkers in our belts, bouncing along to this thunderbeat spewing out of the blaster, cutting through this heat and savage light like scissors through paper, the land huge and wild all around us in the long spread-out stretches between the crud, crum and concrete of the shithole towns we pass through, good riddance to 'em.

At one point we're ragging it through this flat scrubland, house-height bushes either side as far as the lamp can zap, sun beating down, and I've got myself a six of swill at the last fuel stop and am swigging away at one real chug-a-lug, when for no reason I can grok Kane slams his hoof through the fucking floor, screeeeee. Burning rubber the Tucson does a 180-degree turn and skids to a stop. The jerk shoots me out of my seat like a cork out of a bloody bottle but the seatbelt jolts me back making me spurt beer from my nosewells. The can flies out of my gropers, does a summerset in mid-air and lands upsidedown on my crotch gurgling and spurting foam. Before I've even had time to come to my senses and pick the fucking thing up to start swearing at him he's out of the car and pegging it real doomsday like some maniac over the embankment towards a spot that's a sort of oasis in reverse, brother, an island of desert wasteland all dirt and gravel in the middle of this jungle of tall grass and bushes and trees and like thick tropical foliage. I stare at him go. What the fuck's he doing? At first I think it must be like a touch of the shits, maybe, the old Tandoori two-step, I mean that last sangwidge he had did reek a bit boggy. But no, brother, that's not it at all, cos what he does now is not crouch for a Donald Trump or anything like that but start whooping and dancing round this smashed up kiddies' roundabout left to rot and rust there lying in the middle of the place, lifting his arms to the sky and crying out to Wanker Plonka over and over, the bloody Keith Moon, just like he done in bloody Wales. I mean, what?

I get out of the car and watch him going round and round this smashed-up old toy for a bit, thinking this is proper brain damage now but not knowing what the fuck to do except stand there gawping at him, it's all so bloody bizarre.

Now he stops saying anything another human being can understand and just starts wailing while he does the here-we-go-round-the-mullberry-bush oonga-boonga dance routine.

When it's over he hurls out one last howl skywards then comes jogging back.

'This is a good sign, Little Turtle,' he says, panting.

'Yeah, well, I'm very glad to hear it but I think I better do the driving from here on in.'

'You should be happy. The circle is good wakan. Every circle is an embodiment of life itself. Everything tries to be round, the world itself is round. The cycle of time is a circle. This is the natural order, and this is why we must sit in circles for our ceremonies.'

'Funny. All I could see from here was a banged-up old roundabout.'

But he just ploughs on as usual oblivious to anything I say.

'The old Sioux camps were always arranged in a circle. This was the sacred hoop within which everything was safe and knowable. The circle symbolises wholeness and helps us to remember Wakan Tanka, who, like the circle, has no end and no beginning, and so it's always auspicious to find a circle unexpectedly like this.'

Unexpectedly is right. I whistle a few bars of the Magic Roundabout theme and get into the driver's seat.

He rhubarbs on. And on. And on.

'...The Ghost Dance came to us after the white man took our lands and made us live like dogs in his reservations. Wovoka, the great Paiute leader, taught us this dance so our dead warriors might come back and speak to us, and showed us the ghost shirts we wear to protect us from danger, even bullets. That's why the Ghost Dance is performed in a circle, because the circle is very powerful, Little Turtle. Lame Deer, the holy man, once said that in the world around us there are many symbols that teach us the meaning of life. The circle is the symbol that holds all others together, and it is divided into the four cycles. Like the wheel with the four medicine arrows on my back. Each arrow shows a direction of thought and a state of being we must strive to attain. The North arrow is Wisdom; the South, Innocence; the East, Far Seeing; and the West, Inner Seeing...'

Yeah, I'm thinking. Like I give a shit.

'This,' I say, pointing at the steering wheel, 'is a circle too, innit? Well how about we just stick to this one for the time being, eh?'

34

CODE RED

We reach the next town along the highway to hell BR 101 and this time we stop a bit longer cos if I don't stretch my pegs I feel I may never troll upright again, brother. We go into a grubhouse set about a hundred and fifty yards back from the road, a real gruey fodderhole for iron-guts desperado drivers only. We choose a table on the right-hand side as you go in and Kane sits with his back to the wall so he can see anyone coming in. The place is half empty. The fly-to-human ratio is about fifty to one in here: no sooner do you swipe away one wave of the fat hairy things than another swarm lands on you from the other side, covering your food and every available surface of the table. Across the way a pair of blobs in sweatstained shirts and faded baseball caps are sat picking their teeth with toothpicks and inspecting their finds carefully before eating them again. A young couple is plotted down opposite them stuffing food into their faces with the sort of concentrated muscular and psychological effort you'd normally expect to find in a boxing ring. Finally there's a shrivelled-up toothless old alky in the corner with lamps like runny eggyolks that can't get a proper fix on anything, glass in his groper and a damp fag-end gummed to his lower lip wobbling up and down while he keeps up this like gloppy drunken warble mumbling quietly to himself with spit-froth collecting in the corners of his jagger. There's a fuzzy TV in the corner showing an old Jackie Chan film dubbed in Portuguese that no one's watching. A wobbly half-loose ceiling fan switched on at the lowest possible speed so it doesn't come down and chop someone's head off is stirring the hot air around to provide miniature thermals for the flies to spiral and glide on. A pimply waiter who looks about fifteen brings us a menu laminated in yellow sticky plastic looks like it's made of frozen honey. I ask for a coke and he brings it while Kane deciphers the list of dishes. Me, I can't sit down, brother, the old Gary Glitter's going like a nest of fucking hornets all hot and sweaty and sore from the long drive so I just ask Kane to get me something nice and simple like and then go and take a troll outside with my can of pop while I wait.

Apart from the dusty road here there's mostly just scrub and in the middle distance a couple of rickety old houses side by side in a fenced-off plot of shit, the houses more like sheds really with a few rags left to dry gathering dust on the sagging clotheslines out front and some dogs and a few grubby nippers running about in the shade round the side playing football. I troll up following the fence as far as the gate on their side and watch them monkey about for a bit then back off when one of the dogs runs up and starts barking its head off at me.

Then I hear a motor coming. I turn to look back at the road. There was a couple of motors parked in front of the restaurant when we arrived, and now a third one is gliding along the narrow dirt track raising a cloud of yellow dust behind it. As I watch the car disappears from view beyond the edge of the fence and five seconds later I hear the engine switch off and the doors open and bang shut, then it's all dead quiet again apart from the occasional fly buzzing in my ear. I shade my lamps and squint up at the sky. It's late pee-em, brother, but the sun's still bloody frying my skin to crispy bacon so I start trolling back sipping at my pop that's already warm and tasting like piss.

I reach the end of the fence, turn the corner and am facing the open entrance to the restaurant about twenty yards away when a burst of shatter breaks the silence and a couple of bright flashes whistle past my bonce real doomsday, missing me by maybe as little as an inch, zing, zing.

I don't have time to be scared and just drop behind the nearest motor, breathing hard through my jagger, heart rate rocketing with all the adrenalin pumping like jellied fire through my pipes. There's a man shouting and desperate screams from inside. I pull out the barker and release the safety. There's a full seventeen-round clip in it so I'm confident if anything comes at me out of the restaurant it's going to get hit and no fucking mistake.

Suddenly shots start going off again like bloody popcorn and it's only now I'm steady enough to remember Kane who's inside and must be taking gory hell in there probably hit maybe even dying or already dead. And then it like hits me that if he goes I am well and truly fucked cos on my own what fucking chance do I have? Still, in a flight-or-fight situation like this the body first screams flight cos you know if you stop one you don't get another stab at nothing, brother, that's it, no rewind or start-again button to save your skin. When you're in this shit for real death feels very close, you're not one of them indestructible cartoon joes get stabbed, jabbed, creamed and fucking steamrollered, burnt to a black frazzle and dropped ten miles off some beetling cliff then flattened pancake-thin only to pop up again right as ringo and on to the next zippy zany gag all laughs and joy. If you die, you bloody stay dead, and it's ugly and very very sad.

Mega-death thoughts are rollercoastering through my nut and here goes the old bullet in the noggin sequence starting up again, bright and in razor-sharp focus like a film being projected in my brainpan, when there's a crunch crunch on the gravel a few feet away, someone running. It gives me a jolt and I'm scranching hard enough to crack a tooth but aiming the barker now ready-steady-go to blow a hole in the fucker whoever he is.

I see a bloke stagger between the cars, fall, get up on his marylebones and crawl past on all fours straddling the far wall. It's the waiter took our order. I catch a glimpse of his dial and it's shiny red and dripping blood.

At this point it's struck me this is like proper code-red danger I'm in and I'm starting to feel kind of ailish, brother, that familiar tight squirmy pressure in my guts, and I'm trying to make sense of this ardle mcardle and at the same time wanting to do a bloody runner out of here somehow, abandon ship, but not knowing if it's a good idea to move at all if you know what I mean.

A couple more shots crack out inside the restaurant and one takes out the big front window, glass suddenly flying everywhere, then there's a volley of rapid-fire in like response, which if I'm guessing right means Kane's still breathing in there, only I also realise there's no way he's coming out of this alive without my help, unfortunately. So without really thinking about it I sort of edge out very alert-like from behind the motor on the far side and make my way round to the restaurant in a tight crouch with my bonce practically between my marylebones. I reach the wall and flatten my back against it, then inch my way towards the shattered window, all extra careful and slow-like so as not to make any noise or raise any telltale dust might give me away. Keeping my bonce low still I can hear someone sobbing on the other side and much closer up two urgent-sounding male voices speaking fast Portuguese. I take off my shades and plucking up some real true-grit bottle now crane my neck swanlike to take a squiz over the edge. It's two of them all right, one stocky, one thin, in T-shirts and jeans, with their backs turned crouched behind an up-turned table, semis clutched tight in their fists. I duck back down and suck in a long lungful of air. My gun hand's trembling so much I have to steady it with the other. I know if I don't do something very serious and decisive right fucking now they're going to get Kane and then bloody come after me. Shit. I fight off the sick feeling and poke the muzzle of the Taurus through the broken window just about where my bonce was a second before. Shit, shit, shit. I hold it there a fraction of a second then I squeeze down hard on the trigger and let them bloody have it, brother, real destruction and no pity. Suddenly it's fucking hellzapoppin bedlam in there with my gun blasting and tables getting knocked over and more screaming and glass shattering and things cracking and breaking all over the fucking place. In the words of Teflon Tony Bliar, maximum death and destruction. When the clip's empty I scarper back to my shelter behind the parked motor shouting *yeeeaah* just in time to avoid a round of shatter from one of the sods has somehow managed to stay alive and reach the window, aiming right for me now raking the ground at my feet so there's bullets kicking up all round and slamming into the wheels and the side of the motor, whack whack whack. When I'm tucked away safe and cosy the shooting stops and I hear glass tinkling like maybe he's climbing over the window. I fumble for my extra clip but am shaking so hard I can't get the empty one out to slot the new one in fast enough. I'll have to make a run for it. Just as I start scrambling for the next car along, two shots blast out from inside the restaurant, sort of dry and flat-sounding, and then there's this total churchyard silence, no cry or thud or return fire, only the tiny tingling in my eardrums from the noise that's suddenly not there anymore mixed with this like itty sizzle of heat I suppose really I only imagine I can hear what with the sun drilling down so hard on everything and coming up off the cars and the beaten sand in like diddy wobbly waves everywhere.

I wait. What's happening out there? Is he fucking gone or what?

I put my bonce down to the ground and take a zap round under the motor. Nobody, all clear, apart from the waiter I can see still slumped against the far wall, not moving except for this twitching groper covered in blood.

I get into starter position, finally manage to feed the other clip into the barker and shout:

'Kane! You still in there?'

There's no reply but I can hear like chairs and crap being shoved out of the way. Then his voice:

'I'm coming out. You can put that gun away now.'

He lumbers out. His left arm's drenched in claret but he doesn't seem to mind. On his way to the car he zaps the waiter lying on the ground and kneels down to see how bad he is.

I troll over and crouch down beside him.

'Who the fuck were they?'

'8's boys, no doubt.' He checks the waiter's wounds, one on the side of the head and one on the back of the groper. 'He's OK. He's just fainted.' He turns to me. 'And you?'

'I'm OK. It's you you should be worrying about.'

I point at his arm and he looks down at it like it doesn't belong to him.

'This? Took a little chunk off, that's all. No real harm done. I was lucky. I told you that circle was a good omen.'

'Fuck me. If this is what a good omen does, I don't want to be around when a bad one comes along and no fucking mistake.'

***

At the next town I stop at a chemists and get plenty of iodine and plaster and a first-aid kit so Kane can patch himself up. He improvises a little tourniquet and the bleeding stops. I've still got the shakes pretty bad so I get myself a little something to calm my Millwall reserves (you don't need no prescription for nothing in Brazil, they don't even pretend to like ask for one, brother). I've got this stiff neck as well from my nocturnal contortions with Zoo-Lady that's been paining me a three-ring horror and getting worse since it's turned to whiplash after Kane's pedal-jam screamer so I also buy ten packets of 500g aspirin, the strongest they have, and start eating the bloody things like they was smarties.

We're close to the border with the next state, place called Alagoas. Kane thinks of dumping the Tucson and taking a coach across to Pernambuco from here but we give up on the idea and decide to chance it cos where will we carry the hardware if we do that? And brother, no way am I parting company with the hardware after what just happened, nix nix.

Well the 101 is in even worse fucking condition along this stretch, full of cracks and lumps and craters now big enough to bury not just a horse but a whole fucking herd and what with mad chickens crossing the road and dozy cows and kamikazi cyclists carrying whole families on their handlebars, the constant swerving and jogging and jolting is making Kane's arm ache right torture-chamber and leak all over the bloody place so we stop at what they call a *pousada* here, a sort of Brazilian cousin to our bed-n-breakfast, to lie low for a day or three till he's recovered a bit and we can get our act together. He's looking a bit pale, is Kane, and I suggest maybe we should get a doctor in to look at his arm, I mean it's a nasty gash, brother, gaping ajar like a real old pro's love-flaps, but Kane he just shakes his bonce. He soaks the wound in some sort of disinfectant he cooks up with iodine and some other antiseptic shit, clamps it shut with great wads of extra strength superglue sticking plaster, and goes on an antibiotic diet saying no, no, he don't need no doctor, it's fine, a doctor'd have to report a bullet wound to the police anyway, he'll rest and pray and drink the muddy tea he makes from the shit in his diddy pouch and Wanker Plonka will see him through all right, OK.

Well he's a nut, no doubt about it, but this much I will say for him, he's a hard fucking nut and no mistake.

35

LOCKE, HUME AND TWO SMOKING BERKELEYS

There's a diddy banged-up TV set in the lounge and I'm watching it the following evening when the news comes on and it's the mess at the roadside restaurant they're talking about. I don't know what the reporter's saying, but there's footage of the place all shot to bits and ID pictures of the two dead gunmen. I ask Kane to come and watch next time so he can find out if there's anything about us but he's not interested. I don't know if it's the wound becoming infected or the heat or if these things just come in like periodic waves (I mean ain't the moon supposed to influence these headcases?), but there's no doubt Kane's behaviour has taken a turn for the seriously peculiar since the shooting. I never see him get out of bed, brother, not sleeping but just lying there staring at nothing all day and all night, but every time I go out for supplies or it might be just for a troll around the *pousada* or down to the village for a drink just to get away from the bloody suffocating locked-in feel and claustrophobia of the room and Kane's weirdness, I come back and find he's somehow nipped out as well without my noticing to buy stuff like a new toothbrush (he's got five of them now), a hand mirror, a cheap fishing rod and a bamboo flute. I mean, what?

But he really hits the fucking apex of cuckoo cloud nine on the third day when I troll in after lunch and find him in bed with ping-pong balls taped to his eyes. The curtains are drawn and all the lights are off except for the table lamp pointed at his dial which is blazing like hell-fire cos he's thrown a red T-shirt over the bulb, and the scene sort of takes the breath out of me for a second, brother, utterly baffled and not being able to make out right away what's going on eggzakly wondering what the fuck's the matter with him and what are these things on his eyes, thinking perhaps it's his eyeballs have burst out of their sockets like eggs when they crack open in boiling water. The scene is made more bizarre still by the sound accompanying it: the radio's on but it's not tuned to any station, so there's just this loud like crackle of static.

I tiptoe to the side of the bed and peer into his dial, making sure what I'm seeing is what I think I'm seeing and not just some trick of the light. The ping-pong balls have been cut in half so they cup round his lamps. There's a funny ronk in the air like factory smoke and I realise it's the dust and dirt on the T-shirt burning under the heat from the light bulb. I zap his heaver and it's moving: he's breathing, he's alive.

'I've seen some strange things in my time,' I say finally, 'but this one definitely takes the fucking hob-nob.'

The ping-pong balls turn slightly towards me.

'What a tiresome little shit you are,' he says.

'I thought you was dead there for a moment.'

He props himself up on his elbow, peels the tape off of the left ping-pong ball so it's dangling down his rosie, and blinks this single bloodshot lamp at me.

'I thought you said you were going out for lunch.'

'I did.'

He glances round him, ticking this over like he don't quite understand something.

'How long were you gone for?'

'Couple of hours.'

He pulls a face.

'Extraordinary.'

I go and sit down on my bed.

'You know, this is just getting too fucking weird. I mean the Native American lark I'm used to by now, but this... I'm almost afraid to ask what the hell it is you're doing.'

'Reliving past lives.'

'Fuck me. I knew I shouldn't have asked.'

'It's a simple technique. It's called the Ganzfeld effect. You shut out all external stimuli, nothing to see, nothing to feel, nothing to hear but white noise. Without the clutter of sensory perception, the spirit is free to explore its own antipodes, the memories of its past lives, things buried so deep that most people don't even know they exist. You should try it.'

'Me? I don't even know what antipodes means, let alone want to go bloody exploring it.'

He zaps me for a long time with his one lamp (the other's still got the ping-pong ball over it), then shakes his bonce.

'Yes, you're definitely a Humean being. Not hum-*an* — Hum-*ean*.'

Well, brother, if this is meant to be funny, perhaps the humour is all in the delivery like they say, cos I'm not bloody larfing, am I?

I give my warble a sarcastic twist. 'I'm sorry. Did you just say something?'

'That is Humean as in Hume,' he says, unfazed. 'The philosopher.'

Bog's baggy trousers, what the fuck's he on about this time?

'People like you are stuck in a constantly changing but ultimately meaningless moment, with no real past, and no future. Half people, little people.'

I take my shoes off and lie back. 'Well, you're right there, mate,' I say. 'This fucking trip feels like one endless meaningless bloody nightmare and no two bloody ways about it. I just can't wake up out of it is all.'

'That statement may be more true than you think.'

'Oh, yeah? And now you're going to tell me all about how I'm one of those people know the price of everything and the value of nothing, is that it?'

'Hume,' he clatters on, 'a mind perfectly attuned and representative of the white man's limited culture, said people are nothing but a collection of different sensations which succeed one another with inconceivable rapidity and are in perpetual flux and movement. He was not describing what they are, however, but what they've become.' He turns his lamp on me again. 'What *you've* become.'

'But I thought you said I was a speck of dust.'

'Locke,' he continues, ignoring me, 'was a sceptic despite himself. He believed we are born with no knowledge of anything whatever, and that it is only experience derived from sense perception that shapes the human mind. Now Berkeley denied the existence of matter altogether, claiming objects exist only through being perceived. God, to him, was only an eye, an ear, and the world nothing but a stream of sensations and ever-changing perceptions.'

I nod and hum and pretend I'm listening. After he's quietened down I say:

'You know, you haven't eaten for three days. I really think you should see a doctor. And I mean pronto.'

So he turns to me and says:

'What do you want to be when you grow up, Little Turtle?'

Oh yeah. Ha ha.

36

GRANDFATHER PEYOTE

Now Kane starts drinking more water than you'd think any-one could take without drowning, I mean bottle after bloody bottle of the mineral stuff, and it's got him in the khazi every five minutes too, but all he says is he's 'cleansing' his body of the bullet's 'bad wakan' and readying himself for the 'healing' of the 'great medicine'.

As for me, every second I spend shut up in this funky bloody room with him I feel like my brain and my heart and my soul and all my internal organs are sort of shrivelling, brother. A black despair it is. I'm starting to get the feeling he's too far gone this time and we're never going after Captain America, never going nowhere, so what the fuck am I doing here still, I might just as well get the hell out of this place and stop wasting any more time with this raging gibbering maniac.

On the fourth day of this like fasting and water diet he starts banging this little toy drum he bought the other day and singing this like droning moaning song just repeats itself over and over, all morning, then gets out his little leather pouch and from inside that these pieces of something looks like dried goat droppings, brother, four or five of them about.

'You will leave me now, Little Turtle,' he says, 'for my Vision Quest requires that I be alone.'

'Well, if you're going to keep up that awful warbling I don't bloody mind if I do.'

'It is the Ukcila Yuta Pi Song.'

'Really? Well, it'll never make the charts, brother.' I point at the goat droppings. 'And what in the name of buggering hell are those things?'

'The flesh of the Ukcila Yuta Pi. Strong medicine.'

'Medicine? How does it work?'

'You eat it.'

I'm giggling now. 'You mean you're actually going to like eat some of that poo, mate? I mean, actually swallow it down?'

He takes a deep breath.

'This is not poo, Little Turtle. It is peyote.'

I just like stop and gawp, brother.

'You having a go, or what? Peyote? How's that bloody medicine? That's like heavy shit, man.'

He makes a gesture for me to sit down.

***

'Close your eyes, Little Turtle, and I will tell you how Grandfather Peyote came to the Indian people. Then perhaps you'll understand. You see, long ago, before the white man came, there was a tribe living far south of the Sioux, in the land of deserts and mesas. These people were suffering from a sickness, and many died of it.

'One day an old woman of the tribe had a dream that she would find a sacred plant which would save her people. The woman was very old and frail but, taking her little granddaughter with her, she went on a vision quest to learn how to find this sacred plant. So they left the camp and walked and walked for hours until they were lost.'

I'm listening to him, brother, and I must admit the telling of it is sort of oddly gripping, I mean not so much the story itself, but the way he like performs it, filling it out and bringing it to life.

'Without water or food they were very weak, and as night fell they lay huddled together, not knowing what to do. Suddenly they heard the wings of a huge bird beating above them. It was an eagle. So the old woman raised her arms and prayed to the eagle to grant her wisdom and power. And as the sun was rising, its rays stretching out across the land like a father's embrace, they saw the figure of a man floating in the air about four feet above their heads, and the old woman then heard a voice say: "You want water and food and do not know where to find it. I have a medicine for you. It will help you." This man's arm was pointing to a spot on the ground, about four steps from where the old woman was sitting. So she looked down and saw a cactus, a large Grandfather Peyote with sixteen segments. She did not know what it was, but she took her bone knife and cut off the green flesh. And there was moisture, the peyote juice, the water of life. The old woman and her granddaughter drank it and were refreshed.'

Here Kane mimes the woman drinking this stuff then pulls a face of like huge blissified joy and gushy relief.

'The sun went down again and the second night came. The old woman prayed to the spirit: "I am sacrificing myself for the people. Have pity on me. Help me." And the figure of the man appeared again, hovering above them as before, and they heard a voice saying: "You are lost now, but you will find yourself again, and you will save your people. When the sun rises twice more."

'So the grandmother ate some more of the sacred medicine and gave some to the girl. And a power entered them through the peyote, bringing them knowledge and understanding and a sacred vision. Experiencing this new power, the old woman and her granddaughter stayed awake all night. And in the morning when the sun rose and shone upon the hide bag with the peyote, they still felt strong. The old woman said: "Granddaughter, pray with me to this new plant. It has no mouth, but it is telling me many things. It will help us in our need, even if it means I have to see the Great Spirit in person to thank Him."

'During the third night the spirit came again and taught the old woman and the girl how to show their people the proper way to use the medicine. The old woman and the girl spent the day filling their bag with peyote. But when night came, the old woman stumbled in the dark and hit her head against a sharp stone. Her granddaughter called out to her, but by then the old woman was dead, her spirit had already fled her body.

'At sunrise on the fourth day once more the girl saw the spirit man, silhouetted against the eastern sky. He pointed out the way back to her camp so that she could return quickly without getting lost.

'Though she had taken no food or water for four days and nights, the sacred medicine had kept her strong-hearted and strong-minded. When she arrived home, her relatives were happy to have her back, though they were sad at the news of her grandmother's death. But everybody was still sick and many were dying. So the girl told the people: "I have brought you a new sacred medicine that will help you. A spirit showed us where to look for it, and Grandmother gathered it for us before she died."

'She then showed the people how to use this Pejuta, as that tribe called it, or Ukcila Yuta Pi as it became known to the Sioux, the holy herb. The girl also showed them the ceremony the spirit had taught her, and told them how the medicine had given her the knowledge through the mind power which dwells within it. From that moment on, they learned to know themselves. Their sick were cured, and they thanked the girl for having brought this blessing upon them. They were the Comanche nation, and from them the worship of the sacred peyote spread to all the tribes throughout the land. — Do you understand now, Little Turtle?'

Well, brother, I said I didn't, but you know, in secret I sort of did, I can tell you now. I mean he was right, the story *had* made me see the thing differently in a twistified tiswas sort of way, and it really like made me wonder about Kane after, like could there be more to him than just the madness, maybe, and wasn't it perhaps just me being too hung up on my own notions of what was normal to notice this before.

Food for thought, brother, food for thought.

* * *

Well, after this I take the motor and leave. Best idea I ever had, too. I spend a peaceful night in another poxy pousada even grottier than the first but away from Kane, at least, cos despite my growing respect for him my main line of reasoning is: if he's a case when he's straight and sober, imagine him tripping on that doomsday stuff, eh? Downright bleeding Godzillic.

But this sneaking suspicion that there may be more to his krazy ramblings than I first imagined is confirmed when I come back next day, brother, cos I have to admit, he's looking much better and the wound does seem to have healed up considerably.

So maybe this Sioux voodoo does like work, then, I'm thinking, I mean, who knows, all sorts of weird shit in this world we don't know about, ain't there, stuff science can't like explain.

Well.

So I ask him is he like feeling well enough to leave but he says nothing. Then in the middle of the night, about three in the ay-em this is, he wakes me up shaking my shoulder and I jump out of my skin thinking he's gone Norman Bates on me, but he just says '*we got to go, we got to go now*', hissing urgent-like in my ear, cos you see he's had a Vision, and it's time to get back On the Road.

But as he's saying it he has the sort of look in his lamps you don't want to question, brother, real doomsday, predatory-like and frenzied, so what can I do?

I go.

37

REEFER MADNESS

We arrive in the capital of Pernambuco state — a place called Recife which Kane says means 'reef' cos of the reef formations, though from what I hear it could just as well be from 'reefer', if you know what I mean, brother — anyway we arrive, as I say, just as the day is dawning in a firework display of bright sizzling salmon pink turning to deep orange then a dazzling 24-karat gold over the sea gently lapping on a long stretch of sandy beach dotted at this early hour by shadowy human forms doing weird geriatric exercises. The air here is even more like a steam bath than it was in Rio or the other states we come through, dense and heavy enough to make any movement a real bloody effort. It's like an illness, this heat, draining away your will to do anything. By six ay-em the light is a million volts bright and every colour like jabs your lamps and screams at your brain real doomsday, but the city revealed by this sunburst is – I can think of no other word to describe it — repulsive: everything lumped together like the buildings and roads was all squeezing and falling over each other trying to get to the front of the queue; cracked, beshittened, littered pavements that sometimes disappear altogether invaded by crumbling piss-stained walls so that pedestrians have to take their chances wading through ankle-deep puddles of raw sewage while they dodge the vicious chaos of the traffic; stubby crap-encrusted houses covered in bathroom tiles like huge public lavatories, everything filthy and in a state of near-ruin, deterioration and neglect; even the fucking trees and animals and people all look like they're in the last stages of some terminal disease, deformed and grotesque. Understand, it's not poverty I'm talking about here – for a start we're in the rich part of town, and I'm certainly no stranger to poverty, brother, having spent most of my bloody life neck-deep in it (and of course no matter what anyone says it is always, always ugly), just as the disease I'm talking about ain't physical — no, what I'm talking about is something that goes deep, it's in the ground and in the water and in the atmosphere, everything thick with treachery, corruption, stupidity and malice, enough to make an honest johnny out of me, almost. I tell you, brother, I've never seen nothing like it, not in the rest of Brazil and not nowhere, and you know I've seen some pretty fuck-awful places in my time. And it's not just what you can zap, neither, it's what you can sense, touch, hear, taste, smell. Even at the speed we're driving the horrorama ronk of like things festering is enough to give your guts a proper kick and make you wish you had no nose. Kane says Charles Darwin came here on one of his voyages and reached the conclusion that it was the worst place in the world. That was over a hundred and fifty years ago. Imagine what he'd say if he could see it now, eh, a paradise for skeeters and cockroaches and a hell for everything else and no fucking mistake.

Well, while I drive Kane's got this map open on his lap but it don't correspond to anything in the real 3-D world and we get hopelessly lost wandering around like a couple of right bollock-brains for over an hour in this fucking swamp till we finally get back on the main road along the seafront and pick out a tiny cheap *pousada* called *Canto do Sol* where we can rest and decide our next move. The gaff is virtually a carbon-copy of the *pousada* in Alagoas, only this time I insist we get a room each. After a good splish-splash and a sam-up I feel a little less depressed and manage to catch the tailend of the self-service breakfarts. I load up on overripe papaya, cold scrambled eggs and coffee. Kane doesn't show.

I don't see him till a couple of hours later when for a change I go banging on his door instead of the other way round.

'I didn't wake you up, did I?' I say, hoping for a yawn.

He says nothing. He's looking pasty. I wonder if his wound's not infected. There's no chair so I plot down on the edge of the bed. It's made, not a crease on the bedspread, so either he's not lied (laid? lain?) down at all or he's done it on the floor wild-style.

'Do you have the file on Tobczyk I gave you?' I ask, coming past him into the room.

He cocks his head at me like he's finding this display of initiative on my part a bit of a larf, like I was some knobhead kid playing at being grown-up. But he goes and gets the file anyway.

I riffle through it and find what I'm looking for.

'I've had an idea of how we might find him. This list contains the names of all the people that we know who work or have worked for Tobzcyk, right? Some of them I met a couple of times like I told you, but I got the names from the Tank. Now, what I was thinking is Tobzcyk wouldn't be stupid enough to register anything in his own name down here, but he has to live somewhere, right? So if he's bought or rented any property he's probably registered it under one of the names on this list.'

'Possibly,' says Kane, unimpressed.

'So what I can do is run a check on all property deals carried out in the last twelve months in the state against these names. Whatever comes up is bound to be where he's at.'

'And how exactly do you propose to run this check?'

'The Internet. Heard of it? I know a couple of geezers in London can find anything you want, anytime, anywhere. They've worked all sides of the game, white, black and grey hat, and I'm telling you there's nothing they can't bloody do.'

'Do they speak Portuguese?'

'They don't have to, do they? All they need is the name of the government organ responsible and an online translator to find the right section. Once they're in the system, click, it's just names and numbers, brother, easy as piss.'

'And these names on your list, do they all check out?'

'Well, there's no way of telling how many are genuine, if that's what you mean. But it's a place to start, innit? Otherwise we might as well be looking for a fucking polo in a snowstorm.'

'I noticed there wasn't much in the file about these Quintana brothers, Miguel and Benício. What can you tell me about them?'

'Well, we don't know much. Like it says there, Captain America knew the older one, Benício, when he was still in America and hired him way back. But he's a real sneaksby, this geezer, keeps a very low profile. Miguel joined a bit later. He's the Cap's watchdog, from what I hear. But it's the older brother, Benício, who's Tobczyk's wank-hand. He never travels anywhere with him, though, not when there's important meets and stuff, so they're never seen together. Clever really, if you think about it. I only met him once, in Rotterdam. Why?'

'How do you know he's Puerto Rican?'

'That's what I was told. Everybody knows.'

'And who told you this? Tobzcyk?'

'Well, yes.'

'So you don't really know doodly-squat about his closest associates, yet you think your hackers in London will be able to trace Tobczyk to an address here?'

'Why not?'

'Because,' he says.

'Well bloody hell if that's how we're going to think I might just as well ask you how can you be so ruddy sure Captain America's here in the first bloody place.'

'Algebra. What Lima said and what 8 said and what I found out about the girl. It adds up.'

'What girl?'

'Carla, the bondage artist.'

'You think he's here just because she's here?'

'That, too.'

'And how can you be sure this is where she came?'

'She has a boyfriend.'

'Yeah, so?'

'He told me Carla came here. He said she was coming to see her best client. He knows who Tobzcyk is.'

'Why didn't you just get an address from him?'

'He didn't know where she was staying. She didn't know herself. They were going to pick her up at the airport and take her to the house. All part of the confidentiality agreement they have.'

'How do you know this boyfriend wasn't lying?'

'Because of this.'

Kane screws up his lamps and shows me his knife, a huge thing with a curved blade.

'OK, OK. So what do you suggest we do? Go knocking door-to-bloody-door? This is a huge fucking state, mate, Tobczyk could be anywhere. Easier to find an ant's bollock on the bloody beach.'

'Do you know, that's the first sensible thing you've said all morning. Oh, and just to put you in the loop, the Quintanas aren't Puerto Rican, they're Mexican. Belonged to a gang called Los Zetas before hooking up with Tobczyk. Still have the tattoo on their left arm, right next to one of Santa Muerte.'

'Who?'

'The patron saint of death. All those Mexican gangs are into it. They build shrines and mark off their territory by mounting severed heads on poles and hanging bodies from bridges which they offer as sacrifices to her.'

'Really? And how come you know so much, then?'

'I did all my homework back in London.'

'Remind me to give you a medal when we get home.' I get up. 'Now if you'll excuse me, I'm off to find an Internet connection.'

'You're wasting your time.'

* * *

Well, brother, I tell him to fuck off in so many words and get a message out to the IT lads back home and answer a few e-mails while I wait for their answer. It's six pee-em in London so they'll be glued to their screens. Sure enough, the reply comes through in a matter of minutes and I give them the names on the list and a few guidelines. Now all I have to do is wait till tomorrow ay-em and rub Kane's nose in whatever they come up with.

* * *

I don't see Kane for the rest of the day. I take a troll out to the beach just before sunset. The tide is up and there's only a tiny strip of dirty sand for the rats and cockroaches to play around in. I have an early dinner of ham sangwidges and pop at the hotel and turn in. Next ay-em after breakfarts I check my e-mail. No answer. I go out and troll about the hot, stinking streets for an hour then go back and check again. Still no answer. I repeat the procedure twice more before the message finally comes through.

And the bloody answer is nix, brother, they haven't found nothing on anyone, half the names don't even fucking exist, it's all been a total waste of bloody time.

Smeg.

Like he knows this already Kane's waiting for me when I get back.

He takes one zap at my dial and says:

'What did I tell you, Little Turtle?'

I shrug my shoulders in defeat.

'What now, then?'

'Now we book into a five-star hotel.'

He's starting it again, brother, the old tom-n-jerry routine. He's just waiting for me to ask why.

'I won't say no to a bit of luxury, of course,' I say cautiously, 'but how's that going to help us find Tobczyk?'

'It's not going to help us find him.'

'It's always the same stupid word-trap with you, ain't it, always the same itty game. Well, fuck this, I'm not saying nothing any more, you yampy sod.'

But he tells me anyway:

'It's very simple, really. You see, if we can't find him, Little Turtle, then we let him find us.'

Gog all bloody mighty I should've known.

* * *

The place he's chosen for our new accommodation is the Atlantic Plaza Hotel, a towering building overlooking Boa Viagem beach, lit-up like a fucking X-mas tree with blue-tinted mirror windows and an outdoor lift winking blue lights and a huge swish foyer with a slippery marble floor absolutely crawling with people when I arrive. I have two questions. First, what's a massive luxury hotel like this doing in a shithole of a city like Recife? Second, what fucking difference does it make where we're bloody staying? But I might as well be asking the bloody rash on my bum for all the answer I get, brother. Still, a bit of style and comfort never hurt no one, did it? I go for something called the executive suite, about five times the size of my room at the *pousada* and done up in tasteful pastel mauves and like umber and amber and filbert and shit, with American-style naugahyde upholstery, a chrome minibar, a work desk with a swivel-chair, a 40-inch TV set, a jet-black Jacuzzi and diddy Belgian chocolates on my extra-mega kingsize pillow.

I don't know what sort of room Kane's picked out for himself and frankly I don't bloody care. This is the first real bit of comfort I've had in bloody yonks. He comes in just as I'm enjoying some footie on cable washed down with a hugful of minibar goodies and spoils the fun saying there's one last thing has to be done before we can lay our trap (his words, brother, not mine).

We drive back to the *pousada* where he says he has something I need to see.

Well I remember arriving, brother, and I remember going up to our old room, but I sure as fuck don't remember coming out again.

38

DEEP FRY

Wassat? *Let me sleep. Shmsh. Christ. Who's that bloody talking? Belt up and fuck off, you sod, you... Leave me alone. I just... Hang on. That's not...*

Eh?

I'm too stiff to move. When I try to open my lamps I realise moving any part of my phiz is going to involve more pain than I'm willing to endure. My brain's frozen solid, throbbing, thudding, making everything hurt like when you stuff too much icecream into your jagger: skull, cheeks, jaw, my lugs even, all aching proper doomsday. The voices – there's clearly more than one – are louder but coming through all warbly-fuzzy like someone speaking into a cushion, fwomf fwomf. Gog, my stomach feels like something's crawled in there and fucking died. One side of me is getting hot, and the other half's not cold but there's a definite breeziness about it, sort of drafty like.

Suddenly I'm fully awake, staring up at a circle of dark bonces peering down at me. The light behind them feels like I'm having acupuncture done on my eyeballs. Who the fuck are these people and what are they doing in my room?

Only I'm not in my room cos that's the bloody sun up there and those are clouds, so where the fuck am I?

I get a hinge propped under me, raise myself an inch and lift my bonce. It weighs a fucking ton.

What in the name of smeg? I'm on the beach, brother, lying on the sand like some bizarre specimen of marine life spat out by the ocean in disgust, and there's about two hundred people standing around gawping down at me. I don't have any bloody clothes on. That's right. Naked, brother, bare and in the bloody raw. I look down at my shrivelled dong lying there like some diddy dead bird coated in sand like it's about to be deep-fried. I'm so utterly betwattled I don't even have the presence of mind to cover it up. A couple of the men are skriking at me real doomsday they're so shocked and appalled (haven't these fucking gringos no sense of decency, this ain't bloody Germany...) I stare at them like some demented twonk not knowing what to say, do or think. I mean, I don't even understand what they're screeching about, and I very much doubt they're going to understand anything I can blubber out in my state neither.

And it's about to get worse, brother, cos here come the fucking cozzers.

* * *

One of the cozzers covers the family jewels with his cap and they hoist me to my feet. There's kids hooting, girls cheering, and some of the men are trying to punch me now and have to be pushed back. A couple of chancers have got their mobys out and are taking snaps of me in all my glory. Most people are just cracking up. The cozzers shove me about a bit and ask me questions. I shrug and look confused. Someone brings a towel and I wrap it round my waist. They put a pair of plastic snaps on me and troll me up the beach. The crowd's following and now there's a couple of professional photographers clicking away too. One journalist actually tries to interview me with the cozzers' consent. He only gives up when he realises I can't twig a fucking word and wouldn't answer anyway even if I could. I get thrown into the back of the van. They take me on a ten-minute drive to the local copshop. There I'm interrogated again, with the same results. Eventually they find someone who can scrape up a few words of English and I explain what happened – or rather I explain what didn't happen, cos I've no fucking idea what happened. Apparently what they're thinking is I'm just another drunk gringo who thinks he can do whatever he fucking likes in Brazil and get away with it. My interpreter tells me I have broken a law and then explains something called Article 233 in the Brazilian Penal Code which forbids lewd and indecent behaviour in a public place. It's three months to a year in nick or a fine of about a thousand reais, which in round figures comes to about 350 pounds. OK, I say, I can pay the bloody fine only this is not a case of indecent exposure, at least not intentional, and give me a fucking breathalyser test if you think I'm euaned. But he doesn't understand no matter how I say it, no one fucking understands, and this mad infuriating confusion just goes on and on and on. What I've got by this stage is not a headache, brother, but an ACHE, and my fucking bonce is inside it. I'm trawled before various people who keep asking me the same bloody questions over and over again. I suspect the interpreter is making a right mess of translating what I say and is only making it worse for me. I feel like I'm going deaf, brother, it's like the air here's too thick, too hot and too heavy with humidity to carry sounds right, and so they have to struggle through layers of this goo to reach your bloody ears. No one understands anything anyone else is saying. I ask for a phone to call the hotel but it takes about forty minutes for someone to do something about my request. The fucking interpreter keeps harping in my ear about 'documents, documents' and I do my best to pretend he ain't there. I finally manage to get someone from the hotel who speaks English on the blower and explain to her what's happened. She's a while taking it all in but after it's clear in her mind she just says:

'I'm not sure what you want me to do, sir. I'm very sorry, I can't help you.'

Can't? Won't, you divvy cow, fuck you and your hotel.

But there's a bloke in a doctor's coat before me now with very bright and clear lamps glinting behind the polished lenses of his gigs (it's the face of new young prosperous democratic Brazil) and he starts examining me taking my temperature and blood-pressure and poking about my nooks and crannies and noting stuff down on his jotpad on the desk and turning round to the others to explain whatever medical marvels it is he's discovering about me.

After a few minutes of this he looks up and surprises me by saying in handicapped English:

'You have not had no alcohol to drink.'

From his intonation I can't tell if it's meant as a question or a statement.

'No,' I say, 'I haven't had no alcohol to drink.'

'Why you were on the beach without no clothes?'

'I don't know. The last thing I remember I was in a hotel room with a friend. Next thing I know I'm lying there on that beach the way they found me.'

He squints at me over his gigs and chews on the end of his pen for a bit, ticking this over.

'Have you any sickness? Are you on medication?'

'No.'

'Any history of psychosis, mental problem?'

'No.'

I say 'no' to about twenty more of these ruddy questions before he's satisfied. More people come in and go out, I'm shuffled here and there, my dabs are taken, and I sign two copies of a document no one bothers to translate for me. On the doctor's evidence they have apparently reached the conclusion that I am most likely the crime's victim and not its perpetrator as originally surmised. But there's still the problem of my 'documents, documents'. I get on the blower to the hotel again and finally lose my patience with the

English-speaking bint on the other end. When I get stroppy she goes all patronising telling me to calm down, sir, there's no need to get nervous, sir, we are here to help, sir. I want to tell her to shove the phone up her arse sideways but give her permission to enter my room instead. I tell her to bring me some clothes. Twice. She asks me what clothes. I tell her any fucking clothes for fuck's sake as long as she has taken them from my room and they're mine. She hangs up. I'm escorted to another room, an office the size of a washing machine stinking of sweat, dirt and decades of corruption. It's fucking hot, too, proper armpit, and what with my towel it now feels eggzakly like a sauna. I sit down to wait in a toy plastic chair wobbling on a dicky leg. A couple of flies keep me company. Overhead the stained tube of a fluorescent light flickers with a soft hum. My clothes arrive an hour later in a paper bag with the hotel's insignia printed on the front.

I get dressed quickly and two of the cozzers picked me up on the beach take me to the hotel in their banged-up copmobile. During the short drive I'm thinking: Kane, where the fuck is that harpic bastard? Did he have anything to do with this? Or has something happened to him too?

I try to remember last night but apart from stepping into his room it's all a dead bloody blank.

I draw stares and sniggers from the hotel staff when I come in accompanied by my two new chums. I get my key and we go straight up to my room. Everything's just as I left it, with the exception of my documents. What I mean is they're gone. They're fucking gone. The world does a doomsday zoom effeck and cartwheel and for a moment I stand there numb except for the dead rat burbling in my guts. Then I go berserk pulling out all the drawers, up-ending my case, shaking open my bags, tearing the sheets off the bed. I even look inside the minibar and in my bloody shoes. The two bizzies shake their bonces and pout as if to say, 'this ain't looking good'.

You can fucking say that again, brother.

But not all hope is lost. I tell them in sign language to come back downstairs with me, we must drive to the *pousada* where my friend is staying, maybe he has my documents. Impossible to tell how much of this, if any, they understand, but of course by this stage their expressions are starting to look a lot like they did back at the beach, fearful and suspicious, giving me narrow side-glances and threatening zaps. On the way down they keep a tight grip on my arms. I come out of the lift like Public Enemy No. 1. When they see this, the Plaza staff ain't sniggering no more, not nearly.

We arrive at the *pousada*. The bird behind the desk recognises me but says nothing. I'm at the foot of the stairs about to make my way up to Kane's room when the manager comes out of the itty office at the back and seeing me says:

'No, Senhor. You friend is depart.'

I do a fly-catcher. He waves his groper like he's brushing crumbs off his trouserleg.

'Depart,' he says again. 'Depart.'

I can't fucking believe this.

'What do you mean, depart? When?'

His eyebushes crawl up his forehead. He doesn't understand.

'When, when!' I say, pointing to the spot on my wrist where my Jaegre-LeCoultre should be.

'Oh,' he says, twigging on. '*Ontem a noite.*'

'What?'

He jerks his thumb over his shoulder a couple of times, then taps his watch. I pull a face. He snatches the fold-open calendar off the counter and jabs a finger at a date.

Well, fuck me. Unless I'm very much mistaken, brother, he's trying to tell me Kane left last night.

My two friends are shaking their bonces again, 'not good, not good...' And so it's back to the copshop, pronto. More questions, more shuffling. The interpreter is wheeled back in. Who, why, where, how? Pass. What, which, when? I don't bloody know. So this time *they* phone the hotel. The manager comes on and assures them I had my passport when I arrived and yes I had a valid visa but they don't have to take his word for it they can check for themselves it's all in the system, full name, passport number, arrival date, etcetera, etcetera. The room? Yes, he can confirm that I am staying till the end of the week and that my accommodation has been fully paid for in advance, yes.

OK, that's quietened things down for a bit. But I am told I'll have to file a police report giving precise details of everything that's been stolen. I am also advised to contact the British Embassy asap to notify them of my loss and arrange to have new documents issued in my name. I am requested not to leave Recife until the matter has been cleared up.

As Frank might say, this is a right clusterfuck this is.

39

SEACHANGE

'm trying to get a fish on the line here, brother, any fish, but they just ain't bloody biting. I mean, what the fuck's going on? Back at the Plaza I go through my tackle again but there's no sign of my passport. The passport and press cards in the name of Clifford Fuchs are missing as well. But I do find my Jaegre-LeCoultre, at least. I put four calls through to England, each to a different number. I have to let the Tank know what's been going down. But no one's seen him, no one's heard from him, no one knows where the fuck he is. I get Derek on the line and to say he sounds evasive is like saying water feels sort of wet. I leave messages with everyone saying how the Tank can get in touch with me and wait in my room for his return call. Nothing happens. I text the Tank then a couple of the lads asking what to do. Nix. Vicky's not answering neither. I wish Zoo-Lady was with me, and wonder where she is and will I ever see her again. There's a real ache thinking about her, warm, dark and heavy. I stare out of my spotlessly clean bedroom window. I've got my forehead pressed and cooling on the pane. The air-conditioner's on in the room and I can feel the heat pressing against the glass from the other side like it's trying to get in. Outside there's no wind and the world is sagging under the muggy armpit heat. Out at sea a few *jangadas*, the rafts used by the local fishermen, seem hardly to be moving at all. They look like folded napkins on a snot-green tablecloth. The hours tick by and still no bell from the Tank, no word from Vicky, not a sign of life from anyone. It's like I've fucking died and gone to limbo.

After midnight I lie down and close my lamps and wait for sleep, but it don't come till streaks of blush-pink light have appeared far away on the horizon.

* * *

I'm up late next ay-em and my bonce is aching worse than ever. I still manage to catch breakfarts but there's another surprise waiting for me downstairs. It's in the local paper. Splashed there on the front page is a smudge of yours truly being escorted from the beach in shame and confusion, a black stripe hiding my tackle from the prying eyes of the world.

That's all I fucking needed.

I go to the desk and ask if there have been any calls for me. No. — No messages? No. — When I turn my back the receptionists turn to whisper and one of them lets out a squeaky giggle. Fucking great, this is. A sleb at last. Get me out of here.

I try the phone numbers in England again, get the same answers and leave the same ruddy messages asking for the Tank to get in touch with me. Ditto Vicky, but with less hope.

Well it's ringing. Once, twice, and click: 'Sorry I'm not in right now. Leave a message after the tone and I'll get back to you. Promise.' What? Answer, you bitch! Didn't you hear my last fifteen fucking messages? I'm dying here! I can't believe you're not going to answer the fucking phone! Vicky!

Beeeep.

Then I wait. Again. After lunch I'm lying in bed watching telly when I get treated to another nasty shock. Guess what, brother, I've made the local news programmes. There's some shaky moby footage of me leaving the beach and one of the cozzers who arrested me is interviewed. On another programme, a puffed-up popeyed git in a shirt two sizes too small for him introduces the same footage, only this time there's comic sound FX and saxophone striptease music playing on the soundtrack. Fuck. It must be all over bloody YouTube by now.

And still not a fucking dickybird from the Tank or anyone else.

* * *

Soon it's darkmans again. What happened to the bloody day? Where'd it bloody go? I lie in bed brooding. I start to get the feeling that this time I'm not going to be spared, that there's no dodging whatever end is planned for me. My luck's out; my reserves have run dry. To numb the panic welling up inside me I resort to the national poison, cachaça. It's made from fresh sugarcane juice, fermented and distilled, and not from molasses like ordinary rum. It tastes like piss. I try it in the caipirinha first, then just have it straight with ice and a lime wedge. I lie back on my pillow wondering what's going to become of me. The world's gone so quiet the clinking of the icecubes sounds like the ghostly ringing of crystal bloody bells. I work my way through two-thirds of a bottle of the premium yellow stuff – aged in chestnut barrels it is – and get sozzled enough to think an evening swim's a good idea. I get two legs into one hole of a pair of surfing shorts, fall flat on my arse, get it right the second time, fill another glass to the brim and zigzag out of the room towards the lifts. Downstairs in the lobby I pinball my way round the other guests and make it to the street without too much hassle or spilling more than a quarter of what's in the glass. The night's what you might call balmy, nice salty breeze blowing, a sliver of moon in the starlit sky, and across the street the beach is in comfortable darkness. I get across and onto the sand and don't stop till I'm in the water. It's incredibly warm, slapping up against my ankles. I drain the glass as I wade in deeper, then a wave clouts me one across the chops and knocks the glass clean out of my hand. What a larf. A bit further and I've lost my footing. Water's a bit colder here, especially below the knees. I start to paddle, gargling salt water. Shark bites me now it'll be like eating the olive off a fucking cocktail. Only there *are* bloody sharks here Dodger you twat. I've stopped larfing. Getting tired now, heavy. Let the waves carry me, had enough of carrying myself. Float about like a turd, don't care what happens at least I'm out of it, flushed out of this fucking life and its misery. It's an odd combination of fear and recklessness I get, feeling myself sucked out further and further by the current, pissed and alone in the immense cold mysterious Atlantic Ocean. A million light years from everyone. Wonder where Vicky is right now. Can she really have forgotten me this quick? And where's Zoo-Lady? I miss her, I miss her more than seems right or reasonable. I feel like an abandoned child, betrayed by everyone. And Frank, who I thought looked out for me, who I thought of almost as family, an older brother, putting me out like some fucking cigarette stub. I have more respect for Kane than for that fat cunt. At least you know where you stand with him. Christ, what a cheap, stupid, dirty little life I've made for myself. I don't want to struggle no more. Maybe I'll meet Pinto down there somewhere.

At this point I've given up in my mind, brother, really given up, only my body somehow hasn't got the message and begins splashing about like some demented out-of-control mechanism about to short-circuit. Panic is just setting in nicely when I find myself suddenly tearing back towards shore. It's a wave, brother, a fucking monster of a thing. I give out a drunken yell of it might be joy or is it fear, I've no idea, only to have it choked by a huge jaggerful of water. I'm spluttering and coughing but the water just keeps pouring in cos the wave's taken me by the scruff of the neck and is tossing me about like an old sock in a supersonic tumble drier, spinning me every which way. I go down hard and for a couple of minutes I don't fucking know which way is up or where my arms and legs are in relation to my bonce, everything mad, bad and helter-skelter.

I don't remember much of the next part, only that I had these like crazy images flashing in my pan: of a deep well and me lying in a coffin and Zoo-Lady washing my body while Mum watched and sang, and then Kane was dancing his Ghost Dance, this drum beat thud-thudding in my head and his grunting and huffing and stomping was throbbing inside me like it was blood pumping through my heart and I realised what he was doing he was calling my spirit back from the dead like he said.

After a million years the wave finally spits me out on the beach. My jagger's clogged with sand, there's salt water pouring out my ears and I have a couple of real horror-film scrapes on my knees and hips that I know are going to sting like hairy fuck next ay-em. But at least I'm still breathing. I'm alive.

I lie there gasping for a long, long while.

***

My zeds are troubled and my dreams ugly and when I wake up next day feeling like minced shit I find myself curled up on the floor of my room with my face pressed against the leg of the bed-side table. What I have is not a hangover, brother, there's got to be another name for it, like acute megacrapulence syndrome or terminal dipsonecrosis. Zombified by pain I manage only the simplest vegetable movements. How did I manage to find my way back from the beach last night? Fuck knows. A bloody miracle.

When eventually I return to a more-or-less human state I remember the mess I am in and check my moby for messages and missed calls. Nix. I phone down to ask if there have been any calls or if anyone has come in asking for me, but there's still no word from Kane and nothing from across the pond neither. Ditto into lunchtime. Well, I'm thinking, either the Tank's done a Lord

Lucan or he doesn't want to talk to me. I lean towards the second hypothesis, brother, and it's bloody doing my nut in. I mean, is this all a fucking set-up or what? But if it is, just who's setting up who? And why, for fuck's sake?

Well you know what, I tell myself, feeling a little of the old confidence returning, fuck Frank, fuck Vicky, fuck Kane and fuck Captain America, I'm not bloody hanging around here like some sitting bloody duck waiting to find out, that's for bloody sure. In this game either you're dead careful or you're dead. Simple as fucking that.

So I chew down some aspirin and get on the Internet to see about reporting the theft of my passport and applying for a new one. I google 'British passport stolen abroad' and get on to the Foreign and Commonwealth Office website. If you're abroad, it says, you have to report any passport losses or thefts to the local plod in the country you're in as soon as possible. OK, done that. You'll also need the crime reference details for something called the LS01, a Lost or Stolen Notification form which has to be filled in and signed after reporting the theft to the UK embassy, consulate or high commission. I make a note of the relevant phone numbers. But there's still more crap to wade through before I can leave the country. First, the record of the theft has to be forwarded to something calls itself the Identity and Passport Service so they can cancel my passport to stop anyone else using my identity. Then the FCO will issue me with 'replacement travel documents' cos I can't get another passport till I'm back in the UK. Then and only then will I be allowed to purchase a plane ticket out of this shithole.

As I walk out into bright blinding sunlight my bonce is swimming and I'm thinking: how long will all this take? I could be here for fucking weeks, months even.

* * *

But when I get back to the hotel and ask for my room key at the desk I find there's a message finally been left for me. At first I think it's the Tank who's called the room while I've been out but no, it's a note from Kane. It says to meet him at nine pee-em sharp before the side entrance to an abandoned building site at the Federal University of Pernambuco campus. I am to take a taxi from the hotel at 20.15 and ask to be dropped off at the Arts Faculty, a place called 'cack' and spelt CAC. I'll be able to spot the construction site from there. He will explain everything to me when I arrive.

Well, he fucking better, brother, cos I've had just about as much of this bloody cloak-n-dagger crap as I can bloody take.

***

Back in my room I start ticking things over more carefully and in greater detail, cos it just don't make any fucking sense, none of this feels right, brother, not by a long bloody shot. If I go to this place at all, I decide, I'll go early and I'll go well tooled, cos there's no way I'm trusting any of these bloody bastards, least of all Kane.

Just before sunset I walk round to the square a few blocks down the road from the hotel facing the beach. Set up round an ugly blue church in the middle there's stalls selling souvenirs and snacks and stuff and there's a lot of people milling about. At one end a group are doing a square dance of some sort to squeezebox music from a couple of squawking crackling loudspeakers. I glide over and scan the crowd for a certain kind of dial is recognisable anywhere in the world. It's mostly in the lamps, a certain look that's unmistakable. I spot a few but am not quite sure which one to approach first. I'm trying to decide when I feel a tug at my sleeve. I turn round and zap a bloke in a red-and-green Che Guevara T-shirt and half-formed dreadlocks holding a display tray full of handmade hippie trinkets. His chinpuff does a diddy wag: would I like to buy one? Well, he's not quite what I had in mind but he'll do for a first crack. He's got the look. I buy a couple of bracelets off him, then ask him where I can get cigarettes. He slips out a packet from his back pocket and offers me one. I take it and, sniffing at it meaningfully, ask if he doesn't have anything stronger. I raise my eyebushes at him in an obvious sort of way. He twigs on real fast and asks me to follow him. Just at the corner of the church there's a stall selling white pancakes made of manioc flour and coconut which they call *tapioca*. Sitting on beer crates round the stall are a fat old bird making the pancakes and a couple of cool geezers dressed up in Rasta gear: Haile Sellasie shirts, striped tam hats, rings on every prong. My cigarette friend whispers something to them and one takes a crumpled packet of Marlboros from a rucksack at his feet and places it on my friend's display tray. He turns to me, winks down at it and holds up five fingers. I hand him the fifty reais and take the packet. I walk off a couple of steps, stop, then go back as if I've just remembered something. Leaning down close to his ear I say one word:

'Revolver?'

It's a universal rule: where there's dope there's shoot, sure as shite is shit, brother. It takes my friend a second or two to tumble, then he zaps me for a couple more, just to make sure. But he's not wondering why the gringo wants a barker, no, he's calculating just how much he can squeeze me for. He holds up the five prongs again, then adds the five of the other hand. This is cheap. Too cheap. But what can I do? I shrug, then nod and slip him fifty from my wallet, indicating that I'll give him the rest when I've seen the goods. He jerks his bonce meaning I am to follow him again and we make our way across the mampus to a taxi stand on the other side of the church. There's a line of taxis waiting on the kerb and the drivers are all napping, smoking, eating or playing dominoes along the top of a low wall that skirts the square. My friend signals one of the drivers over. He's a right lardyboy, this one, with thick folds on his neck and a gut like a bloody tractor tyre hanging halfway down his crotch. He lumbers over towards us in a thick-thighed waddle plucking his shreddies out from between his arsecheeks. Stopping before us he flicks his head back and darts a zap down his misshapen hooter at my cigarette friend. It's a look in which I detect blunt disdain and authority. My friend shuffles from one foot to another, gives a self-conscious grin and in a piddly warble very different from anything's come out of him up to this point explains what I'm after. The driver turns his lamps on me for what feels like a mucho long time while his face goes through a repertoire of sneers. I lob them right back at him. Then he waddles to his cab parked at the end of the line, opens the back door, and darts a glance at me over the slope of his shoulder. He makes a clicking noise with his tongue like I was a horse in need of encouragement. I get in the back and he shuts the door, then crabs round and plonks himself down in the driver's seat. The inside of the cab smells like a rugby changing room after a difficult match on a hot day. A plastic Virgin Mary dangles from the rearview mirror beside a toy mascot in the shape of a lion representing lardyboy's football team. Grunting and huffing he bends forward reaching for something under his seat. He brings it out and peels back a succession of dirty red flannel cloths to reveal a plain old .38 in worse fucking condition than he is: battered, scratched, stained and with patches of rust all over the muzzle. I reach out to grab hold of the thing and instanter he goes all frantic huffing and wriggling and waving his hands about. Ah, I geddit now. The hundred was just for the contact. He'll let me have the barker for 500. I give him a Private Pyle up-from-under stare. A full monkey for this piece of junk? It's indecent, brother. But there's no time to go after anything better so I take it. I ask for hornets and he gives me a box with a dozen 148 grain thirty-eight specials. Since I'm already sat here I also ask if he can pick me up from this eggzak same spot in an hour to take me to the Federal University campus, UFPE. I manage to make him understand this on my third attempt.

Right. All set. I get out, pay my cigarette friend his fifty, then make my way back to the hotel with a new extra bulge in my strides.

40

QUE SERA

ong experience tells me to dress all in black, so that's what I
do, brother, black jeans and a long-sleeved button-down black
shirt hanging out to help hide the loaded barker tucked under
my belt. I troll over to the square at the appointed time. Lardyboy's
there as promised. Before getting into the cab I go round the stalls
and buy the only black cap I find for sale. It's got 'PIMP' written
across the front, if you can believe it. I mean, what?

He guns his motor and we drive inland plunging almost
immediately into heavy traffic with the usual demonic hooting,
flashing headlights, dodgy manoeuvres, shouted threats and
manic start-stop-start routine. It thins out only after we get on
the motorway at the edge of the campus about a half hour later.
We come off the motorway, duck under an overpass and take a
roundabout so bloody fast the Virgin Mary swinging on the rearview starts to do a lambada with the mascot lion while I have to
hold on to the bloody sides not to fly out the fucking window. Like
shit off a chrome shovel we shoot off the roundabout into a long
deserted stretch of road that I soon realise is the main entrance to
the sprawling university complex. UFPE is spelt out in huge block
letters on a patch of grass at the head of the strip dividing the two
lanes joined at the ends in a u-turn like it might be a long racing
track. There's a cabin checkpoint on either side going in and coming out, but the guard inside the one near the entrance stretches,
yawns and barely turns his bonce as we pass. Apparently strikes

are common here most of the year round and this latest one's lasted for over a month so it's no wonder that at this late hour there's very few lights on in the buildings (which I'm guessing is why Kane chose this for the meet in the first place). The dim yellow glow in the guard's cabin stands out like a beacon in the dark. In the middle distance everything is pitch bloody black except for the faint glimmer of three lampposts peeping out from behind a huddle of stunted trees. There's no other motors anywhere as far as I can zap apart from a couple parked on the opposite side look like they've been there so bloody long they've fossilised.

We drive to the end of the road. On the corner to our right the shape of a large building looms over us out of the darkness, solid black against an off-black sky. Lardyboy points.

'Cack,' he grunts.

I get out and pay him. He stares down at the money, grins and shrugs. Sorry amigo, no change.

Yeah, nice one.

I pull on my pimp cap and, squinting into the shadows up ahead, make my way across to the building site on the other side of the road, all black and gutted like something bombed-out with only the bare skeleton of the floors and a few alberts standing, some with huge gaping holes and bent reinforcement bars sticking out like ribs on a cut of meat and everywhere full of crumbled chunks of concrete and like junk and abandoned building stuff. Set up all round the site there's a chicken wire fence and behind that some hoarding made of rain-warped wooden panels and I find a spot round one side where there's a bit of a gap and climb over the wire and manage to squeeze in between two panels.

And I'm in, brother. It's dark as shit in here. Whiff of the boneyard about the place. I slide a stick of gum into my jagger and chew on it listening for a second to the din this makes in the dead silence, nyak nyak, then cross the yard to the front of the building proper where a couple of long planks form a ramp takes me up from street level to what would've been the ground floor. Kicking myself for not thinking of bringing a flashlight, I grope about waiting for my lamps to grow like accustomed to this zero visibility. Obviously I want to be in a position where I can see Kane arrive before he can see me, so I make my way towards the back of the building hoping to find some way up to the floors above so I can be on the crow out over the ledge zapping down into the street.

I come upon a column of iron rungs embedded in the concrete leading up to a square hole cut out of the ceiling and climb up. The rungs continue through to the next floors so I go up one more.

On the second floor I go back to the front of the building and step up right to the edge to look down and across. There's the empty street and the dark shapes of the buildings opposite and the tiny light of the guard's cabin winking in the distance. Not a leaf stirring anywhere. I crouch down behind a column in a position that's a bit more comfortable but from which I can still zap anything coming this way from either side of the road. I cop a feel of the barker nudging up against my thigh under the shirt and pull it out. The weight feels good in my palm. I turn my gaze back to the street, scanning for any sign of movement, and get a bit of a jolt when suddenly from the shadows of the trees across the way these diddy like sparks light up and begin to float about in the dark as it might be a cloud of twirly dreamy ghostified fairy lights. Some go out and others come on sort of like something you might get on an X-mas tree. I stare at them a long time wondering what they can be and so I don't clock right away a pair of HID headlights giving off a glow like a blue gas flame gliding slowly down the road on the opposite side. They haven't come all the way from the entrance but have turned off into the main road from some side street halfway down. While I'm watching and wondering whether it's Kane driving the headlights go off, though the motor's still moving. It swings round the bend with hardly a sound cruising in bottom gear at maybe 5 mph max and starts coming back the other way on my side of the road. Before it reaches the building site it pulls onto the grass and disappears under some trees. The engine stops purring. I tighten my prongs round the .38. For about five minutes nothing else happens. Then I hear the sound of the car door opening and shutting with a soft click like someone is trying mucho hard not to make any noise. Expecting to see Kane step out into the road I inch my way closer to the edge. Down below a pair of legs appears from under the treeline, then the rest of a man's body. It might be Kane, I can't really tell, but what's more worrying is there's another bloke following close behind him. And they are definitely coming towards the building site.

What a stupid fuck I've been.

I lose sight of them for a bit behind the hoarding, but I can hear the dirt crunching under their feet and the creak of the wood panels being lifted. A moment later the beam of a flashlight probes the shadows of the yard below, then swings towards the upper floors. I jerk my bonce back just in time to avoid it. I slide noiselessly to a spot behind the pillar furthest from the ladder and wait trying to hold my breath down and my barker firm.

Their footsteps on the concrete of the ground floor are creeping nearer. I can't tell which way they're moving but it's not long after I realise they're on the floor below me. I poke my nose round and zap the beam of the flashlight waving to and fro through the ladder hole. It's getting brighter. They're climbing up. I'm fucked, totally fucked. My groper's shaking and the dead rat's somehow managed to crawl back inside my guts. I realise I'm still grinding down hard on my gum making too much noise so I take it out of my jagger and glue it to the side of the pillar thinking: here's the last of Dodger: a wad of dry gum on the wall.

Then it hits me for no apparent reason: *fireflies*, that's what those diddy lights are. But in an instant it's out of my bonce again cos they're here, brother, ten, twelve feet away. I try to remain very, very still. The flashlight cuts slices out of the dark all round me. In the glow I zap a barker with a silencer in the fist of the bloke walking in front. They make their way cautiously to the edge and peer down over the side. Their silhouettes are clearly visible now against the blue-black rectangle of sky and when he turns his bonce slightly over his right shoulder I recognise the profile of the one holding the gun: a long hooter coming down in a straight hard line from his forehead without so much as a curve, just like the dials on them figures you see in ancient Greek vases. And it's not Kane I'm looking at, brother, it's Benício Quintana, Captain America's man.

My nutmegs climb up into my throat. They're bloody in this together!

I bring my barker in a two-fist clasp bending my knees at the same time like you're supposed to and take aim at Quintana's bonce. I take a deep breath to steady my shaking hand and squeeze the trigger. But guess what? That's right, nothing happens, the bloody thing doesn't go off, doesn't even click, the hammer doesn't bloody budge. I can't fucking believe it.

A church choir starts up in my brain, brother, complete with pipe organ, and the words to the hymn are 'Fuck, fuck, fuck almighty', I am that saxified. I mean total black shitless despair. Now there are several blows to the body I know of that can incapacitate an attacker, and most of them can prove lethal if applied properly and under the right conditions — the temple blow, which can cause unconsciousness; the nasion or top-of-the-nose blow, which can kill; the philtrum or upper-lip blow, which usually proves fatal; the hook-to-jaw punch which can snap a neck easy as piss; the Adam's-Apple blow which can cause arsephyxiation; the small-of-the-back blow which can cause the backbone to break; the cerebellum or base-of-the-neck blow which kills instantly; the brain buster; the Russian omelet; the heart punch — the list is as long as my ruddy schlong, but Gog help me if I can remember a single one as I'm stood there behind the pillar trying not to puke. True, brother.

So this funk's like sizzling through me real doomsday when from the other end of the building there's another noise like the pop you get when you open a bottle of fizzy drink. It echoes and bounces off the walls and the two men spin round just as a large lump of a projectile (a brick or a stone maybe I can't be sure) comes flying out of the dark like a bat out of hell and wallops the one holding the flashlight right smack in the mush with tremendous force making him lose his balance and stumble backwards over the ledge still holding on to his bloody flashlight. And hup, over he goes. He doesn't even have time to let out a yell before there's the dull wet crack of his skull breaking open on the concrete twenty feet below.

At the eggzak same time this happens a bright flash tears a hole open in the dark. It's Quintana firing his barker, which on account of the silencer gives off a phut instead of a bang. For a moment I'm blind, zapping only blobs of colour. A second later I hear a grunt and then the sound of shoes scraping hard against the concrete floor. When I can more or less see again Quintana's no longer standing upright but bent down doing a sort of shuffle-shuffle two-step and brother it don't half look fucking bizarre cos now he's got not two, as you'd expect, but four bloody legs swinging under him. What? But then the second pair of legs like detaches itself from him and I realise of course it's another person. Quintana crumples to his knees. There's no sign of the barker in his hand. What's going on? The other figure is standing beside him looking down and doesn't move. Suddenly Quintana spreads his arms out and slowly lowers himself to the ground like he's gone to sleep.

I hold my breath and try to keep my heart from beating cos it's just making too much bloody noise. After about a minute the figure standing turns towards my pillar and says:

'You can come out now, Little Turtle.'

***

It don't need no explanation, brother, and Kane ain't bloody offering any, but it takes me a while to credit how this was all like worked out from the word *beach*, right down to making sure Captain America'd know eggzakly where to find me and when. Fucking bait, I was, and didn't even know it.

Well, Quintana's buggered worse nor a Quentin's asterisk on Gay Pride Day but still breathing, just, and once Kane's got him strung up all cosy and secure-like he splashes a bit of cold water from a bottle into his lamps and the big bad Mexican hombre wakes up out of it spluttering.

'You fuckin' dead, man, you fuckin' dead all of you!' is the first thing he says, so Kane fetches him one hard across the jagger then tips him over the edge of the building bonce-first holding him just by his ankles.

'Fuck you!' Quintana says, dangling upside-down. But it's not coming out quite so full of beef somehow, if you know what I mean, not nearly.

'Where's Tobczyk?' Kane asks.

'My brother he gonna kill you, you fuck!'

'Where?'

'I'm not sayin' nothin'. You crazy if you think I tell you anythin' you fuckin' motherfuckers.'

But he does, brother, in the end he does.

***

Now as you probably know identifying unknown corpses is one of the hardest things a forensic pathologist has to do. Of course DNA is a dead cert as it's found in almost every cell and can be matched to personal effecks such as razorblades, toothbrushes and even combs and hairbrushes. Samples can easily be gathered from a package by doing a cheek swab or leaking a little claret. But if, as in the present case, no one reports the victim as missing in the first place and there are no witnesses, even wunnerful amazing DNA is of no bloody use. What are you going to compare it against? Now it's a fact that here in Pernambuco they don't even bother with DNA. They go for dabs and maybe dental work and that's it. If after a week or two a body matches no missing-person reports they just say fuck it and that's that, off with you to a hole in the ground somewhere with an anonymous tag on your big toe.

But you know Kane, brother. Just to make sure, he strips the two johnnies down, snips off the ends of their prongs at the joint with wirecutters and then yanks all their teeth out with a pair of pliers. What's left he bungs into the boot of the Corolla they come in. He's going to drive it somewhere he's already got ready and says by the time they're found we'll be long gone. The clobber and bits of finger and bloody dominoes all go in a plastic bag. To be rid of later, perhaps. Or, who knows, maybe the mad fucker wants them as souvenirs. I mean you never can tell with him, can you brother?

Me, I take the motorbike Kane rode here on and head back to the Plaza to get ready for the long tomorrow.

As they say, what will be will be, even if it never happens.

PART FOUR

Why should I mourn the untimely fate of my people?
Tribe follows tribe, and nation follows nation, like the
waves of the sea. It is the order of nature, and regret is
useless. Your time of decay may be distant, but it will
surely come, for even the White Man, whose God walked
and talked with him as friend to friend, cannot be exempt
from the common destiny. We may be brothers, after all.

Chief Seattle of the Duwamish (1780-1866)

41

THE AMERICAN AGE

So here we are finally, brother, in this itty shitty cagmag tup-peny-ha'penny town called, of all things, Nova Jerusalem, sat smack on the edge of what is known as the Dope Polygon, a 25,000-square-mile area deep in the heart of the Pernambuco backlands that's become like synonymous with drug production, trafficking and wild-west violence. This is what's known as the *sertão*, brother, the mean, dirty badlands where the *bandido* is king. Road signs in the region are all riddled with bullet holes like in some cheap western and any road traffic coming through stands a fifty-fifty chance of being held up at gunpoint. Night travel is fucking suicide. Coaches are a prime target. After being robbed any surviving passengers are usually stripped and left naked by the roadside. Unprepared, understaffed and ill equipped, the local plod can do little but take backhanders and give their support to the outlaws. Occasionally the Federal lads are brought in for a big clean-up operation, but for every gang member they manage to nick, at least three more spring up to take his place, and for every plantation they manage to burn down at least two more go into bizniss within a matter of days.

But Nova Jerusalem itself is the land that time forgot, quiet as the bloody grave and almost as exciting but not quite. I learn from Kane that it's called this cos every Easter the townspeople put on their own open-air theatre version of the Passion of Christ, complete with cardboard Roman armour, plastic helmets and ketchup blood, and if you could see the place you'd understand why, brother, cos the geography don't half look Biblical, if you know what I mean, all sort of arid and desert-like with huge parched stretches of sunbleached scrubland dotted with cactus (cactuses? cacti?) and weird lunar rock formations harbouring the sort of wildlife you definitely don't want to cuddle: scorpions, poisonous lizards, rattlesnakes and whatnot — especially whatnot. Apparently, in recent years the passion play has become something of a local tourist attraction, but for the rest of the year the town's just another airport for flies. To look at it you'd think at first this would be the last ruddy place a vain drugstar megalo cunt like Tobczyk would want to be holed up in. I don't know what the eggzak population is, but I bet you there are more bloody horses living here than people. But when you think about it, it's perfeck really: only a four-hour drive from the capital Recife, totally ignored by the federal, state and municipal plod, property prices so dirt cheap he can afford to build himself a fucking fortress here, and dead at the gateway of the Polygon.

We come to the edge of the main road running down the middle of the town like a hair-parting but don't actually get on to it so as not to draw attention. Two gringos in a big motor they've never seen before at this time of year is sure to raise a few eye-bushes. The road's long and wide but there's not much else either side of it: a straggle of shabby houses, a crumbly church, a fly-blown petrol station and a few larger properties on the outskirts tucked away behind long whitewashed walls. Tobczyk's gaff is not actually in Nova Jerusalem but some miles further west towards the sierra visible from anywhere down in the valley, a line of low mountains or high hills with jagged edges, sharp peaks and steep sides look sort of purple in the distance.

I let the car roll slowly to a stop. Kane's nodding to himself, scanning the country all around, satisfied. Finally he says:

'We're here. Really here. Close. Can you feel it? It's like we were inside the belly of the beast. It can feel every move we make...'

You fill in the blanks, brother.

But we need a few supplies so Kane who's darker-skinned and less conspicuous gets out of the car and trolls off down the lane where we're parked and into the main road. He's dressed sort of scruffy in old jeans and a striped short-sleeved shirt and he's got a straw hat and his cheap cheaters on so he's not attracting too many curious glances. The houses are all diddy and plain and painted different rainbow colours like vivid green and pink and baby blue but all faded and slightly yellowed from the sun frying everything down here like we was under some huge invisible magnifying glass concentrating the beams. It's not humid like in the city but still I don't think I've ever felt heat like this, brother, mid-pee-em and forty degrees in the shade with everything blistering and wrinkling like paint under a bloody blowtorch, you included. My sniffer's glowing like fucking radium and the back of my gregory's redder nor a monkey's arse and twice as sore so every time I turn my bonce my shirt collar feels like a ruddy cheese grater.

Kane goes in and out of two or three of these itty shops they have like old-fashioned grocers and the like, then trots back to the car carrying all these brown parcels and plastic carrier bags full of food and water and bug repellent (and that's the important one, brother, I can tell you) and all the other stuff we'll need cradled in his arms.

When he gets in he lets out a long breath and turns to me and says:

'Do you like living in the American Age? It's almost over now, you know.'

Yeah, I think, and one of these days you'll set off and meet yourself coming back, mate.

He's still looking at me, not blinking.

'Are you scared?'

I let out a puff of fake larfter.

'Scared?' I says. 'Me? Only on Wednesdays, mate.'

'Then I will tell you a story,' he says.

Christ, I think, bend over, Dodger, here it comes again.

'One day, when the world was still very young, The Great Spirit gathered all of creation and said, "I want to hide something from the human beings until they are ready for it." And when they asked him what this secret was the Great Spirit said, "It is the understanding that, like me, they can create their own reality." So the eagle said, "Give it to me, I will take it to the moon." But the Great Spirit said, "No, one day they will go there and find it." And the salmon said, "I will hide it at the bottom of the ocean." "No," said the Great Spirit, "they will go there too." Then the buffalo said, "I will bury it on the great plains." But the Great Spirit answered, "They will cut into the skin of the earth and find it." Then Grandmother Mole, who lives in the breast of Mother Earth, and who has no physical eyes but sees with spiritual eyes, said: "Put it inside them." And the Great Spirit said, "It is done."'

'Nice one,' I says. 'But I'm still scared shitless.'

So then we drive off east a few miles away from town and find a spot deep in the scrub hidden from view of the road.

Now all we have to do is wait until dark.

42

WARPATH

I am gasping with my throat in my stomach, my bonce back-to-front and my legs twisted round the wrong way and only after a second do I tumble that I'm still in the car and it's Kane nudging me from this nightmare I been having where I'm chased by reptiles with human eyes. But when I wake up all the way and realise where I am I don't know which is worse, brother, the bloody nightmare or waking reality. It's a toss-up, I tell you.

'Time to go,' he says.

We take our shoulder bags out of the back. I'm carrying the Beretta, binoculars, a flashlight, a first-aid kit, a folding camp chair, a couple of tubes of repellent, some cheese sangwiches and mineral water. I've also got a thermos of caffeine-rich energy drink to help keep me awake and on my toes. (You don't want to be caught napping in a situation like this, do you brother.)

Gog knows what Kane's carrying in his bag.

It's a steep narrow winding track and getting steeper, narrower and windinger with every bloody step. There's a slice of yellow moon giving off a sickly light just bright enough for us to get a dim sense of where we're treading — sort of. It's much cooler at night here than in the city and I reckon the temperature's dropped by at least half since daytime but the fucking skeeters don't know this or don't care cos they're twice as bleeding ferocious as anything I've encountered so far in Brazil. I rub repellent on what I think is every square inch of exposed flesh till it's a thick gooey paste but it's only later I realise I've forgotten to do my bloody eyelids.

The track leads between dense clumps of rough thorny bushes sharp as fucking needles and these rubbery plants look like stuff you see growing under the sea sprouting out between the weird rocks they have in these parts which in the dark take on the shapes of huge impossible animals waiting to leap out at you. The ground's hard bloody going full of loose stones and sudden bumps and lumps and unexpected depressions and uphill the entire bloody way so I have to stop to like catch my breath a few times but Kane never bloody stops he just tells me to get a move on.

It takes us over an hour to get within sight of the house. By this time my right hand is bandaged from a cut and I've got so many scratches there's bandaids fucking all over me. For the last half-mile we can see the dirt road converging towards our track, a pale glow beyond the scrub.

We set up our stake-out on a sort of mound rising just above scrub level on one side of the track. There's a knot of trees at the top and the thickest makes for a good observation post. Kane climbs up and I get my chair open below to zap the property through my binoculars in relative comfort. But my eyelids have started itching from the skeeter bites so I squeeze gobs of repellent on them and then of course they start stinging like fuck cos you're not supposed to do that and for about fifteen minutes I can't see a fucking thing.

Kane is very, very quiet up in his tree.

'What about snakes?' I whisper up into the dark. 'I heard they have coral snakes here.'

'Shut up,' he says. 'Don't make so much noise.'

When I can see again what I zap is just the sort of ostentatious layout you might expect from a geezer like Captain America, an ultra-modern looking pile of shit full of sharp angles everywhere and stacks of geometric shapes in different shades of what in the dark looks like grey but could be almost any colour, like an ugly cubist painting miraculously swollen out into three dimensions. Only thing kind of stands out different is this big white horned skull of a bull staring down from the crossbar over the main gate like it might be one of them ranches in a John Wayne movie (in fact we come across a skull very like it on the way over – a bad omen). As for the house itself it's got a terrace and thick wooden columns and an L-shaped swimming-pool glinting in the moonlight and around that rows of expensive-looking white sunloungers and deckchairs and round tables with parasols stuck through their middles. There's diddy lights on round the pool and at the foot of the house pointing up and a few bigger brighter ones set up round the eletrick chain-link fence surrounding the grounds and one over the bull-skull. The fence has signs on it every few feet showing diddy bolts of black lightning warning of the electrickery and on top rolls of barbed-wire like a bloody concentration camp, and I'm thinking well how the fuck're we going to get in there, then. At first I don't see anyone but they're there all right, brother, two goons in the shadows keeping watch, then one more comes out round the back and joins them for a chat and a smoke, tips glowing in the dark. Even out here a million miles from nowhere Captain America knows he's not safe, he knows what's going down and is just waiting for the crunch.

Kane whispers down:

'You see them?'

'Yes.'

He climbs down.

'Keep an eye on them,' he says, 'I'll be back in a moment,' and vanishes into the scrub.

He's gone a long time. I just sit there counting my feet. After about twenty minutes all the lights around the house suddenly go out. Even through my binoculars I can't see a thing, it's so bloody ink-like. But by contrast the night sky seems much much brighter than before, brother, sprinkled with like a trillion stars like I've never seen and down the middle a long trail of like white mist and for the first time I twig why it's called the Milky Way and all that.

All dead quiet. I don't hear Kane come back and start like a kicked mog halfway out my bloody chair when his dial suddenly looms up not two feet from me out of the liquorice soup. It's painted blood-red with jazzy yellow zigzags down the rosies and black stripes across the lamps and jagger like a bloody slasher clown in a horror flick or it might be Satan's own bloody carnival mask, a real screamer.

'What in the name of holy arse is that?' I ask, finding my warble again.

'This is my Death Face,' says he. 'War paint. The red is for strength, and blood. Black is because I am a warrior, and have proved myself in battle. And yellow is for life, my life, to show that I am willing to give it up, and fight to the death.'

I gawp for a bit taking this in then start to shake the old bonce muttering all sorry and bleak-like to myself, deep depression stuff it is like 'I don't believe it Gog all bloody mighty what the fuck am I doing here this is it bloody cunting hell we're bloody done for,' that sort of thing, brother, cos it's at this moment that the true pure atomic madness of the situation hits me, right between the bloody lamps and hard, if you know what I mean, real shock and horror.

I mean, it's going to be a bloody massacre, and sure as shish kebabs it's not us going to be doing the massacring.

Then he walks off a little ways, and I can just see a faint outline of him holding his arms straight up to the night sky, and if I strain my ears I can just make out the prayer he's mumbling out:

O Great Spirit,
Whose voice I hear in the winds,
And whose breath gives life to all the world,
Hear me.
Let my eyes behold the beauty of both sunrise and sunset
With the same wonder and pleasure.
Make my hands respect the things you have made
And my ears sharp to hear your voice.
Let me learn the lessons you have hidden in every leaf and rock.
I seek strength, not to be greater than my brother,
But to fight my greatest enemy: myself.
Make me always ready to come to you
With clean hands and straight eyes.
So when life fades, as the fading day,
My spirit may come to you without shame.

***

'The lights in the house have all gone out,' I say after a long, long while.

'Yes,' he says. 'I followed the electricity poles carrying the service cables from the house. I found the distribution transformer.'

'Ah,' I says. 'And now what?'

'Now we wait.'

It'll be daylight soon.

'Yes.'

But you know, soon's a long time coming, brother.

43

DOOMSDAY

Dawn. Like someone's torn itty strips off this huge wallpaper painted with the night sky to reveal grey-pink plaster underneath and a bunch of other colours with no names. Birds twittering all about now and larger insects buzzing and making my life more of a misery than it already bloody is. My joints are locked stiff from sitting in this fucking chair and my ankles is itching like the itch out of hell from ant-bites (the bloody ants here love repellent, brother, they can't bloody get enough of it), but my despair's so black it's left me numb and ready for just about anything. Everything's in slow-motion now, shimmering and wobbling in the heat. From under a rock not three feet away a pus-yellow scorpion darts out, takes a good look at me, and vanishes into the scrub.

Kane, king of the wild frontier, is still up in his tree.

Sunshine creeps towards the house, glittering on the pool and tiles and roof. As it gets brighter the two goons at the door are joined by two more moving about outside. They're all dressed the same in jeans and T-shirts. And I'm thinking: right, so there's at least four of them, and Gog knows how many more inside, and this whole bloody idea ain't bad, brother, it's fucking cataclysmic, cos if I go down there I'll be committing suicide and no bloody mistake, proper Dodgerloo and fucking final. Know what I mean?

But I'm in a right giddy strange mood at this point, brother, so I don't fucking care about anything no more, not Captain America, not the Tank, not bloody Kane and not even myself, I'm tired is all, bloody totally nanxed in body and mind, and I just want to get whatever it is I got to do over and bloody done with so I can lie down somewhere and go to sleep or die or whatever just as long as I can get some rest and forget I ever bloody existed.

I glance up. I can see Kane now wrapped round his branch like a huge snake. He's got the rifle's telescopic sight (and it's not just any old sight, brother, it's a Hensoldt ZF6x42PSG1 scope with an illuminated reticle, real state-of-the-arse stuff) pressed to his lamp scanning the place out measuring distances, establishing targets and estimating ranges.

I point my binoculars down at the house again. After a bit the front door opens and a diddy fox-terrier bounds out onto the lawn followed by this bandy-legged bird in a short towel-robe carrying a glossy magazine and a steaming mug. She walks straight past the goons without a word and, taking the little stone path across the garden, parks her arse on a sunlounger by the pool to read. The dog tears about wagging its stub of tail, barks and jumps at the legs of one of the goons, then goes and takes a coily dump by the flowerbeds. The woman yawns and flicks over the pages of her magazine licking her prongs. Her nails are painted bright deficit-red. She looks Oriental but her skin is tanned to a deep olive. Several feet behind her in the shaded terrace a uniformed maid comes out and starts laying a long table for breakfarts. Nothing more happens for a bit. Then suddenly there's movement from the other end of the house. Two of the goons are climbing into the big black 4x4 parked in the gravel driveway at the far end of the main block. The car reverses a few yards, does an arse-about-face on a broader stretch of gravel then heads for the front gate. The gate doesn't open automatically when they get to it cos, courtesy of Mr Kane, there's no electrickery, so one of the goons, swearing, has to step out of the car to open it by hand.

They vanish down the road leaving a cloud of nicotine-orange dust. Then even that is gone.

I go on watching. Nothing. My brain is melting. I swing my binoculars back and forth, then point it straight up at the sky. There's dots there, black dots wheeling and spiralling far, far up in the blue beyond the wispy clouds. Vultures, they are.

I put my binoculars down. None of this makes any bloody sense. What are we doing? What's he bloody waiting for?

Ten, fifteen minutes go by without change. I finish the last drop of energiser in my flask and stand up. I got to take a slash. I find a spot a little way off and let rip. The piss splashing on the dusty ground and dry leaves sounds dangerously amplified in the dry dead silence.

I'm just thinking this and squeezing out the last drops and dribbles when a loud crack goes off behind me. I jump three feet in the air and spin round dripping piss on my shoes still holding my tadger in my hand like some bollock-brain. I zap round looking for Kane and find him lying on top of the stake-out mound with his arms wrapped round the stock of the Heckler & Koch mounted on its diddy tripod and with the muzzle pointed down at the house. As I'm watching he squeezes out another round and I see his shoulders judder from the recoil. The cartridge casing flies off the rifle sideways almost bloody hitting me in the chest. I scramble for cover, remember my binoculars, go back to my chair for them, then point them down at the house.

The goon by the front door is crouched down waving his barker about and swivelling his bonce trying to understand what the fuck's happening and where the shatter's coming from. The other one is on his hands and knees near the woman's lounger by the pool. She's screaming with her hands shaking round her ears but too terrified to bloody move, but the goon takes no notice of her, he's just crawling slowly on all fours, bonce down like he was looking for something very small on the ground as it might be, inching forwards across the flagstones. He reaches the edge of the pool, gives a diddy shudder and dives in over the side bonce-first. Splash. Where he falls a dark stain immediately starts to spread, flowering out all around him. His bonce doesn't come back up for air.

Kane fires again. I try to see if he's hit the other goon. From behind the edge of the wall there's a magnesium flash followed by two dull bangs. The goon's shooting back. Kane's next shot takes a chunk of masonry off the edge of the wall as big as my fist. The goon fires another shot but it's way off target. Then for about three minutes there's total scrotum-squeezing sphincter-tightening silence. The woman by the pool has scarpered into the house and everything's still as outer space. No sign of the dog but I can hear it barking as though from a long distance away. I realise I'm sweating cos it's started dripping down into my lamps and I have to blink. I start breathing again and tumble to the fact that without thinking I've somehow pulled my barker out of its holster and am gripping it hard in my fist.

Down in the house the dead goon in the pool has floated out almost to the middle and the water has gone bright orange. The goon behind the wall pops off another round but this time he tries to see where he's aiming. There's a slice of face an inch wide and the corner of an eye peeping round the edge of the wall. Crack. Kane's shot gets him right through the cheek and he flops down sideways on to the lawn with his arm stretched out still holding the barker. The next shot smacks him in the chest but apart from the jolt of the impact he doesn't move.

There's someone coming towards me and I jerk round pointing the Taurus.

Kane says, 'Put that thing away, you idiot. We're going down.' He hands me the FN P90 carbine out of the shoulder bag. 'Take this and spray anything that moves. Is that one fully loaded?'

'What do you bloody think?'

We start down the slope towards the house cutting through the sharp scrub moving in a sort of zigzag. About halfway down I hear two gunshots that sound like they're coming from a mucho long way away carried by the wind but one of them rips the dead leaves off the top of a tree not five feet away from me and the needle goes right into the fucking red. There's no trail of any kind and we're just stumbling through and I'm getting fucking shredded cos it's all cactus and thorns and dry twigs and sharp fucking blades and a lot of dead wood. There's more shots coming from the house now and they sound closer but I don't see where they hit. We go the last few yards on our stomachs using the undergrowth for cover but it's hell cos now there's not only the stuff tearing at my bloody face but there's also dust jamming my throat and midges flying in my lamps.

The impression that the universe has decided to wipe us out is very strong with me now. The cogs are moving again, pushing me on; the events of the past weeks have all conspired towards this, plunging me into this hellzaskelter orgy of murder and madness that somehow I know is going to end today, here in this no-man's land at the end of the world, as senselessly as it began.

Suddenly Kane's tugging at my shirtsleeve dragging me sideways. I squint up through the thick cake of dust and tears clogging my lamps and zap the foot of the gate across the dirt track.

'I'm not fucking crossing that,' I say.

But before I can say anything else Kane's haring it across the road in a rugby-tackle crouch and giving off a Chief Crazy Horse 'Hoka hey!' kamikaze Indian war whoop means something like 'it's a good day to die' (not the best battle cry to like encourage the troops, eh brother?). I watch him and just shake my bonce in like dumb despair. I mean, fuck. There's more shatter coming at us from the house and now I can see where they smack the road near his feet kicking up these diddy sprays of dirt, fwup fwup.

Reaching the other side he throws himself down with a body roll behind the bit of wall at the foot of the chain-link fence and with his Taurus starts shooting the shit out of the lock on the main gate. There's pieces coming off it and sparks flying and smoke. When he brings his arm down everything suddenly goes very still again.

A minute ticks by, two. Kane's waving to me to cross over. 'Fuck you,' I say in dumbspeak. I hope he can lipread. He throws me a yampy stare and gets up and walks — not runs, brother, not dashes or bloody sprints, but fucking *walks* up to the gate as cool as you like and gives it a kick with the heel of his boot.

It swings open and he looks back at me.

So what do I do? Like a git I run across the bloody road, that's what.

But nobody tries to shoot us till we're more than halfway down the drive and coming up level with the swimming pool. Then it all starts happening at once. We hear the sound of the 4x4 behind us coming back up the road and an instant later it's on top of us as we tear across the lawn. Real charge of the bloody light brigade, it is, only now we have to stop and run back the other way cos there's shots coming from the house hissing past our bonces and I'm trying to understand what's happening but it's fucking impossible nobody can make sense of this sort of shit while it's happening, brother, nobody, not even bloody Kane.

It's Condition bloody Red. My teeth are clenched, my arse-cheeks are clenched, my stomach-pack's clenched. I'm fucking clenching muscles I didn't even know I had, brother. Even my bloody hair is clenched. I feel there's like a steamroller going over my chest pressing down so hard on my lungs that I have to suck deep down all the way to my bloody socks for a breath of air.

I'm running nine ways from breakfarts here, real Tom and Jerry, when out of the corner of my lamp I zap the goons out of the car behind us.

I have just time to think: *this is fucking it.*

And then everything just opens up, brother, shatter flying all over the bloody place so I can't even fucking tell where it's coming from or where it's going, kicking up dirt and grass and sharp flitches of stone all around me hitting my legs then my arms and dial as I try to like scrabble blindly on all fours to find cover only there is no fucking cover. I've almost reached the flowerbed when there's this loud slap of a bullet hitting flesh. I don't feel it going in, just the impact, like I've been kicked in the arse by a fucking mule. I do a nosedive, all the air sucked out of my lungs, and land in a tangled heap a few feet from where I was a millionth of a second ago. Something between my chest and my stomach like churns and burbles horribly. My gropers go flying all over my windmill feeling for the bullet-hole I know must be there letting my blood out, only it's all so sticky and wet back there I can't fucking find it. In a panic I scramble to get up to start running again but there's something wrong with my legs and I trip over my own feet and collapse like a soggy bag of shit. I can't move. I raise my bonce shouting but I can't hear either cos there's too much fucking noise and there in front of me is a dead face staring up at the sky. It's the goon Kane shot half-past dead with the sniper rifle. There's flies coming out his jagger and dirt on his eyeballs. The lake of blood under his head is so deep the fucking ground can't drink it up fast enough, brother.

I'm staring at this when something grabs me by the ankles and I try to fasten on to the grass but it's too dry and too short so I'm dragged back screaming shredding my nails. The pain in my windmill is like an illogical bloody scramble of numbness and burning so hot I'm not sure if it's heat really or bloody freezing cold. There's still swarms of gunfire blasting everywhere an inch over my bonce and instinctively I push my dial hard down into the grass but it's not bloody grass anymore it's stone fucking steps with hard bloody edges and I get four or five great crunching knocks on my jagger bouncing up and down off of them and break a domino as I'm pulled up backwards into the house.

Once inside I feel my legs being dropped and roll over on my side just as a window shatters. The hornets hit the wall, a row of coin-sized holes appearing as if by magic in the plaster.

Kane grabs hold of my shirt and shakes me.

'Stay awake! Grab your gun and fucking start shooting!'

He turns me over, slips the carbine off my shoulder and plonks it in my hands. All I can think of is how thirsty I am. The noise is totally deafening with shots tearing non-stop into the room ripping pieces off everything.

'You're OK,' he shouts in my face, pointing at the open door we've just come through. 'Shoot! Shoot!'

And then there it is, brother, the old bullet-in-the-canister sequence going round on a loop in my innermost, proper doomsday, only now it's a hundred times more real in widescreen bloody Technicolor Blu-Ray sharpness with Dolby Surround Sound: this time I know — I *know* — I'm going to die. I'm going to die... the next second... I'm going to die...

Now.

A shadow crosses the doorframe and without even knowing what I'm doing I squeeze down on the trigger, then again, hard as I can, and get a jolt not from the recoil but of fright when this heavy limp lump comes crashing down across the threshold and smashes its bonce on the floor with a sound to make your jacobs shrivel and crawl up into your guts. And now I see what it is: a zombie out of a schlock horror flick, with half his face blown off and bits dangling down his cheek all black and red.

I'm shivering now and it gets so bad it starts to seem a bit comical somehow so the more I shiver the more I feel like larfing even though I'm still blasting away with the carbine.

Kane's somewhere near the back of the room shooting over me lying on the floor at his feet. But now I'm larfing so hard I don't even know what the fuck I'm doing anymore and it's only when he pulls me up off the ground and fires off a shot close to the side of my face that I stop cos that bang is worse than any noise so far producing this instant loud ziiiinnnnng in my right ear that completely drowns out every other sound and drives me completely mad. I start to shout out of control.

'I'm deaf! I'm fucking deaf!'

But next moment I have to shut up cos through the haze of smoke I now zap this new bloke who's in the room with us and he's staring at me coming closer step by step but I can't tell what he means to do cos it's not like a threatening look at all and his rosies are all sort of bulged out like he's trying not to ralph and all the time he's groping and tugging at his shirt real desperate like trying to get at the bullet holes in his chest still smoking as if he could still do something about them. He totters a little and blinks, once, twice, looking straight at me then through me like I'm made of glass. But he can't hold it down no longer, brother, and his jagger sort of comes loose at the corners sagging open and then this like tidal wave of thick black blood just all pours out gushing through his choppers and over his chin and down his neck as he slumps to his marylebones like he's been unplugged.

I don't see what happens to him then cos I'm half-puking myself, toppling backwards through a door leading further inside the house with Kane pulling me hard by the collar.

And I'm actually greeting now, boo-hoo-hooing hot brine into my bloodstained gropers, and it's only when I calm down enough to peek between my sticky prongs that I tumble where I am and I see it's a big living room with two long yellow sofas and a couple of armchairs and a coffee table everything full of gaudy decorations and like ornaments and whatnot all rather swish in that expensively cheap way typical of a certain set of people like Captain America with absolutely no taste, only I see all this only over a length of time in like twisty slow-motion and not all at once slumped face-down on the sofa where Kane's put me. I'm still deaf in one ear only now there's this noise inside my skull like something's scraping and scratching to get out. It feels like there's not enough air in the house and I'm breathing very hard but after a few seconds of zapping the room this gets better and my pulse rate goes down a bit cos now it dawns on me that the shooting's stopped and I'm still alive.

I'm still alive.

Problem is, brother, the calmer I get the worse the wound in my arse aches. So I lie there worrying about losing too much blood and about the possibility of infection and did any cloth get in the wound cos I remember reading if it does you're fucked and then I start wondering where the nearest bloody hospital is and do they have good doctors and so on and I don't know how long it is before the bird I seen through my binoculars reading by the pool trots in with Kane squeezing her arm.

'Sit down here,' he says to her. He jerks his chin at one of the armchairs. 'And don't move or make a sound, or I'll be forced to kill you.'

Her lamps is swollen red and her lashes all wet and there's a snot-bubble coming out her left nosewell and she's shuddering and shaking all over with these great deep sobs wracking her from the ribs up but you can see she's trying to hold it all down terrified of even glancing at Kane or me.

'Keep an eye on her, Dodger,' he says to me.

An eye on her? I can barely fucking breathe, you fucking maniac.

But all I say is:

'I need a doctor.'

My voice sounds like piss trickling out of a cracked empty bottle.

He walks off.

A long time I lie there concentrating on not concentrating on my pain, if you know what I mean. The bird doesn't move in the armchair beside me, and the whole house's is creepy quiet, till from somewhere inside comes this like hoarse shout or croak. I turn to the bird and she's looking at me too now but the moment she zaps me glancing at her she swivels her lamps down and starts blubbering again very low and like trying to swallow it down.

What made that noise? What's going on? Where's Kane? I'm so thirsty now it feels like my clapper's stuck to my teeth and the sides of my throat are glued together. I don't want to go anywhere or do anything. I can't keep my lamps open they're so heavy but I'm starting to feel the panic return too cos I've started to think that if I shut them I won't ever open them again but somehow that thought in itself is helping me to stay awake, but not as much as I'd like.

44

CUSTARD'S LAST STAND

I don't know how long it's been. A second, an hour. Far away but getting closer there's someone whining high like an ambulance siren and my lamps ungum and flutter open. The sound moves past me, fast, along with a body that blocks the light for a split second. I blink and another whizzes by, faster than the first. I roll over and try to focus.

And there on the carpet, not four feet from where I'm lying, is Captain America.

He's completely naked except for a pair of pointy-toed cowboy boots. He's panting hard and his face keeps on crumbling then pulling itself together again, like it can't decide whether to collapse completely in like panic, horror, despair, or to hold onto that slender invisible thread of hope and sanity that says to him something like hold on, pal, there may still be a way out.

Kane's standing over him, legs set wide apart, head tilted back, his own face a mess of paint and sweat and grease and gory splatters, his body soaked all over in blood and dirt like some primitive great God of Death.

For a long moment the Captain can't take his eyes off him and doesn't even notice me or the girl. He doesn't blink or breathe. Nothing in the world can distract him from this savage presence before him, holding his fate in its hands, the decision to give life, or snatch it away.

The Captain's looking for something there in Kane's eyes, his gaze trying to push through the hard crust into something warm and soft underneath, some sort of recognition and understanding, as if to say, *can't you see a little of yourself in me? I'm just a man, like you, can't you see...*

Only he's not finding it, brother.

Finally he blinks, and his face crumbles again. He turns it away, sees me now. He doesn't remember me, has no idea who I am, but it's like suddenly he's found a brother, cos at least I'm human, not like the supernatural horror standing over him, and it lights up another ray of like diddy hope in him.

'There's no need for this...' he mumbles. His lips hardly move as he says it, like he was the ace ventriloquist. 'Please, let's just stop this madness...'

He pulls himself back, face gone cold custard now all soft and yellow, holes sagging open, dragging his bare pink arse across the carpet trying to get away from Kane. But he's still looking at me, hardly nothing left at all in his lamps now but raw primitive animal terror.

'I'll work it out with Frank,' he says, still talking to me, his tone very like sober and serious to show we're all reasonable men, here, we understand each other. 'I didn't know what I was doing, I was out of my mind... But, I know him, we're like brothers, he'll understand... Just... Let me just talk to him, I'll phone him—'

Kane swings a leg forward and instantly this like body-quake starts inside the Cap, rumbling up from his thin white thighs all the way up to his frecklesome stooped shoulders, all quivering and juddering like he was a huge human vibrator.

'Wait,' he says, his warble gone runny as a pat of butter hitting hot iron. 'Please, don't...'

Kane swings the other leg forward to join the first.

'Look you guys, this is crazy. I'm just a businessman, that's all I am...' The Cap's Adam's apple's working now, big and pointy like he had a chicken bone stuck through his neck trying to poke its way out, just at the height where the brown chafe marks form a sort of ring of darker skin. His lamps fill with tears. 'Okay, I'm not denying anything... But—' The tears spill out onto his rosies. '—But it doesn't have to be like this... You're in the same business, right? We can work this out.'

I have to confess, brother, I feel a twisted twinge of like guilt at this. He's right. In many ways, I'm no better than he is.

He finally lets himself glance up at Kane again. 'What do you want? I'll give you anything you ask... Go on, just name it...'

So Kane pulls out his hunting knife.

Captain America starts yelling, and the girl, who up till now has been watching in a sort of stupor, starts yelling too, only her warble's dread shrill, like old dry chalk scraping against a blackboard, eeeeeeee. And suddenly the stroppy fox-terrier tears in out of nowhere and parks itself on the edge of the carpet in front of the Captain and starts barking too, proper freaked. After a second, even I feel like bloody barking and yelling.

And Kane? Well I can see his lips moving, brother, but it's to himself, no sound coming out, praying like I seen him do on the plane over.

Now the Cap's cowboy boots are scraping away at the floor as he tries to push himself back away from the huge knife, but all he's doing is making rucks in the carpet and getting nowhere. Then suddenly his yelling sort of takes shape, like it's hit home that he's not going to get out of this, that there's no last moment reprieve, no cavalry charge, no moment of mercy, no bargain, no deal, no offer, no exchange, no threat, no nothing that's going to save his skin, and so he allows himself this little spurt of rage to cut through the terror, his last chance to get back at the man who's going to murderate him in cold blood, even if it is just a few lame insults he can fling.

'You fucking Limeys! You're *nothing*, you fucking dumb motherfuckers! You can kiss my ass and go to hell! You hear me, you can all go fuck yourselves, you cocksucking—'

Then suddenly he's up, chunky boot-heels skidding on the bare floorboards as he swivels, stumbles and swings a right through the sliding doors. He bolts outside, naked and screaming.

Kane gives a whoop and leaps after him, knife in the air.

I feel myself sinking, right through the sofa, through the floor and the earth beneath it to a place deep underground.

***

Last thing I remember is Kane standing over me with the diddy fox-terrier in his arms trying to lick this thing like a punctured pink balloon covered in grey hairs all wet and matted with blood.

What was it?

It was Captain America's scalp, brother.

45

AFTERMATH

Someone's throwing these hard bright slices of broken light straight at my face, all sharp shards and smashed glass-like, making my lamps throb so bad I have to look away and down and shut them and then I lose my balance and when they're open again I zap these like dirty trekking shoes moving in and out a hundred miles below me on tiny pencil legs and it takes me a mucho long time to work out they're my own bloody feet trawling through dirt and scrub and kicking up dust in puffs like itsy atomic bomb blasts that sort of fascinate me. Then my feet aren't swinging beneath me any more but I'm still moving just floating along while they drag behind, dead things scraping up the dust in even bigger clouds.

That's when I start to feel this right vomitsome pain everywhere and not just in my lamps and arse and upper leg but all over my bloody body like a thick heavy oily ache sliding and crawling through every muscle and fiber and nerve ending, brother, with hot razors for teeth. I groan and start to disappear.

'Stay awake,' says the bloke carrying me.

I know that warble. Head's just a blur, but I definitely know that warble.

'Kane?' I says.

'All right, easy now,' he says. 'Don't try to speak.'

Next thing I know I'm trying to explain to him that I could stand resting for a bit cos I can't go no further not with this fucking pain it's too much it's making me feel sick and strange. But it's no use, I'm making a total mess of saying anything another human being can understand.

'Quiet, now,' he says. He hands me a canteen and I take a swig of water. It's piss-warm but the best drink of water I've ever had, brother. The world still looks like I'm seeing it through the bottom of a pint glass, but this time when I try to speak again I at least manage to squeeze out whole words:

'I'm cold... It's fucking freezing out here...'

'No it isn't. You've lost a little blood, that's all.'

'What the fuck happened?'

'Don't worry,' he says. 'You'll be all right. When we get back to the car I'll see to your wound properly.' He pats his shoulder bag. 'I brought the first-aid kit.'

I'm totally awake now. 'Why didn't we just do it back at the bloody house?'

'Too dangerous to hang around there any longer.'

I'm staring at him. There's great smears of fresh claret just out of the tin very red and wet all over his shirt-front splattered like a bloody butcher's apron and his hands is covered in the stuff, dark and sticky. I'm about to ask him is it all mine when I hear the sound of a car horn in the distance, blasting full urgent like, chopping through the silence like a meat-cleaver.

'Who the bugger's that?' I gasp.

He takes a few seconds. 'Miguel Quintana, maybe... I checked all the bodies back at the house and I don't think any of them were him. He must have been out while...' He looks at me. 'I shouldn't have left the girl behind. She's told them. They'll be coming after us.'

The horn starts again, then stops dead. We both hold our breath to listen for the sound of a car engine starting up but hear nothing.

'How far to the bloody car?' I ask, whispering now.

'At least an hour, more in your condition.'

'Bloody hell.'

A sudden like despair grabs hold of me. I stumble forwards in a mad rush shuffling and jerking my giddyup blast-buggered all to bits and almost trip over myself. He comes up behind me and props me up like before with my arm hooked round his neck.

'Steady,' he says. 'We can make it.'

We manage to get into some sort of rhythm, but a few yards on he hears something I don't so we stop again while he cocks his ear to the wind.

'What is it?' I ask, breathing hard.

'Shh,' he says, holding up a prong.

I listen. Nothing.

'OK,' he says finally, and we move on once more.

I'm making a huge effort here dragging myself along, bit by bit my body is dropping away from under me, brother, sagging, getting heavier and heavier. Finally I just give up and say, 'I can't bloody go on.'

Kane stops, shaking his bonce. 'We can't risk a fight now. We'll just have to hide and hope they give up searching before too long.' He looks round, then nods at some bushes over a low ridge. 'We'll take a cut through there and see if we can find somewhere you can lie down and I can take a look at that wound again.'

He gets out from under my arm and turns facing me then gets into a half-crouch like he's going to take a crap in the middle of the track. He comes towards me with his bonce down in a rugby tackle and before I know what's happening throws me up over his shoulder in a smooth fireman's lift like I was some molly duffel bag. It fucking hurts too, but when I yell out in pain shouting 'Put me down, put me down,' he tells me to shut the bloody hell up or he'll knock me silly.

'You want them to hear us?'

'But where can we go?' I say after a bit, fighting down the agony, my bonce hanging halfway down his back. 'There's nothing out here. I'll fucking bleed to death.'

'You're not that badly hurt,' he says. Then he sort of chuckles to himself. 'Anyway, blood's good for the earth, Little Turtle, makes it happier and greener, helps things grow...'

Yeah, cue the canned fucking laughter, brother.

Well, after that I sort of stop struggling altogether and let myself go, feeling the pain close in around me like a hard wossit-called cocoon. It's all ruggedy-rough terrain these parts like I said, mucho dry and thoroughly thorny and full of like loose rocks and bumps and jagged edges, and we've been darting proper ziggery-zaggery, up, down and every-which-ways, Kane grunting under my weight even though it's mostly downhill now, but I hardly notice any of it any more. I'm too done in.

The outside world starts to go dim.

I'm just slipping off completely when we hear the car again. Not too near, but near enough and that and a sudden movement from Kane jolt me wide awake again. He loses his footing on the crumbly slope we're on and we begin to slide and topple over. I hear him snarl trying to keep his balance but we fall anyway. I land on my side and roll over scrambling trying to get up again right away scared out of my wits and hurting twice as bad as before but the world does a couple of cartwheel turns veering madly and I have to just like lie back flat on my back again right away to hold down my puke. I shut my lamps and swallow a lump of dry sandpaper big as a fist. The pain in my nut now is like nothing in this world, brother. It's like nothing in the next neither.

I'm moaning so Kane comes and clamps a paw over my jagger fast as anything then manages somehow to heave me up again still telling me to keep quiet as we listen for the engine. It's still there, but doesn't seem to be getting any louder nor fainter, the noise just like hanging there in the air, hovering round our ears.

What's worse is it's totally impossible to tell which direction it's coming from.

With me back on top of him Kane scrambles down the slope and under some gnarled dry midget trees that scratch the bloody skin off my arms, keeping to a low crouch as much as possible and trying not to make too much noise.

Darting in and out where there's space between these like sharp claws of dead branches and twigs tearing at us we make it out into a clearing where there's one-third of an old brick albert still standing, part of a house or hut long ago abandoned and left to crumble and rot in the middle of all this nothing.

'Wait here,' Kane says, putting me down. Then he creeps along this narrow ditch right down to the foot of the wall and has a peek over the edge. 'OK,' he signals back, and I totter down to join him.

On the other side of the wall now I can see we're inside the space where the house used to be if ever in fact it was, and there's bits of the other walls around us forming a sort of square, just a foot or so of blackened bricks half-hidden in the low-growing scrub.

He sits, I lie, with our backs to the wall, listening.

Nothing.

'You think they're gone?' I ask after a bit.

Kane pulls a face. 'No telling,' he says.

'Do you have any idea where we are now?'

'Not really.'

'So we're lost then, lost out here in the middle of oblivion like two... like...'

He frowns. 'The only place you can be really lost is in your head, Little Turtle. Now turn over and lets have a look at your bum.'

* * *

It's around noon I guess hot as fucking Hades and I'm not cold no more just lying there staring dumb-eyed at the shadows all razor-sharp and black as oil-spills stark against the blinding glare bouncing off the sand and grit and dry earth waiting for the world to go round and time to pass. Nothing comes out in this, brother, not even the fucking ants. But I'm patched up at least and feeling a bit less like a sack of rat vomit now that I've rested and had all the magic aitch-two-oh in Kane's canteen and munched on a couple of crunchy NRG bars. Kane says it was a clean wound and not deep so I can bloody well stop whining.

No sign of the car or any kind of noise or movement anywhere any more just us two breathing and existing so I ask:

'Why don't we just go? Get back to the bloody car and get the fuck out of here?'

Kane's doodling in the sand with a broken twig and doesn't look round to say:

'No. They're still out there. They may even have found the car by now.'

I let out a long tired breath full of misery.

'We just going to wait here, then?'

He nods slowly. 'Until nightfall, at least.'

Well Gog all bloody ruddy mighty.

***

I've dozed off and woken up a dozen times at least and am looking up at the vultures circling above us again, little black crosses in the sky hoping patiently just praying for us to die so they can have lunch. It's been a couple of hours at least and the shadows are stretching longer and every now and then these diddy lightning lizards with tough leather bodies dart about the ruins shopping for insects to kill and eat. I begin to wander what they'd taste like roasted, these lizards, even though they're so itty, thinking if we stay here much longer it might just bloody come to that cos food-wise we've gone through everything what was in the bag. I'm zapping one of them perched totally like paralysed on top of a rock imagining it skewered over a BBQ then skinning it and the tiny bones crunching between my gnashers when there's a loud snap from the bushes.

My pulse stops.

Shit.

In half a blink Kane's crouched by the edge of the wall with his barker tight in his fist.

And I don't feel the heat at all no more, brother, not even a bit: my blood's turned to fucking pack ice.

Something's moving out there. I concentrate all my being on listening to it, trying to give the sound a shape.

Then everything stops. The sound's gone.

We don't move.

After a long long time I whisper quiet as I can to Kane, 'Did you see anything?'

He waves a hand behind him.

'Keep qu—'

Dakka-dakka-dakka.

The noise cracks out from everywhere and nowhere at once totally impossible to tell which bloody direction the acoustics all krazy but the automatic weapon shots zing clear right beside the wall just inches above my bonce and smack into the bushes on the other side with a crackle of splintering wood.

My jagger hangs open. I scramble about in one spot not knowing which way to turn or where to hide.

'Stay down,' Kane shouts behind me.

I hit the dirt, literally, with my face.

In the silence I can hear the blood thundering inside my head.

Waiting, waiting for the next—

Dakka-dakka.

The shots kick up stalks of dirt not three feet away from my left shoulder in a straight line. I zap back more or less at where I'm guessing the shatter's coming from, squeezing my lamps squinting against the terrible glare and sweat that's blurring everything, searching the trees and scanning bushes madly, blinking, seeing nothing.

Silence.

I push myself back hugging the wall as close as possible pressing my legs together and my arms curled up under me making myself as small as I can but I feel huge, lumbering and totally exposed with my soft tender insides all pink and helpless quivering just waiting to be torn apart.

'Get back here!'

It's Kane, only I don't know where back here is or which way I'm facing any more.

Dakka-dakka.

I hear the thunks where the bullets smack the wall and then the bits crumbling off falling to the ground somewhere near me. With sweat totally rivering into my lamps now I zap round again and see Kane crouched down right at the other end of the wall with his bonce over his shoulder pulling ugly faces at me. I get on my knees and lizardwise crawl fast as I can towards him. The moment I reach him he opens fire, three quick rounds into the bushes.

Suddenly from a long way off a high-pitched warble shouts out in a comic Pancho Villa desperado accent:

'You fuckin' gone, gringo! No way you comin' out of this alive.'

Then all dead still again.

'You see them?' I ask, gasping for breath.

'I saw one of them,' Kane says, then pushes his heavy shoulder bag back towards me with his foot. 'Grab the Beretta and some ammo.'

I'm rummaging in the bag when the air suddenly rips apart around my ears. They're shooting the wall to bloody bits and Kane's shooting back. I fall to the ground lying on my side holding the Beretta up against me with both hands praying for a fucking miracle, my chest heaving I'm breathing so bloody hard.

Then it all stops again and there's that sudden absolute complete heavy silence, a total absence of sound like it's all been sucked out of the air making you feel like you're suffocating.

After about a minute Kane says very quietly, 'I think there's just two of them.'

'So?' I squeak. 'What the fuck are we going to do now?'

He glances round.

'Nothing.'

***

And that's eggzakly what we do, brother, No-Thing. I strain my ears but if they're moving out there they're doing it very bloody quiet and wrapped in cotton fucking wool.

Five minutes go by, ten, fifteen. It's fucking torture, imagining what they're up to, waiting for the shooting to start up again and not knowing where it'll be coming from this time and what it's going to hit.

Then it happens. There's this loud messy rustle of dry leaves and breaking twigs very close and these heavy like clop-clopping footsteps just over the wall and four or five shots crack out hitting the bricks on the other side. And I don't know who the fuck it is out there but the sound is definitely not human, brother, a deep pained bellow right out of this fucking world.

Then Kane says, 'Oh shit, it's a cow.'

46

SPERM TO WORM

A nd you know what? It is, brother, a bloody cow. I take this light-speed squiz over the ruined albert just long enough to catch a lickety-flash of an image like a snapshot in the brainpan: horns, sad eyes, big wet nosewells and a square body full of ribs sticking out, all wrapped in patchy flyblown fur.

Well, I mean, what?

'It's stuck,' Kane says. 'The rope's caught in the branches.'

The cow moos.

Dakka-dakka.

Bits of wall sprinkle down over my head and shoulders like fucking hail.

'They're going to kill it,' Kane says. 'Those bloody bastards are just going to—'

Dakka-dakka-dakka.

The shots ring out rippling through the air for a long time after, drawn out till I can't tell if the sound's out there or only inside my head. The cow's mooing away totally like desperate now and I can hear its thick hoofs clomping and scraping at the ground trying to get away.

'Fucking bastards,' Kane says.

'Where the bloody hell are they?' I ask.

Dakka-dakka.

Then Kane says to me, 'Start shooting,' and runs out. — That's right, brother, he fucking *runs out.*

I'm shooting and at the same time shouting, 'Kane! Come back!'

He's there jumping twisting scrabbling at the fucking rope pulling and tugging hard as he can bullets flying all around.

'You mad fucking bastard what the fuck are you doing?'

I'm still shooting but I don't bloody know what at I can't see nothing only bushes and crap but around us everywhere it's fucking chaos shots blasting bits flying dirt stones bricks twigs leaves smashed all to smithereens like so much confetti and the world a nightmare of noise.

Kane gives the rope a huge final yank losing his balance as it comes loose stumbling backwards and the cow's free tearing away tottering and bellowing and almost collapses I think hit somewhere on its side with blood running down its leg but still managing somehow to dive into the brambles but only barely. I can hear it bolting away through the brush, still mooing, then it's gone.

There's a sudden hush, a second of total silence.

I cut through it with:

'Kane!'

Dakka.

This time there's no dirt spraying or brick breaking only a wet thud. When I look he's limp on his back wheezing and coughing and I see on his chest this like rosebud of flesh, brother, puckered, blooming with a great gushy fountain of blood.

'Jesus Christ! Kane!'

He groans, saying something I can't hear.

Shock and helplessness are sucking on my insides, milking them dry, shrivelling them down to nothing. My arse feels loose and soggy.

I crouch down behind the wall. I can hear him. A tiny gurgle, a hiss.

In that instant I feel something unexpected, brother, not just the jolt of tumbling to the fact that he's had it, but also this huge sense of loss, like the stuffing's been vacuumed out of the world, cos something important's been lost here and can never be got back.

Of course I know, *I know*. It's over. He'll go first and then it'll be me.

I look round at the dry twisted plants and the yellow hard earth and then at parts of myself: my feet here on the end of my legs and my knees trembling and my cock and my stomach and juddering hands and wonder how much longer I will have them for. A great sweet longing sadness overflows inside me spilling through my chest and up into my songbox then my lamps. I picture for some reason the lace curtains in Mum's bedroom window blowing in the summer breeze the day after she died, just like they done when she was still alive, and Corrie which she never missed is on in the next room, no different, cos some things don't change, you're gone but the world goes on, it doesn't care. And why should it, eh, why the fuck should it?

No Mum. And no Kane. The world seems very empty now. And in another few seconds no me neither.

I try to work it out in my head but it don't make no sense. I can't believe he's dead. Why did he do it? For a cow.

A cow.

And now there's a huge hollow in my chest too a black emptiness eating itself inside-out sucking everything around it like a black hole: the ultimate fear, brother. I don't see anything but I have this impression of everything happening at once the start of life like a dot then a jumble of every moment in my life all the way to now and after, when I'm just a bag of decomposing hamburger.

***

I don't know what happened then eggzakly or how long I sat there in this like twisted mind-mess, I only remember that breaking through the dream there was this very crisp distinct click of metal close by like a key turning suddenly in a lock and then someone whispering and the next instant I'm not sitting down any more but somewhere else running into that darkness that started out inside me and now is outside sucking everything into it so the sun is gone and the heat and even the air has vanished. I can't even tell if it's really me running or it's this thing sucking me in but there's no fear or despair and no hope neither only maybe the sense that this is the end, the very end, but no clear thought at all it's like I'm this wild animal with my lamps bulging and spit drooling a yard down my chin, a savage prehistoric beast with instincts buzzing raw and primitive like I could tear flesh with my teeth and drink blood.

There's faces looking at me but I see them only in bits, especially the eyes, staring wide and hard. There's a lot of noise but it seems to be booming out of my head. Something incredible is happening now cos I'm not running any more my feet don't even touch the ground I'm just leaping through the air, higher, flying.

Then I fall. And when I fall, the kick to my bonce knocks me back to sanity, or the present, or reality, or whatever you bloody like to call it. A world of pain.

I lie there for years, very very still, hardly breathing. Nothing interests me.

And as I become aware of my own weight pressing against the ground, of the dust in my nosewells, of the stabbing pain in my arse and the deep silence all around, I wake up to the fact that my miracle has just happened.

There's a hand close enough I could reach out and touch it. But I don't want to. I let my eyes crawl up to the wrist and notice how hairy it is. The arm is also hairy, very thick and brown. And totally dead.

I get up. It's like trying to lift six of me. Death is hugging me very close like a good friend or a lover but I feel very alive, more alive than I've ever felt. I want to scream. I start to laugh. I think about Zoo-Lady. We're lying naked on a carpet I've never seen before and I'm knobbing her brains out. Then her hand is pressed over my heart. It's beating very hard and fast, I'm in love and I'm crying. It lasts a fraction of a second.

One of the blokes I've killed is looking at me. He is smiling. I smile back at him. We're like old friends.

The other one can't smile cos he doesn't have a mouth any more, or even a proper face.

I feel very strong. I feel like I could eat the whole world for breakfarts.

Then I hear...

What's that?

Someone's singing.

He's singing, brother, Kane's actually singing. Very soft, very quiet, blood bubbling up through his lips. It's his Death Song. Two days ago he was telling me I should have one, too.

I come closer and listen to him, the sound getting fainter and fainter. Then he stops the song and says in this warble that's like someone sucking up the last drops of his drink through a straw:

'Enough, enough... Rest... My poor girl, my...' He shuts his lamps, breath coming very shallow now. 'Bring me my ghost shirt and chanupa, Little Turtle... Let me make my journey with honour.'

It takes me a moment to understand. I find the shoulder bag and dig out the shirt and pipe and put them in his hands. I don't think he even felt them.

The last thing he said was:

'I'm a ghost now.'

47

THE MARK OF KANE

I did everything like he'd asked me to back in the motor when we was coming over: if he died leave him where he was, don't bury him. No stone to mark his grave. Nothing. Take everything he had, leave him in his togs only. And if at all possible — and if I thought I could like stomach it — stay with him four days.

It wouldn't take long in that heat for the bodies to start stinking. I dragged the other two away into the bushes as far as I could and left them there for the vultures.

Then I sat with Kane. His face looked very ancient, like something from another age, made of stone. At first I felt nothing specific one way or another. I wasn't even tired or hungry or thirsty. I just sat there, brother, like I was fossilised, a part of the landscape, turned to stone.

Later, the second day I think it was, I cried. A little. It was like I was sobbing for I'd lost long ago, brother, or something I'd never had and always wanted, only — and here's the yampy part — it was Kane. Not in a dirty way, mind, but a feeling very solid like, so pure and simple.

Then I lay my hand on his cold forehead, brother, and shook and wept till I thought I'd bloody dehydrate. I don't know, I must've been weak from losing so much life-juice, I guess. I would've hugged him, too, but he was in no state for it.

That same day I saw maggots crawling about in his chest. It was as it should be.

My wound wasn't too bad, but not better neither. Then I remembered him back at the hotel after he'd got shot. I found the dried peyote buttons in the shoulder bag and ate them.

* * *

I heard voices, brother, all fangled and crackling, people inside and of myself, and I saw Kane, a warrior angel of death like at the Cap's house but also an angel of life, smelling of rotten fruit, phiz painted blood-and-guts-red and tar-black and a dazzling white of zigzags, doing his geometric circular ghost dance to the four winds. I danced, too, flesh gone all raw-eggy, and felt a real mind-mingle pass between us, like we was brainblendixed. Then this anteprehistoric granddad come hobbling along in his flip-flops, shlep shlep, Granddad Peyote, singing a mad moonlight sinatra, turned-in eyes milky blind, his face a no-face, if you can under-stand that. And it was sort of sweet, too, this old song he was trill-ing, even though it was so chopped-up and his warble nothing but a cracked deathrattle all choked up with like sand and dust and dirt. And I stood there staring at him and at Kane and every-thing that was going on, the world suddenly buzzing and sizzling with life, staring till my yogi stood on end, brother, literally, cos like all these feelings were rushing over me at once, a tidalwave, it was, proper tsunami, every emotion known to a human bean: pride confusion happiness hate love horror pleasure sadness joy and so on, the bleeding lot.

I felt very wise after, like I'd been there bloody centuries, but at the same time I was still only this fertilised eggthing in mum's womb. And I zapped inside myself then, seeing all the diddy tubes and wossits and grokking how they worked and how they connected with what was outside, then I zapped hard into the ground x-raying all and the trees and leaves, seeing the veiny nerves and mickle itty subatomic stuff in everything, all very biochemiphysiolololological. And I even sort of twigged the stoniness of stones, brother, the wotness and isness of it all and space and time all like looping soft and jellified, proper play-doh.

And I realised the sky was really on the inside of my skull, and the moment I understood this there was this explosion like a bullet crashing through my brain, but not just killing me, it was also like making love, you understand, this like mixture of love and pain.

And then I saw myself inside a long black coffin, I was both inside it and outside looking at myself lying there, totally dead. People standing round, decked out in black, long faces mourning. The Tank was there, with Derek, Keef and Porker and some of the others. A moment later I was being carried to the boneyard to be buried, and I could see the trees passing by overhead. The inside of the coffin smelled of shit and dead flowers. Someone's hand touched my cheek, Zoo-Lady's or Mum's, I think. Mum was crying and I tried to tell her not to, but I couldn't speak cos my jagger wouldn't open. Then I floated up above all those people, and saw my phiz there on the corpse that was still lying there in the coffin, hard and cold and white like a slab of marble, but the next instant I forgot all about it as I floated up higher and higher, seeing the streets and cars and houses gone very itty far far below. Up and up I went, like a kid's balloon, till I passed the clouds and reached the furthest reaches of like outer space. And there in the vast black interstellar ocean I looked back and I saw this monster thing holding up the earth on its back. And when I got closer I saw it was a turtle, brother, with a great splendourifical multisectioned shell bejewelled and showing like a googol of megacolours, all impossible, redgreen and smurfblue and pinkpurple, and its skin was made of scaly chips of starmatter and glittering like ultrabright cosmik dust. And as I was looking at it it sort of came to me that I was on the verge of some dobbing great truth, here.

Cos I knew that turtle. *I* was the turtle.

And the rest, well, it was like an unknowing of everything that had gone before, brother, which was needed to start over again totally different. And, well, words just cannot tell. I mean, they just can't.

48

BACK TO ZERO

A nd like a shot it hits me, brother, ka-pow, right in the marbles: Krazy Kane, in his cracked twistified way, *was* a great man. I mean, he wasn't famous or anything, and he didn't change the world, nothing like that, but he was still your classic cheez whiz radical gandhi, a true wossitcalled, visionary. Of course I realise he was also a vicious bloody killer and like totally radio rental and all, but at least he stood for something in life, and on the only terms that actually mean anything: his bloody own.

Come to think of it, I really don't know why it only dawned on me then, so late in the game. Understanding some people takes time, I suppose. (Look at how it was with Vicky. After I got back I said only two words to her, both of them very short and to the point.) And my mood and the setting helped a bit, too. Just picture it, brother: there I was adrift in the middle of the sprawling great city like a bloody ant lost in the ocean, alone as anyone could be in the world, ripped loose from absolutely everyone and everything — work, love, family, friends, the old life and all the old ambitions — when suddenly I come over all soulful and like thoughtsome as I look across at the dirty old river in the distance, the mighty Thames, flowing so sad and slow and oily out to Gog knows where. The sight of it does something to me, brother, sets me winding back the thought-tapes to find just eggzakly when it all began, this seachange in me, BC-to-AD, the big bang absolute point zero. Was it after I got shot and thought I was going to die? Or was it when Kane popped his clogs? No, perhaps it was long before that even, that night I almost drowned, or earlier still, when I first met Kane in Wales...

But you know what, brother, the further back I go, there's always a moment before when I get a sense that something in me was already pulling me towards this moment, this transformation. Weird, or what?

So then I sort of squiz up at the barbed-wire trees above, the depressed carbon-monoxized birds nursing hangovers in the dread twisted branches, shitting on the heads of the workaday humanoid hordes shuffling back and forth across the windy pavement below all assembly-line and like trying not to look at each other's cardboard phizzes, and I think: well, here's another ordinary cold grey pee-em in the Big Smoke for you, no doubt a day like any other for all these mass-produced good citizens, my fellow Babylondoners, each and every one a modern civilized Humean Being, like Kane once called me, going about their daily bizniss, and they don't know, can't see, and couldn't bloody care less, cos they don't know what it's like to zap out over the far edge into the long cold goodbye and see themselves arsy-versy outside-in and in the red red raw.

No, and they wouldn't want to, neither, I'm guessing. Only you really have to learn about these things if you want to understand, brother, if you want to know about Living as opposed to just *a* Living. You do. And the truth is, if it hadn't been for Kane, I'd still be one of them, just another dumb chancer jam-packed full of ordinary diddy dreams and hopes like everbody else, hungry for the Big World even though to me it was all dead dead dead.

I didn't know it, of course, but then I didn't know where the centre of things was — and believe me, there is a centre, oh yes, most definitely.

And now here I am, brother, watching the zombies shuffle along the pavements like there's no tomorrow, not interested in the smile on my face nor its reason for being, the odd bit of newspaper or plastic bag, blown by the wind, catching at their ankles; the world around them coming slowly to an end. They don't mind.

But me, I'm almost free.

Without thinking, I pull the Jaegre-LeCoultre duometre a chronographe off my wrist and throw it down hard as I can on the pavement, giving it a couple of real doomsday heel-stomps for good measure. Why? I dunno, brother, it just seems like a good idea. And it feels bloody great. I then squint down at the smashed pieces, tennis-matching the bonce all like well well, sort of golly gobsmacked by the sheer stupid sight of the bloody thing, and you know it puts me in mind of the wise words of old wotsisname, Lame Deer, the great Sioux Holy Man Kane told me about, who said we see in the world around us many symbols that can like teach us the meaning of life. And about bullseye bloody right he was too, brother, cos I immediately tumble to the fact that the broken watch and my wounded arse *are* symbols, I'm sure of it, Symbols with a capital bloody ess too, no less. Only I'll be buggered if I know what they actually mean.

Kane would've known, though. Yes he would.

Does this make sense?

I then step over the smashed remains and tell myself: okay, one last thing to do, one last, and then...

I walk on, not paying mind to anyone around me, totally like focused. The sky, huge and splashed with black and silver, a doomsday sky, is staring down at me, I can feel it, the eyes of the great Wakan Tanka egging me on.

And I think: twelve weeks. What's twelve weeks? Less than a hundred days, less than two-hundred-and-fifty hours. But enough to turn the world arse over elbow.

Well well well.

***

So I take the train from Waterloo. You see it's off to Kempton Park for the twilight flat gee-gees. Yeah. Doo-dah. Frank's got himself the Lanzarote private suite, which can accommodate up to fifty guests. It's his favourite. There's four large tables and a bar and king-size glossy snaps of horses and riders on all four alberts. I come in expecting a crowd but he's sat there on his jack, nibbling on chicken liver parfait and crusty bread slices, with just Derek and Porker at a table nearer the back waiting for him to tell them what to do with themselves.

I draw closer and see now there's two places set at Frank's table, and for a moment I think he's going to invite me to sit down.

'Ow do, Dodger. Thought you wasn't going to show up there for a minute.'

'Trains running late, Frank.'

'Yeah, course they are. How's that wound healing up?'

'It's fine Frank, thanks.'

Just then a tidy blonde in the highest heels ever wombles in from the bogs straightening her skirt and plonks herself down next to Frank giving off a mushroom cloud of industrial strength perfume. There's barely room behind the table for her ballooning fake tits. Frank doesn't bother to introduce us. He gently pushes her out of the way to poke his bonce round at Derek and Porker.

'Here,' he says, 'did you know, Dodger can shit twice as fast as any man alive now? Some Brazilian tore him open a new arsehole.'

Derek and Porker larf a bit at this, but I can tell it's just canned. I used to make eggzakly the same mechanical sound at Frank's limp-cock jokes.

'Tell you what, though,' says Frank, turning back towards me. 'Whatever it is they got going over there in sambaland, it's done

ou good, boy. I don't know if it was the sun, the food, the birds or the fucking bullets, but you don't look half the mummy's boy you used to.' He turns to the funbags and digs a huge elbow in her side playfully. 'Eh, Janette? What d'you think? Doesn't our Dodger here look handsome in his new tan and bullet hole?'

Janette doesn't so much as glance at me. 'Yeah, luv,' she says, showing a cosmetically whitened smile that could swallow your head.

'You see, Dodger? Even Janette thinks so. And she knows a thing or two about goodlooking men. Don't you darling?'

There's a professional knock on the door. Two crisp starched waiters waltz in doing balancing tricks with trays. Frank's having chargrilled sirloin steak and chips, the gourmet.

When the waiters have gone he snicks a big dripping chunk off his meat, rare-done and bloody the way he likes it, dips it in the béarnaise sauce and starts chewing down hard and loud while he speaks.

'That was good work you done for me over there, Dodger. And to prove I mean what I'm saying, I've got you a little token of as it were my appreciation.' He raises his fork and flicks it in the air, getting a drop of béarnaise on Janette's hair. 'Bring it over, Derek.'

Derek hands me a glittering cube. I tear off the wrapping thinking maybe's it's another watch. The box is about the right size. I open it and feel a grin of loathing spread slowly across my face.

'What you have there is an S.T. Dupont Ligne 2 palladium plated lighter,' says Frank, the words muffled by the chips rammed in his jagger. 'The best there is. No, no need to thank me. You've earned it, Dodger. That's for a job well done, that is.'

Looking back at my old self, I can understand how them butchered soldiers must have felt getting their Purple Hearts. I mean, I don't even fucking smoke, brother.

'Now, what the fuck's happened to that fuckwit Kane? You know he hasn't even been round to collect his second half yet.'

I shrug. 'He'll turn up, I expect.' This time I know my lamps are giving nothing away.

'Yeah,' says Frank, squinting. 'And if he don't, so much the better for me, eh?'

And I'm thinking: oh yeah, you can fucking say that again, you fat sad wad.

But Frank's locked onto me now, on the scent of something not quite right, noticing something's changed, and trying on one of his inter-skull electromagnetic brainmatising Rasputin mind-bogglers. Only this time it ain't working. He meets the dead blackness, then, slowly, feels it turning in on him, gazing back into his own ugly nut. And it frightens him, brother, I can sense it, like I had antennae and his fear was little waves making them tingle.

And instantly there's a taste of danger in the air, like hot iron, cos in his world how you deal with fear is through violence. But me I'm almost smiling again, brother, cos what I realise more than anything else, what really strikes home for the first time in all the years I've known him, clear as clingfilm, is the fact that he bloody bores me. The fat old fucker bores me fucking stiff.

I let my gaze stray to a pile of magazines on the next table. On the top one, in red grot letters, a headline reads:

Security fears in lead-up to Brazil World Cup 2014

Frank tries to larf it off, asking mock-bright and right chumly-sounding:

'You in for a flutter today then, Dodger?'

I swivel my bonce round, very slow and deliberate-like, and zap him again, straight in the piggy lamps.